"So, what do you want?" Adriana asked, conscious of his closeness and the sense of his body's restrained strength. "You deliberately wore the ring today so that I would see it, didn't you? Why?"

"I wanted you to know that I already have something that once belonged to the Falcone family. Soon I intend to have much more." Thorne's hand captured her chin and his thumb caressed her lower lip. "Including you, Marchesa."

"I've been threatened before, Mr. Weston." She jerked away from his grasp. Her body burned where his hand had touched. "In ways far beyond your limited imagination."

Slowly and deliberately, he examined the tiny derringer in his hand. "Then I suggest, Marchesa—" he tossed the gun to her "—that the next time we meet you make sure this gun is loaded."

"Fresh and original, exotic and entertaining, a sweeping panorama of the world of cruise ships and international intrigue. I predict *Ports of Call* will be only your first stop on a Sally Fairchild suspense and romance tour."
—Paul Levine, author of *9 Scorpions*

"Between the high hills of Italy and the high seas of luxury liners, author Sally Fairchild spins a riveting tale of lust, greed and mystery."
—Jeremiah Healy, author of
The Stalking of Sheilah Quinn

Watch for the newest blockbuster from
SALLY FAIRCHILD

Available October 2000
only from MIRA Books

PORTS *of* CALL

SALLY FAIRCHILD

MIRA

MIRA

ISBN 1-55166-505-0

PORTS OF CALL

Visit us at www.mirabooks.com

Printed in U.S.A.

DEDICATION

To Louis Magrini, Seattle's "Editor On The Hill," who first nurtured my writing muse with assignments for the *Capitol Hill Times*. Apple pies are a specialty of mine primarily because of one such article, "Baking My First Apple Pie." After twelve pies, I finally got it right.

While living on Long Island, I was fortunate to meet Barbara Bretton, who not only became a dear friend, but encouraged me to write my first novel. She celebrates each of my book sales with me by sending a beautiful basket of flowers.

A move to Florida brought a new circle of friends. We've shared career highs and lows, passed babies around luncheon tables while deciding on book titles, wrote long into the night, knowing we weren't the only ones on a deadline, and supported each other at book signings, graduations, weddings and birthdays. I'm so thankful and honored to call Judy Cuevas, Joan Johnston, Barbara Parker, Diane Plasencia, Heather Graham Possezzere and Sherryl Woods my friends.

Special appreciation and thanks go to Dianne Moggy, Amy Moore-Benson and Damaris Rowland who always believed in me and *Ports of Call*.

And especially Rudi Schoeneweiss, who introduced me to the world of cruise ships and who has always been there to support me.

1

Julia

Tuscany, 1967

It wasn't easy to leave a lover.

In the early-dawn light, Julia crossed the cobble-stone courtyard of the ancient villa. Olive trees hugged its stone-and-stucco exterior, and the lemon trees in the nearby hills scented the air. Soon, she knew, church bells would summon the estate workers and villagers to morning mass. When she reached her rented Fiat, she stopped and turned.

Her gaze sought and found the arched window—tucked in the eaves of the villa and nearly obscured by vines—still shuttered from the night air. Despite two days and nights spent with Piero on the other side of that window, the same room where more than twenty years ago they had pretended to be husband and wife, Julia was no closer to knowing whether she should reveal the secrets she had kept from him.

Was it wrong to try to recapture the past?

Julia opened the door of the Fiat and tossed her purse onto the passenger seat. Something cold touched her calf and she jerked around.

Relief washed over her at the sight of the big fawn-colored dog and she laughed softly. How silly, she thought, to still be so suspicious, so on guard. She was forty-three years old and all traces of the war that had ravaged the area had disappeared. But on this visit to Piero's villa in the Tuscan hills it was as if time had stopped centuries before and the past was simply yesterday. Impulsively she knelt beside the mastiff.

"Buon giorno." Julia rubbed the dog behind his ears, something that she had learned in her two days here the dog loved. "I'm going to bring a little boy back with me. Tonight we will all walk in the vineyards together."

She cupped the dark muzzle in her hand and looked directly into the dog's doleful eyes. "Take good care of the marchese for me." She glanced at the villa and whispered, "You see, I love your master, too. "

With a whirl of her full-skirted stylish shirtwaist, Julia slid into the seat of the car. After rummaging in her leather bag for the key, she inserted it into the ignition and started the engine. She risked another glance at the window behind which Marchese Piero Falcone slept.

The decision that had prompted her to leave the warm bed she had shared with him for the past two nights still troubled her. If she was wrong, the journey she was about to embark on would have terrible consequences for those she loved.

Julia found her memories, so carefully locked away, returning. Memories of Piero. And the nights they had spent together. First during the war and then again eleven years ago when she had come to Europe for the wedding of Grace Kelly and Prince Rainier.

A few days ago she had impulsively contacted the Falcone offices in Genoa and asked for Piero. "I'm in Rome," she'd blurted. "Is it possible to see you?"

Julia had held her breath. Piero was married. She thought she had long ago accepted the fact, only to abruptly realize she had not. Feelings of jealousy and possessiveness had welled up. She'd sighed with relief when she heard his answer.

"I was planning to leave the palazzo here in Genoa and spend the weekend in the mountains." He'd cleared his throat. "You remember the Falcone villa in Tuscany?"

"Yes." *How could she have ever forgotten?*

Now Julia heard the distant chime of the village church bell. Jerking her gaze from the villa and checking that the mastiff was out of harm's way,

Julia stepped on the gas pedal and sped out of the courtyard. She didn't have far to go, only to the village where she had left Thorne, the dark-eyed, dark-haired boy she wanted Piero to meet. But the road was narrow and treacherous, bordered by steep ravines, and Julia let up on the gas pedal. It was just that she was so anxious to collect Thorne and return to the villa. She had been apart from him for two days. And her confession to Piero was long overdue.

Soon, Julia knew, loaves of freshly baked *pane toscana* would be pulled from the villa's kitchen ovens and Piero would awake to find her gone. Her note had been vaguely worded, saying only that she would return later that day with a surprise for him.

She was suddenly aware that the upcoming curve was approaching too rapidly. She stepped on the brakes. Nothing happened. She began to pump the brakes. Still nothing.

Julia had eluded death in these hills and valleys often enough to recognize the metallic taste of fear in her mouth.

Not now! she thought, fighting for control of the car. Especially not now. I have too many reasons to live!

Just as the sun rose with all its blinding brilliance on the far horizon, a force greater than her own wrenched the wheel from her hands and the Fiat was suddenly airborne.

* * *

The light, whiter and brighter than any she'd ever known, beckoned. Despite its powerful pull, Julia was reluctant to move toward it. She was a woman who had always put loyalty and duty before her own desires.

It was strange yet remarkable to see herself, like a broken doll tossed on the rock-strewn ravine, her long golden hair tangled and windblown, her blue dress soaked with blood, a slim leg twisted beneath her body.

The light grew even brighter and drew Julia closer. Shadows formed and seemed to take shape. But then there was a movement below and Julia's focus shifted back to the scene beneath her.

Standing on the road by the spot where her brakes had failed and sent her hurtling into space. Disbelief filtered into her with crushing force. How was it possible? Julia thought they had been so careful; now she knew they had not.

Oh, God. Thorne…was he safe? Her thoughts, like butterfly wings, beat and fluttered in panic.

She turned again to the light. Now she could distinguish the shapes in the light, faces she recognized. Her grandmother smiled encouragingly when Julia hesitated.

How could she leave Thorne and Piero when they were in such danger? While her enemy—and theirs—still lived?

* * *

Miles away in the courtyard of the Falcone villa, the mastiff suddenly rose and howled, its mournful wail sending shivers through the inhabitants of the villa and echoing throughout the valley.

2

The Christening

Miami, Florida, 1999

"Welcome to the Port of Miami." The white-haired director of one of the world's busiest ports placed a lush bouquet of yellow roses in Adriana's arms. Angling his stocky body to allow the photographer kneeling before them to take an official picture, he added, "It is an honor to have you and the Falcone Line join us."

Then why was it so difficult to get docking space for my ship? Adriana thought. She forced a smile, holding it a fraction longer than necessary to allow the scrambling photographers on the pier below the newly erected scaffold to get their shots. "It's a pleasure to be here," she responded with all the diplomacy gained from having spent years in the public spotlight. *It should be a pleasure. It cost enough.*

Mentally Adriana tallied the expense for the new Falcone Line terminal and the permanent berthing of one of her ships—and one man's determined efforts to undermine her every step of the way. "There were times I wasn't certain this event would take place."

"As you can see—" he made a sweeping gesture with his hand "—it most certainly has."

Miami's power elite was out in force, as if the arrival of yet another cruise ship in the port was not an almost everyday occurrence. Standing on the wooden platform with Adriana was a host of city and county officials, including the mayor of Miami and several city commissioners. Her personal assistant and a company publicist were her only buffers from the press of bodies.

It was midmorning and the busloads of departing cruise-line passengers were nearly gone. The nearby terminals stood empty of luggage. Porters joked and smoked while cruise ship personnel took advantage of the lull to attend to duties, largely ignoring the group of invited guests congregating on the pier below Adriana.

The huge turnout had nothing to do with the ship—one Adriana had risked a portion of her personal fortune to finance—or the christening ceremony about to begin.

They had come for one reason and one reason only.

To see her.

Or rather, to see the Marchesa Falcone, former

Vogue model known as the "The Face" until her storybook wedding to a man more than twice her age had turned her into an international celebrity spokesperson for his Genoa-based fleet of ships. Tragically widowed and heir to the centuries-old Italian Falcone Line, she was now more widely known as the Queen of the Seas.

Adriana could feel their eyes on her, probing for flaws but willing to settle for any imperfection. A wrinkled dress. Chipped nail polish. Dark roots on her cap of hair, evidence that the spun-sugar color wasn't real. Anything. Once—God, how she could have been so naive?—she had reveled in the exposure. As an Arizona-born college girl turned runway model, she had loved the attention. Until the day she had learned the terrible consequences of being public property.

If she had a choice now, which she didn't, it would be to live a secluded life, perhaps at the villa in Tuscany. Now she lived by the sea in Genoa, where the ocean's constant ebb and flow reminded her of all that life had given her. And all that life had taken away.

The process of acquiring a terminal and berths for her ships at the booming Port of Miami had been a nightmare, an endless series of obstacles including bureaucratic red tape, regulations and one man's insidious opposition. Whether the enormous expenditure of capital and man-hours and the headaches would compensate for it was yet to be seen. But for a few hours on this lovely late-spring morning, with the intoxicating scent of roses filling her nostrils, Adriana wanted to simply enjoy the thrill of being acknowledged for her accomplishment.

She was another step closer to fulfilling a promise.

"Do you see him?" Carla, her assistant, whispered in her ear. "He's supposed to look like Richard Gere."

"You've seen too many American films." Adriana smiled. "Besides, he's absolutely the *last* man I want to see today."

Since reaching the decision to open a terminal in Miami and position a Falcone Line ship in an American port, Adriana had heard Thorne Weston's name mentioned far too many times. Now even Carla seemed in awe of the man who not only owned the largest and most successful cruise line at the port, but appeared capable of orchestrating everything to his own advantage.

Or trying to.

A gentle nudge from Carla reminded her that she had an important role in the ceremony. Following the port director's brief welcome speech, Adriana handed Carla the roses and accepted the oversize bottle of champagne, a jeroboam specially commissioned for the christening. The bottle was warm from the sun and heavy in her hands. The crowd became quiet as Adriana stepped up to the fragile railing that separated her from the cruise ship looming over them. She adjusted the bottle's heavy weight to be certain she would not let go of it too soon. A short expanse of water separated the ship and its gleaming white hull from the platform. Perhaps it was an old seaman's superstition, but she wanted no mistakes, no second or third tries. It was necessary for the bottle to swing across and crack cleanly.

"I christen this ship..."

Adriana paused, the moment a poignant one. The ship represented not only a chunk of her personal fortune, but a graveside promise to her late husband, Piero. The ceremony was the culmination of years of hard work and the beginning of a new era of renewed prosperity for the Falcone Line. Taking a deep breath, she released the bottle. As it swung across the chasm, her voice rang with confidence and pride, "The M.S. *Castello*!"

The bottle shattered on impact. The smack of breaking glass was accompanied by a burst of applause, suddenly replaced by a collective gasp of shock.

The ship's white hull had been christened, it appeared, not with champagne, but with blood.

Shocked by the stain of crimson on the ship's hull, Adriana rigidly maintained the impression of composure. Without missing a beat, she motioned for another bottle, determined to finish what she had started. Stepping away from the railing, she registered Carla's quick intake of breath. Her assistant's horrified gaze centered on her midsection.

Adriana looked down at the dress she had carefully chosen for its simplicity and American designer. The white linen dress was splattered with blood. It looked like she had been shot.

Has the horror of the past somehow followed me here to this new country, this new beginning?

Adriana forced back the bile in her throat and willed her legs to remain steady. And then somehow managed to smile into the clicking shutters of a multitude of cameras. The next ten minutes were critical. No trace of the fear uncoiling like a sleeping serpent in the recesses of her mind could be evident. She must fulfill the pledge she'd made to her husband at his graveside. She could not, would not, jeopardize all she had plotted and worked so hard to achieve.

Adriana waited while stewards hastily attached another champagne bottle and handed it to her. Her heart in her throat, she let the second bottle fly. It smashed and champagne spilled, mixing with the blood.

Adriana let out the breath she'd been holding and turned once again to face the crowd.

They had gotten what they'd come for.

She wasn't perfect after all.

* * *

Thorne Weston's gunmetal-gray limousine sped along the palm-lined drive on Dodge Island, slowed for the automatic wave-through at the customs checkpoint, bypassing waiting trucks, taxis and cars that weren't as fortunate, and minutes later veered to the left. Dead ahead was the Falcone Line terminal and the newest addition to its fleet, the M.S. *Castello.*

Although ships of this size—the impressive equivalent of a twelve-story hotel—were a familiar sight to Thorne, it was impossible to ignore it. The Falcone Line colors of black and gold were a distinct contrast to his Blue Ribbon Cruises colors of yellow and blue, which dominated the port. The *Castello*'s funnel was distinctive, too—black with an oval inset containing the Falcone crest, a golden falcon.

Thorne instructed his longtime chauffeur to pull up beside the several other limousines parked in a reserved and guarded section on the pier alongside the docked ship. The scaffold from the christening ceremony was already being dismantled.

The ship, the first of two sister ships commissioned by the Falcone Line and built in a German shipyard, had just completed the crossing from Bremerhaven. For promotional purposes, the christening ceremony had been postponed until its arrival in the ship's home port of Miami. The day before a flotilla of pleasure boats had escorted the ship into Government Cut, a man-made channel dredged frequently to allow cruise ships passage.

Thorne Weston seldom adjusted his agenda to attend a rival company's function. But Falcone was not just any rival.

As the owner of Blue Ribbon Cruises, the most successful cruise-ship operation in North America, there was nothing Thorne wanted that he didn't get. Those who considered themselves part of his inner circle joked that he had merely to think of something and it appeared—or disappeared.

But he had been unable to wish away the M.S. *Castello* and its owner.

Thorne climbed out of the limo. Slinging his sport coat over his shoulder, he'd taken no more than two or three steps when his attention was snagged by the woman walking up to him.

Nevada Sinclair was striking enough to stop traffic, and sometimes she actually did. Almost six feet tall and wearing a severely tailored navy suit, she was still as much a showstopper as when Thorne had first seen her in a Las Vegas revue. He had never regretted persuading her to return with him to Miami.

In the years since, she had risen to the position of vice president of his sales and marketing department. It was still a toss-up whether her most important assets were her business abilities or her long shapely legs and perfect breasts.

"If that suit is supposed to keep a man's mind on business," he said, "it's failing miserably."

Nevada was not only gorgeous but tough. As a kid, she'd had to fend for herself, and now, instead of schoolyard bullies, she took on the corporate world and usually emerged the winner. She might look like a lady, but Thorne knew she had bigger balls than most longshoremen.

She laughed, and although he noted the slight darkening of her brown eyes, he ignored his physical reaction. "Seen the new Falcone terminal?" he asked.

"Nothing distracts you, does it?"

Recognizing the thinly veiled dig at their long-standing feud regarding his business-before-pleasure mentality, Thorne acknowledged the barb with a slight smile. "No," he said, and began walking.

She pivoted on her signature five-inch fuck-me heels and swung into step beside him. "To answer your question, no, I haven't toured the ship yet. Luke went on ahead. Said he'd meet us there."

"What happened?" He nodded toward the *Castello* where a crew was at work, hosing down the side of the ship.

"You're late. You missed the show."

Thorne slowed his pace, curious. "I've seen a dozen ship christenings."

"Not like this one."

"Did the marchesa use a more expensive brand of champagne?"

"Not exactly. She christened the goddamned ship with blood."

The small group had been hastily assembled in Adriana's luxurious stateroom. Captain Angelo Funari was the last to arrive, and when he did, Adriana walked to the bar for a drink. She took her time, adding ice to a crystal glass and pouring bottled water into it. Although she had changed her blood-stained clothing, her hand still trembled. She stalled for time by plucking a fresh slice of lime from a dish, leisurely squeezing its juice into the water and dropping the rind into the glass. Then she placed the glass on a monogrammed napkin and picked them both up. At last she took a deep breath and faced the group.

Captain Funari and his Italian first officer were both strikingly handsome in their uniforms, white a perfect foil for their dark complexions. The captain had not chosen a seat but had remained standing, politely waiting for her to invite him to sit. His face tightened when he realized her failure to issue the invitation was not an oversight, but deliberate.

"I would like to hear your explanation for what happened, Captain," she said.

"I have none," he replied.

"That's not good enough." Captain Funari's ears reddened but Adriana had no pity for him. "What *can* you tell me?"

"I can only guess that whoever tampered with the bottle wanted to cause you embarrassment."

Would he dare?

"I don't have to tell you how important this week is to the Falcone Line. An incident such as this has the potential to become a public-relations disaster. I've already instructed the public-relations department to mingle with our guests and, if necessary, treat the incident as someone's idea of a joke."

Adriana paced to the window to look out at the waters of Government Cut. Her stomach was jumpy.

"I have taken steps to ensure nothing further will happen," the captain said.

Adriana glanced at the diamond-encrusted watch on her wrist. "We're already running late, Captain Funari, but I expect you to have some answers for me before this ship leaves port. Whoever it was had to have help—someone in your crew. Find him."

He nodded and moved toward the door and escape. "It is nearly time for luncheon to be served," he said. "Will you join us as arranged?"

"Of course, Captain. When have I ever shirked my duties?" There was an edge to her voice and, at the sudden quirk of the captain's eyebrow, Adriana realized she had allowed the strain of the morning's events to show. "I just need a few minutes with my assistant," she said. "I'll meet you on the promenade deck."

"Certainly, Marchesa." Nodding stiffly, the captain and his first officer left the suite.

It was only when the door closed behind the two men that Adriana realized her hands were trembling again.

From a nearby lounge chair, Carla conspicuously cleared her throat. "Why do you insist on being so polite? Why don't you get tough with them for once? Say, 'Who's running this motherfucker?'"

"It's not my style."

"You haven't lived in Italy long enough, that's the problem."

For the past five years, Carla had functioned as Adriana's personal assistant, a position that sometimes seemed more like that of a good friend or, at moments like this, a far-too-outspoken friend. Tall and big-boned with a long face, Carla rose, juggling a leather notebook stuffed with paper and notes. "Take my advice and quit being such a lady," she went on. "Just remember, there's only one place where a man's best on top—and even that's open to debate."

"You should know."

"Now you're getting there, Marchesa." Carla checked her lipstick in a gold-framed mirror, part of a custom-crafted built-in against a nearby wall. Carla's gaze connected with hers. "For once let some of these guys see the claws I know you've got. A scratch or two wouldn't hurt any of them."

Adriana placed the crystal glass on a silver coaster. "After the fiasco today, I may take your advice. A new country may require a new attitude."

"Start with that gift I gave you yesterday. Have you opened it?"

"Yes, but it seems ludicrous." Adriana picked up the box containing a revolver tiny enough to be strapped to a thigh. "And looks uncomfortable."

"Who knows?" Carla shrugged. "Maybe it will save your life. Especially since you refuse to have a bodyguard."

"I don't need a bodyguard."

"With an enemy like Thorne Weston you do. Hell, I'd want all the protection I could get. I'm betting he'll show up. He hasn't caused all this commotion for nothing."

Adriana shook her head. "I don't understand it. Why does my opening an office in Miami gall him so much? After all, what's one more ship in port?"

"That's simple, Marchesa." Carla preened in the doorway. "The ship isn't his."

Except for several waiters picking up empty glasses and rearranging chairs, Thorne was alone on the Lido deck of the M.S. *Castello*. Nevada had gone to the reception area to greet the writer from a national magazine and explain why he, Thorne,

couldn't do the interview he'd promised right now.
She'd lots of experience at it, since Thorne had little
time for the press and often cancelled—or as in this
instance postponed—appointments.

Thorne was glad to have a few minutes alone. His
shirt was open at the throat and the breeze coming
in from the bay ruffled his dark hair. Some might
find the noonday sun too intense, but he reveled in
it. He loved the feel of the sun on his skin, the scents
carried by the ocean breeze and the sight of the sparkling blue water. Legs slightly spread, he felt the
gentle motion of the enormous ship, as familiar to
him as his own heartbeat. Although it happened far
too infrequently, one of his favorite activities was
walking the deserted decks of one of his ships late
at night, with only the starry sky overhead for company, and feeling the power of the huge throbbing
engines displacing tons of water as the ship plowed
through tropical waters.

Like so many others, the magazine journalist
probably thought he had it all. Power. Wealth. Pres-
tige. Each year, his name moved higher on the
Forbes 500 list, making it harder for him to maintain
his privacy, his distance from the seekers who
wanted more from him than he cared to give. His
private jet, with its own pilots and stewards, was
always ready to leave with an hour's notice. And
the *Lady Julia II*, his two-hundred-foot yacht, the
second he'd had built at a renowned Finnish ship-

yard, was docked in a heavily guarded slip in Fort Lauderdale. One phone call and its engines would be running, ready to take him anywhere in the world he wished to go.

But today there was no other place on earth he'd rather be than on this Falcone ship.

His plans had been in place for months, and he fully expected to achieve the desired results. He stared up at the Falcone crest on the ship's funnel, the stack rising like a cylinder from the heart of the ship. The proud bird seemed to mock him. But he would have the last laugh. Soon the marchesa's ship would belong to him. And when it did, he would obliterate the symbol of what he hated most in the world—the Falcone name.

Leaning on the railing, Thorne surveyed the Port of Miami and Government Cut—his kingdom.

"Decided to come, after all?" Thorne asked

"Yeah, well, you know me when it comes to beautiful women. I couldn't pass up an opportunity to meet a legend."

Thorne smiled, not surprised that of all people Luke would be the first to find him. For Luke knew him well. At the conclusion of a six-month-long voyage, he had stepped off a chartered yacht and bumped into Thorne on the dock. Five hours and twice that number of beers later, Luke had agreed to work for him.

Like Nevada, Luke had joined Blue Ribbon

Cruises when Thorne was still struggling to make the payroll every week. Now Luke could well afford the hairstylist who attempted to tame his curly hair by brushing it off his forehead and, as a concession to Luke's love of surfing, left the back layer long enough to brush the shoulders of his Armani suit. Outgoing and athletic, Luke was not only adept at managing the operations end of Blue Ribbon Cruises but extremely sought after for community fund-raisers, particularly bachelor auctions. Although tinted sunglasses hid his gray-blue eyes from view, Thorne suspected that Luke found his change of plans amusing.

Luke shifted, draping himself along the railing beside Thorne.

"I hear they call her the Queen of the Seas," Thorne said. "Suppose she is?"

Luke frowned. "What does it matter, Thorne? Your plans only include ruining her."

"Not getting cold feet, are you?"

Luke stared straight ahead. Thorne knew that everywhere he looked he saw only what the two of them had built together over the years.

"If I had cold feet, I would never have accepted your job offer," Luke said. "I guess it all comes with the territory, doesn't it? It's just that sometimes I wonder when it will stop. When will enough be enough?"

"I don't know, Luke. I do know that the time

hasn't come yet." Thorne shoved away from the railing and his glance swept over the decks, noting the perfection of everything he saw. "Today I've moved a step closer. This ship is going to belong to me—and a lot sooner than you or the marchesa thinks."

"Where's Nevada?"

"She's meeting Sandra somebody, from *Insider* magazine. Wants to do some sort of piece on me. You know, the usual."

"I thought you were going to keep a lower profile this year," Luke said.

"I was, but her editor is a friend of one of our board members and it's a favor to Harry, so what the hell." Thorne touched the ring on his finger, a ring he'd chosen to wear for the first time that day. "I guess it's about time we got this reception started."

3

The Ring

"How soon can I leave?" Adriana asked Carla.

Faces and names were beginning to blur. The two-story showroom was filled with guests and Adriana felt as if she had talked to all of them. Huge buffet tables overflowed with elaborate foods, and white-gloved waiters circulated with goblets of champagne. Muscles stiff from the strain of maintaining a perpetual smile, Adriana said, "I don't know how much longer I can stay here. I'm dead on my feet."

"Jet lag," said Carla, who always managed to hover nearby. "You'll recall I urged you to take an earlier flight to allow time to rest up."

"I told you the meeting in Bremerhaven was important. In case you've forgotten in all this hoopla, I've signed a multimillion-dollar contract that includes a sister ship to this one, currently under construction, and taken an option to build a third ship. Construction at the shipyard is going too slowly and

I had hoped to find out why they're so far behind schedule.'' Adriana stifled a yawn. ''Is there anybody I haven't met yet?''

''You've had a chat with the mayor, and three of the county commissioners have confirmed travel on the upcoming cruise-to-nowhere,'' Carla ticked off. ''Oh, and over there, the tall, rather portly gentleman, he's—''

''The publisher of the *Miami Herald*.'' Adriana caught his eye across the room and smiled. ''We have a luncheon appointment next week. Their travel editor is booked on the first cruise with a front-page Sunday follow-up.''

Carla flipped quickly through a small notepad, held discreetly in the palm of her hand. ''That's about it. Except for—''

''Mr. Weston.'' Adriana kept her tone cool and impersonal, though she was anxiously awaiting his appearance. ''I'm glad he had the decency to stay away.''

''Oops. You spoke too soon.'' Carla nodded toward the lower entrance to the showroom. ''If I'm not mistaken, that gorgeous hunk who just entered with an entourage is none other than your Mr. Weston.''

''Not *mine*, Carla.'' Adriana held her assistant's gaze. ''You've obviously fallen under the spell of this tropical climate and forgotten that the beautiful blue waters around us are filled with sharks.''

"Well, if you're going to pass, Marchesa," Carla said, fanning herself with the notepad, "I'd love to get bitten."

"No doubt you would." As she turned to follow Carla's rapt gaze, Adriana briefly envied her assistant's ability to live in the moment. The seriousness of her own life left little room for laughter.

Or lovers.

One look at Thorne Weston and Adriana completely understood Carla's breathless excitement. The description of tall, dark and handsome fitted him to a T. He also had that indefinable quality that made him seem larger than life, a charisma that overshadowed those around him, even the equally attractive man who accompanied him and the tall striking woman who touched his arm lightly and nodded in Adriana's direction.

Thorne Weston had presence. Adriana had known only a few such people in her life, but all had shared similar characteristics: supreme confidence and unshakable faith in themselves. Now, as he separated from his group and moved in her direction, she felt a sense of hushed expectation.

He moved through the crowd like a head of state, quietly shaking hands, nodding a greeting or two and occasionally rewarding some lucky recipient with a smile. He was dressed casually in a sport coat, slacks and open-collared shirt. But there was nothing else casual about him; he moved with determination and purpose.

As Adriana stood waiting for him to reach her, his gaze fixed on her, roaming from the tips of her Italian leather pumps and lingering on her legs and breasts.

Adriana struggled to remain impassive under his scrutiny.

When at last he stood before her, he looked her in the eye and said, "Adriana Falcone, I presume. I'm Thorne Weston."

He moved a step closer and she resisted the urge to step back. She frowned as she realized she'd seen his eyes—or eyes just like his—sometime in the past. A rich dark brown and long-lashed. "Have we met before, Mr. Weston?"

His firm lips curved in an indulgent smile. "I doubt there is a man alive who would forget meeting you, Marchesa."

"I'm surprised you found time to join us."

The curve of his mouth disappeared. His tone was cool. "I'm always interested in a new ship."

"I'm well acquainted with your interest in someone else's ship, Mr. Weston." *Not to mention the money and aggravation you cost me.*

"But I'm remiss." His dark eyes remained fixed on her face. "Let me introduce you to my friends."

She'd been so focused on Thorne that she'd forgotten his companions.

"Luke Benedict and Nevada Sinclair," Thorne said.

As she acknowledged the swift introductions, Adriana knew Carla was noting their names for future reference. She needed to know everything possible about Thorne Weston, including his close associates. Thorne paused, allowing Ms. Sinclair to introduce an older, well-dressed woman, who'd come up behind them.

"Marchesa, this is Sandra Nelson, a journalist doing a feature article for *Insider* magazine."

"It's a pleasure to meet you, Marchesa. I'd consider it an honor to include you in this piece—it's about the growing popularity of the cruise market." The woman's face was flushed with excitement. "Especially your decision to position your new ship in Miami rather than your company's home port of Genoa."

Uncomfortable, Adriana took a step back and Carla smoothly interjected, "The marchesa does not do interviews, Ms. Nelson. However, I'd be happy to make an appointment for you with the head of our public relations department."

"Oh, but—"

"Excuse us." Thorne Weston addressed himself to no one in particular, but his hand closed on Adriana's upper arm. Before she could protest, he said, "There are a few matters I'd like to discuss with you. Is there somewhere more private?"

Guests were everywhere in the tiered showroom and touring the various decks. Perhaps because she was tired and had planned to adjourn to her own suite, Adriana decided it afforded the privacy they needed. And she would be on her own turf. She turned and motioned to Carla. "Please make sure Mr. Weston's associates get everything they need," she instructed. "Also, have a bottle of champagne sent to my cabin."

Moments later Adriana ushered Thorne Weston into her lavishly appointed suite, a combination living and dining room, large bedroom with bath and private veranda. She'd personally chosen the soothing tones of cream, beige and soft gold. But, as the door shut behind them, even these failed to soothe the tense knot that had formed in her stomach.

"You're an unusual man, Mr. Weston." Adriana waited for Thorne to choose a love seat and then sat on the matching one opposite him. "After all the obstacles you placed in my way, I confess I'm more than a little surprised to see you here today."

He stretched his arms out along the back of the seat and studied her. "I thought it was time we met."

"Actually we just missed meeting each other ten days ago." She noticed a subtle shift of his eyes. "You left Bremerhaven at about the time I arrived. From a distance, I saw the megaship you have under construction and understand you're considering having yet another vessel built at the same shipyard.''

"You shouldn't listen to rumors.''

"I spoke with your people in Bremerhaven.'' She toyed with the gold bracelet on her wrist.

"Well, I may do future shipbuilding in Helsinki rather than Bremerhaven.''

"What advantage does the Helsinki shipyard have over the one in Bremerhaven?'' she asked curiously.

"Did I say there was one?''

"No,'' Adriana admitted, "you didn't.''

She rose to answer a quiet knock at the door and admitted a cabin attendant with a chilled cooler. She turned to Thorne and asked, "Would you like some champagne? Or something else to drink?''

"Champagne would be fine,'' he answered, rising to join her at the bar and open the champagne. "Although I sincerely hope you don't expect me to toast your success.''

"I trust you don't mind if *I* do.''

He gave nothing away, she thought, searching his stoic expression for some clue to his feelings as he popped the cork. She turned and removed a fluted glass from the tray and handed it to him. "Surely there's room for more than one successful cruise line in the Port of Miami, Mr. Weston.''

"I couldn't agree more,'' he acknowledged, accepting the glass. In the process, his fingers brushed hers. "So long as it's not a Falcone ship.''

"The Falcone name is synonymous with luxurious oceangoing vessels," she said, feeling a spurt of anger.

"Outdated. And undercapitalized. If it weren't for your own fortune, would there even be a Falcone Line today?"

His bluntness had the force of a slap. Her spine stiffened with the realization that Thorne Weston played every game to win. "Enjoy your inch of champagne, Mr. Weston," she said, raising her glass in a toast. "Because it's the last inch the Falcone Line will give you in Miami."

"Don't you consider your recent multimillion-dollar payment to a shipyard on the verge of bankruptcy a threat to such success?" One dark eyebrow slanted upward. "Since you listen so avidly to rumors, I thought surely you had heard the latest regarding the Bremerhaven shipyard."

"Bankruptcy?" For one frozen moment, Adriana saw her worst fears realized and her suspicions crystallized. In the next second, she realized Thorne Weston had outmaneuvered her. "If what you say is true, how convenient for you, Mr. Weston. Is this yet another one of your games?"

Raising his champagne flute, he smiled and said, "It's a small playing field. And getting smaller all the time."

As he took his first sip, Adriana noticed a ring on his finger. A second later she saw it in more detail and choked on her champagne. "Where did you get that ring?"

"Quite distinctive, don't you think?" Transferring his glass from right to left, he extended his hand. Intently observing her, he added, "For years, this ring has hung from a chain around my neck. Today's the first time I've worn it on my finger."

"Take it off!" The champagne in her glass sloshed over the rim as she hastily set it on the bar. "It doesn't belong to you!"

The heavy signet ring was just as Piero had always described it to her: a gold falcon, twin blood-red rubies on each shoulder, against a black onyx bezel.

The Falcone crest.

Raising her gaze from the ring to Thorne's face, Adriana received another shock. His dark eyes, always so enigmatic, now burned with such angry intensity that she immediately regretted being alone with him.

"I don't know how you got it, but that ring belonged to my late husband and I want it back."

He ignored her demand and said, "There's an inscription in Latin inside the band. *Meum et tuum.*"

"Mine and thine," whispered Adriana, needing no further confirmation. "That ring was stolen from my husband. Take it off." She gripped his wrist and her nails dug into his flesh. "Give me the ring."

He laughed. "So you play games, after all, Marchesa." With extraordinary ease, he pried her hand from his wrist and held it loosely in his grip.

Adriana had not felt such fury and helplessness since she'd stood beside her husband's closed coffin. She, who had every reason to abhor violence, finally understood what drove people to commit desperate acts. Adriana's gaze lifted from the region of Thorne Weston's heart to his dark, mocking eyes.

"This ring was given to me by a special woman named Julia and I have no intention of giving it up."

"What do you want?" she asked in a whisper.

"I have one thing that belonged to the Falcone family. I intend to have much more." His hand captured her chin and his thumb brushed the length of her lower lip. "Including perhaps even you, Marchesa."

Adriana jerked her head from his grasp. Her face burned where his hand had touched her. "I've been threatened before, Mr. Weston, in ways far beyond your limited imagination."

He dropped her hand. "Then I suggest, Marchesa, that you examine all the possibilities, especially since I've been told you christened your ship today with blood. Evidently I'm not the only one who wasn't happy to see a Falcone ship arrive in Miami."

4

The Interview

"**Y**ou aren't answering your phone," Nevada said.

Thorne opened the door to his Miami Beach penthouse. Although it was nearly midnight, he hadn't been asleep. He'd chosen to ignore the occasional ring of his private line and deliberately not returned Nevada's calls. As much as he wished to be alone, he knew Nevada would use the key he'd given her if he didn't answer her knock.

"I was working on the blueprints for the new ship." Thorne stepped aside to allow Nevada to enter, but his glance skittered away from the question in her brown eyes. She was dressed in formfitting jeans, a tank top covered with a gauzy shirt left unbuttoned but tucked in. Simple, but sexy as hell. "Things were going well and I didn't want to be distracted. Something I know from experience you're good at."

"It doesn't have to be that way, you know." She

kicked off her heels and walked toward the built-in bar angled on a far wall. "I'm perfectly able to just stop by for a drink and a little conversation. Maybe just look at those plans with you. It doesn't have to be anything more."

"Yeah, right."

Thorne watched her open a bottle of white wine and pour it over ice. The instant he'd seen her sashay across a Las Vegas showroom stage—wearing little besides an exotic headdress, fancy G-string and tassels covering her nipples—Nevada had ignited all his senses. He'd had a devil of a time convincing her to return to Miami with him. She was an independent person.

The first few months they had lived together. Then, when her job at Blue Ribbon Cruises became more demanding, Nevada had gotten her own apartment, saying she wanted a career, not a relationship. Only it hadn't worked out that way. The chemistry between them was just too powerful. So they had both settled for late-night rendezvous, an occasional noontime quickie, but more often, a few days stolen from their busy schedules on some secluded island hideaway.

And they had each learned to look the other way when either one of them got involved with someone else.

Thorne guessed it was just luck—or maybe their own drive and determination—that had kept them both single and relatively uninvolved with anyone else over the years. Not that he had any regrets. Normally he welcomed a nighttime visit from Nevada.

Just not tonight.

Thorne joined Nevada at the bar and retrieved a beer from a nearly invisible waist-high refrigerator. "I've heard some disquieting rumors about the Bremerhaven shipyard, and I want this ship finished as soon as possible."

"Is that what's really bothering you?"

"Sure," he said, tilting his head to take a swig from the bottle. "What did you think it was?"

"Thought maybe you were bothered by the Falcone business." Nevada strolled to a set of French doors, opened one and stepped out onto the balcony.

Thorne followed her outside and stood beside her while she studied the view of the Atlantic Ocean. The air was cool, the sky starry and the horizon dotted with causeway lights.

"The marchesa's been a busy woman."

"So you've seen the news?" Nevada laughed, a low throaty sound that normally delighted Thorne. "I've been hesitant to fill you in on the latest. Besides, I know you've been tied up in meetings with the shipbuilders and didn't want to bother you."

Thorne set his beer bottle on a nearby table, the sound of glass hitting glass so loud that Nevada gave a start. "What's she done now?"

"She's granted an interview to Kathryn Tyson. It's the first time she's allowed an American journalist, let alone a television journalist, to interview her. It's scheduled to air in a week or two."

"It's because of that goddamned photo of her in that blood-splattered dress," he muttered. "It was only cow's blood. Probably put there by two disgruntled crewmen who mysteriously left the ship that day and boarded a plane headed for a third world country."

"There's been a feeding frenzy because of it. *People* magazine's doing a spread in next week's edition. The lucky guy who shot that picture made a small fortune and resurrected that whole bit about her husband's kidnapping and murder. She's hired one of New York's best public relations firms to handle all the requests from the press."

Thorne frowned, considering the implications for his plans. "How bad is it?"

Nevada took a sip of wine, the ice clinking noisily in the goblet, and Thorne, for a brief moment, wondered why her hand was shaking. "I know someone at the agency she's hired. She wants to buy a chunk of TV airtime and they're already working on commercial scripts."

Thorne gripped the iron railing so hard his knuckles turned white. "In other words, it's not going to be as easy as I thought to make the Marchesa Adriana Falcone go away."

Nevada reached out and covered his hand with her own. Her body leaned intimately into his and he felt the familiar stirring of interest.

"The marchesa has leased a place over there." Nevada nodded toward a cluster of distant lights. "On Fisher Island."

Thorne reached for the button on her jeans with one hand and moved the other to cup her buttocks.

Anything to keep from hearing more.

"She's not going to go away, Weston."

Nevada stepped into his arms, her body hot and fluid against his own. Before his mouth could cover hers, she whispered, "The marchesa's here to stay."

Genoa, Italy

Since her return to Genoa, Adriana had made several visits to the archive room. The solitude had been a welcome respite from the frenetic activities of the past few weeks. Tucked in a remote section of the vast Falcone palazzo, the room was dark and austere, its many shelves lined with volumes so worn and old that the books were dry and delicate. Over centuries, the Falcone family's history had been recorded and collected here—births and deaths logged into family Bibles, business journals, logs and formal documents assembled by caretakers.

"What are you looking for in here?"

Adriana glanced up from the dusty archive and

removed her reading glasses. Donatella, a distant
Falcone cousin, stood in the doorway. Married to
Emilio Donato, who ran the day-to-day operations
of the Falcone Line, Donatella had lived in the palazzo since she was a young girl and often acted as
if she was its mistress and owner, not Adriana. She
had once been engaged to Adriana's late husband's
older brother, who'd died in the Second World War.
If he had lived, the palazzo they were in, as well as
all the other Falcone holdings, would have been
hers. Today Donatella was dressed exquisitely, but
severely, in the finest of black cashmere. She strode
into the room.

"I thought I might find some reference to Julia in
these family records," Adriana replied.

"And I told you I don't know anything about that
woman," Donatella said. "The books are fragile
and can be easily damaged by too much unnecessary
handling."

When she reached for the dusty book in Adriana's
hand, Adriana tightened her grip on it and said,
"Since I returned from Miami, I've asked you more
than once about this matter, Donatella. I've heard
that a woman named Julia reputedly lived in or near
this palazzo during the war. There must be some
mention of her in these records."

"I've cared for these records since 1942. If anyone named Julia was mentioned, I would know
about it." Donatella succeeded now in pulling the

book from Adriana's hands. "I'm afraid you've been misled about our family's relationship to this woman."

Donatella caressed the worn volume in her hands, the diamond and emeralds in her ornate ring sparkling, caught in a beam of sunlight filtering through an arched window high above. She put the volume in its proper place on a nearby shelf.

"I *hope* someone's misleading me," Adriana said. "But I could be more certain if I did some research to determine the truth of it."

"You forget, Adriana. It is best to leave the past in the past." Donatella regarded Adriana with flat unblinking eyes. "That woman called again."

Adriana sighed and rose from the trestle library table. "When you say 'that woman,' are you referring to Kathryn Tyson?"

"*Sì.*"

With her slim figure and long silver hair coiled at the nape of her neck, Donatella, in her early seventies, was striking. But her beauty was marred by her disagreeable attitude and coldness. "I don't like you giving her permission to film here in the palazzo."

"It will be fine, Donatella. I thought we'd use the large salon. The publicity alone is worth millions. Since the *Castello* sailed from Miami, our bookings have leaped ahead of projections. This interview could ensure the success of our operation. I needn't remind you how desperately we need capital for the new ships.''

"I still don't like it.''

Adriana shrugged. "It will all be over soon.'' She picked up her small notebook and slipped it into her pocket. There was no need to tell Donatella that she'd found something. A photograph of Piero taken with two young women. On the back were two names: Julia and Gemma. Gemma Sacco.

It was a beginning.

"Relax,'' Adriana said to herself ten days later on her way to her office in town. "Your interview with Kathryn Tyson is done. You don't have to think about it anymore.''

But every time, since the interview more than a week before, Adriana descended the portrait-lined staircase of the palazzo, she felt as if she was under the intense scrutiny of generations of Falcone men and women. Their solemn countenances and pursed lips seemed to reflect their unspoken disapproval of Adriana's allowing the American journalist to interview her.

Ten days before, Adriana had instructed her driver to deliver Ms. Tyson to the Alitalia airline terminal. The Mercedes had pulled away from the palazzo with an extremely pleased TV journalist, who had gotten an interview that not even *she* had expected.

Adriana had been disarmed by her interviewer's

gracious and charming manner, and so had been quite unprepared for the question, "You christened the *Castello* with blood, Marchesa. Is there any truth to the rumor that this was not a prank, as widely reported, but rather a warning to you?"

"A warning?"

"Yes, I understand your Italian cruise line encountered many difficulties when you entered the lucrative American cruise market."

Adriana had shrugged and said vaguely, "Competition is healthy for business, but not everyone always agrees...."

"Some of the photos were, frankly, rather horrifying, particularly the one of you with your dress stained with blood. At that moment, did you regret your decision to position a ship in Miami?"

"My late husband was a courageous man. As long as I bear his name, I intend to carry out his wishes. And Piero dreamed of Falcone ships sailing from American ports."

"Does that include never backing down from a battle, however unpleasant?"

"A battle?"

"I've been told that Thorne Weston of Blue Ribbon Cruises is less than thrilled with your presence at the Port of Miami. He's rumored to be interested in acquiring some of your ships."

Adriana had shrugged again. "But, of course,

there is only one response to this man, and to such an offer.''

''And that is?''

Adriana had looked directly into the camera and smiled. ''No.''

Shaking off the memory, Adriana walked in the door to her office. Carla hurried in immediately and tossed a pile of messages on her desk.

''You've done it this time,'' Carla said.

Adriana dropped her purse and briefcase on a nearby chair and thumbed through several of them. ''*People*? *Vanity Fair*?''

''That's only the beginning.'' Carla plunked down in the chair opposite Adriana's desk and massaged her neck muscles. ''The hounds have picked up the scent. Some of the storylines go like this— 'Another Conquest for the Queen of the Seas?', 'Queen of the Seas Collides with Iceberg Thorne Weston,' 'Will Thorne Weston melt the Ice Queen?'

''They're having a field day with this alleged rivalry between you and Thorne Weston ever since your remarks to Kathryn Tyson were broadcast last night to millions of American viewers. So much for your aversion to the limelight. You'd better get used to the paparazzi trailing you everywhere.''

''That explains the three motorcycles that followed me from the palazzo this morning.'' Adriana unbuttoned her pale blue suit jacket and shrugged out of it.

"I know you don't want advice from me, but you're going to get it, anyway. You'd better forget driving your own car until this dies down. Use your driver and the Mercedes. It's built for your protection."

"You're right, Carla. I don't want advice from you." Adriana smiled to soften her words and shoved the pile of messages toward her assistant. "Take these and decide on several for possible interviews. Once I know what Mr. Weston's next move will be, I'll decide whether or not any of these will be necessary."

Carla snorted. "You're being naive. You'll need them. The only question is when."

Adriana leaned back. "Have you been able to find out anything about that...other matter?"

Carla scowled. "I don't understand how you can bear to employ such an unpleasant man. He was positively rude when he stopped by the office yesterday and dropped off this large manila envelope." She leaned over Adriana's desk and extracted the envelope from beneath the stack of papers and brochures on her desk. "He said if you have any questions, you know how to get in touch with him."

Nico Lintner was an excellent and thorough private investigator, and Adriana had used him on several occasions. But this was the first time she had asked him to follow up on a personal matter, and she was anxious to read the results. She quickly scanned the report. "Can you clear my calendar for the remainder of the week, Carla?"

"Yes, although it will be difficult."

"Do it."

"I hope you have a good reason. Emilio is going to be furious if you miss the reception he's giving."

"This is more important." Adriana carefully re-sealed the envelope. "Book a flight for me to Rome."

5

The Mustang and the Mistress

Miami

Thorne couldn't get Adriana Falcone out of his mind, but he was determined to try.

The day, already hot and sunny but with cooling trade winds, was simply too beautiful to resist, and he'd impulsively reached for the Mustang's keys when he'd left early that morning. The restored Mustang convertible always attracted attention. It had occurred to him that he was as much of an attraction as his car. He was easily recognized, since hardly a day went by when his photo wasn't in some newspaper or magazine.

In shirtsleeves with his collar open, his dark hair blowing in the wind, Thorne could forget about the thousand and one things awaiting his attention at the Blue Ribbon offices in northwest Miami. Elton John's voice on the radio singing about finding the simple things in life struck a chord. He supposed driving the Mustang this morning was his attempt to reclaim the simplicity of a life he'd long since left behind.

He still remembered the thrill of purchasing the classic car in restored mint condition in the late 1980s. His ships had been starting to leave with a full load of passengers each week, and suddenly he could afford such luxuries. He now had a limousine and a full-time chauffeur to drive him wherever he desired, as well as several smaller luxury automobiles for personal use. But when he was behind the wheel of the Mustang, he felt the weight of responsibility lessen, problems diminish and solutions seem not so impossible.

Changing lanes to avoid a slow-moving semi-trailer, Thorne heard an indignant blast of a horn. He laughed out loud as he gunned the engine and switched lanes again. As if cutting someone off in traffic would bother him. As if the possibility of some fist-waving driver reaching for a weapon and taking aim at him or his beloved lemon-yellow convertible would even cause him to blink.

His days were peppered with threats from individuals much more intimidating than those speeding along beside him, all testing the posted speed limits and a few who, like himself, couldn't care less if a policeman decided to pull him over.

After last night, he had only one worry.

What was he going to do about the Marchesa Adriana Falcone?

As evidenced by the Tyson interview the night before, the Queen of the Seas—or, as he thought of her, the Italian Ice Queen—was definitely not afraid of him.

Stomping on the gas pedal, he decided it was time she learned he could be her worst nightmare.

Ten minutes later Thorne tossed his car keys to the attendant in the underground parking garage. "Take good care of her, Tom."

"Sure thing, boss."

Smiling at Tom's whistle of appreciation, Thorne nearly ran into Luke, who blocked his path to the elevator.

"What's with the car?" Luke asked. "Hell, you haven't driven that baby to the office in years. Aren't you afraid someone will scratch it? Or, for that matter, breathe on it?"

Thorne jabbed Luke's muscular arm. "I just felt like a change of pace this morning."

"Well," Luke said, "my car phone rang all the way here with news that the lobby is staked out by nearly every news agency in the country. There's nothing like speculation about a rivalry—both in the boardroom and possibly the bedroom—between one of the USA's wealthiest bachelors and the beautiful but tragic Queen of the Seas to light up the switchboards."

"Damn." Thorne scowled, the pleasure of his drive to the office forgotten.

"The Ferrari would have been a better choice." Luke fell into step beside him. "When you leave the office tonight, you're going to need a fast get-away."

Stepping into the private elevator, Thorne punched the up button. "The marchesa definitely stirred things up."

"I must admit it was the first time I've ever heard a woman say no to you—and mean it."

Standing shoulder to shoulder in the elevator, the two men were almost the same height. Thorne looked at his friend and business associate in astonishment. "She got to you, too?"

Although Luke held his gaze, a flush appeared beneath his tanned skin. "Her 'no' did sound convincing."

The elevator doors opened on the executive level and Thorne stepped out with Luke right behind him. The scene was chaotic, filled with ringing phones and two very frazzled-looking receptionists. The two women looked relieved to see the men, but Thorne gave only a slight nod in their direction before he and Luke proceeded down the carpeted hallway to their respective offices. With his hand on the doorknob to his executive suite, Thorne glanced behind him. "You wouldn't care to make a small wager, would you?"

Luke ran a hand through his thick head of sandy hair. "Look, you know what I meant. She's the first woman I've ever seen who truly doesn't seem interested in you."

"Yet," Thorne snapped. "Now, about that wager…"

"Forget the wager," Luke said, a glint of humor in his blue eyes. "I'm not *that* stupid. If you decide you really want this lady's ships and/or the lady herself, I have no doubt you'll make it happen."

Stepping into his office, Thorne muttered, "Damn right."

Luke heard Thorne's door shut behind him and lengthened his stride. His own office was farther down the hall and he had a mountain of work, not to mention important appointments to keep. He couldn't afford to dwell on this new situation or speculate on Thorne's reasons for wanting to acquire the marchesa's ships. As if there wasn't already enough work and company business to keep them both putting in seventy-hour weeks.

But Luke understood it.

In the early years Thorne's survival depended on success. And he'd brought Luke along for the ride. Luke didn't even know why he'd said yes when Thorne had asked if he wanted a job all those years ago.

It had to have been fate. A reward for surviving

a childhood of hardship and loneliness and giving his life the purpose and direction he'd been striving to find. He just hadn't known it.

Whenever anyone asked where home was, Luke always answered Hawaii. If pressed further, he would say Kailua, a small town on the windward side of Oahu. It was the place where he'd been the happiest, where he'd learned that the cry "Surf's up" meant he could escape his hellish world on a beat-up surfboard. It was the place where he'd learned to love the sea.

He'd played a significant part in the building of Blue Ribbon Cruises. Now, as vice president of operations, he had the responsibility of making sure thousands of passengers a week experienced the equivalent of a trip to paradise.

And with the phenomenal growth had come money. More than he'd ever dreamed of, a greater thrill than any monster wave that every surfer lives to ride.

Record profits.

Record passenger ratings.

Record everything.

The past few years, two buzzwords had driven the company—expansion and acquisition. But nowadays, expanding the fleet and acquiring anything and everything Thorne or he desired no longer gave either of them the same charge it once had.

So Luke understood Thorne's interest in the marchesa. She'd inadvertently offered him a new world to explore.

And conquer.

"Good morning," Nevada said when Luke thrust open the door to his office.

"What are you doing curled up on my couch?" he asked.

Nevada laughed. "It's impossible for anyone as tall as I am to curl up anywhere." She'd kicked off her heels and stretched out on the leather couch, which was so comfortable she could easily have fallen asleep if she didn't have so much to do. "*Sprawl* is a much better word. Since I've been waiting twenty minutes for you to arrive, you could at least say hello."

"Hello." Leaning over, Luke planted a kiss on her cheek. "How's my favorite girl today?"

"Oh, please," she said with the familiarity of longtime acquaintance. She sat upright, swinging her stocking feet to the carpeted floor. "I hope you don't use that line on your real favorites. It's a little old and trite."

"Point taken." Depositing his briefcase on the desk, Luke glanced at his calendar for the day. "I was surprised when my secretary informed me that you were here waiting for me. What's so important that I'm treated to one of your rare visits?"

"I didn't actually see the Tyson interview. I was hoping you'd taped it."

"I did. But why weren't you glued to the TV like the rest of us?"

Nevada flushed. "I was with a friend."

"Thorne?"

She shook her head. It was impossible to explain to anyone, even Luke who understood most everything, why she so often felt driven to date other men.

Luke let out a low whistle. "Well, you're a big girl. I hope you know what you're doing."

"Luke, it isn't as if there have ever been any strings attached to my relationship with Thorne."

"I realize that." Luke dialed the combination to his briefcase. "But we both know Thorne is very territorial."

"Maybe I didn't watch the interview because I *do* know how territorial he is. There's something about this Falcone situation that makes me feel very unsure of myself in regard to him."

"Here's the tape," Luke said, pulling it from his briefcase.

"My VCR is broken. Can I watch it here?"

He made a face, but answered, "Of course."

"Thanks, Luke. It's become such a media event I need to know how much containment is necessary."

"Plenty, if you ask me." Luke's tone hinted at something more than the obvious.

Nevada crossed her long legs and her skirt hitched higher. She felt a small flutter of pleasure at the appreciative glint that appeared in Luke's eyes. Why couldn't she fall for him? He was every bit as attractive and intelligent as Thorne—and just as adept at breaking a woman's heart, she reminded herself, thinking of the steady stream of women he'd wooed and bedded in the years she'd known him.

Luke was intuitive about people and situations. She'd learned long ago to trust his judgment and heed his advice. "Do you know something I don't?"

"Just a gut feeling," he replied with a shrug of his broad shoulders. He crossed to a built-in bookcase and opened a set of cabinet doors to reveal a TV screen and VCR. Inserting the tape, he tossed the remote to her and said, "Move over."

"You'll behave yourself?" she teased.

"I'll try."

He'd never once even made a pass at her, although most men did. Even those who knew Thorne Weston well enough to fear him.

He sat down beside her and stretched out his long legs, one arm draped along the back of the leather sofa. "But that gorgeous body makes it tough on a guy."

Another appreciative tip-to-toe look from Luke's killer blue eyes made Nevada's pulse flutter unexpectedly. "I should stop by in the morning more often, Luke, for an ego boost," she said with a breathlessness she'd never experienced before around him. Not wanting to examine the why of it, Nevada hit the play button on the remote and focused her attention on the TV.

The screen filled with the image of a woman in a formal old-world high-ceilinged room filled with antiques, oil paintings and tapestries. The setting was striking, but the woman was stunning. Nevada's stomach felt like an elevator had just plunged twenty floors. She knew the interview had taken place at the Falcone palazzo in Genoa. It was perfect, just too perfect, she thought with disgust. A public-relations coup.

"She's—" Nevada began.

"Gorgeous."

"You think so?" *God, another admirer.* Nevada felt sick inside. "Pretty, yes. But gorgeous?"

"Beautiful."

"She's a bottle blonde."

"Nope. It's real."

"Since when did you become such an expert on Adriana Falcone?"

"I do my homework, too, and she's a real blonde," Luke insisted. "Even as a baby, she had that white-blond hair. Baby pictures don't lie."

"Well—" Nevada's eyes narrowed "—the boobs are fake."

"Wrong again. Or at least no one's been able to prove she's had surgery of any kind—in case you're thinking the face is too perfect."

"I was. How did you guess?"

"I'm psychic."

"Doesn't this woman have any flaws?" Nevada frowned. "I need to find a chink in her armor. I've got all those profiles on her, but there's something missing. She's *too* perfect."

"Hard for you to understand, isn't it?"

Nevada blinked. Were her own flaws and insecurities that apparent to others? Then she saw Luke's grin and knew he'd been teasing. Relieved, she laughed. Luke was one of the few people she considered a good friend. He also dressed well, she thought, admiring the cut of his suit. Unlike Thorne, who preferred to dress casually, Luke appreciated clothes and loved fine things, custom-made shirts, handmade shoes from Italy and designer suits. He'd shared her devastation over Versace's death since they'd often been guests at his showings and parties, both in South Beach and Europe.

"So what do you suggest I do?" she asked.

"Are we talking company policy?"

She shook her head. "I can handle that. It's the other. I'm rather territorial myself."

"We both know Thorne does what he wants, Nevada," he said gently.

Nevada felt an overwhelming urge to fling herself at him and cry on his shoulder.

"My advice is to do what you always do. Look

the other way for a while. Maybe a few more dates with last night's friend?" he suggested.

She'd had a lot of such friends in the years since meeting Thorne. But the emptiness lingered and lately seemed to be growing. Leaning over, she picked up her shoes and started to put them on. Some perverse whim made her lean a little too far over, giving Luke a glimpse of the breasts that had once made her a star in Vegas. Sitting so close beside him on the couch, it was impossible to ignore the effect that had on Luke. The finest tailor in the world couldn't hide the telltale bulge.

"You know, Luke," she said, her voice low and husky, "someday I may just have to fuck *you*."

"If you want to hurt Thorne, you'll have to find another man to help you."

"No, I—"

Luke stood up abruptly. "Don't play with fire, Nevada." His voice sounded strained. "We're both liable to get burned."

She got up, too, crossed to the VCR and popped out the cassette. "I'll want to watch this again. I'll have one of my assistants make a copy and return this one to you." She headed for the door, then stopped and turned. "I owe you, Luke," she said.

"Big-time," he muttered.

Thorne punched the speakerphone button, disconnecting his caller. He leaned back in his leather chair, disregarding the blinking light indicating another waiting call.

When he'd purchased the land for this new office building and first met with architects, the least of his concerns had been his own office. Opulence was not a word or quality he coveted, but on rare occasions like now, he was grateful for the luxurious corner office with its panoramic views of his city, Miami. Unlike the Mustang, his office was all neutrals, shades of brown and cream with touches of black.

He didn't like distractions.

The incessant ringing of his phone since he'd arrived at the office had progressed from annoying to intrusive to downright aggravating. His public-relations department had taken the brunt of the calls, but he'd still had to deal with too many. The press he'd spent years cultivating in terms of marketing and promotion would not be denied.

Tit for tat was what one reporter had said this morning while probing for the answers Thorne was a master at not divulging.

Thorne rose from the comfort of his chair and strode across the room to the painting on the opposite wall. He didn't look at it often, but there was seldom a moment when he wasn't acutely aware of it.

The painting, bearing the signature P. Falcone, was simple enough. *Rather crude* one would-be critic had offered before Thorne had rudely escorted him from the office. The painting was anything but crude. It was a large canvas, done in oils and depicting the Genoa harbor with its fishing boats and colorful buildings lining the waterfront. The painting was his legacy from his sister, one of the two items he had by which to remember her.

He fingered the second, tucked neatly under his shirt where it hung from a gold chain near the region of his heart. The ring with the Falcone crest.

Until Adriana Falcone had tried so angrily and desperately to take it from him, he'd had no confirmation that it had ever actually belonged to Piero Falcone. Now he knew for certain it had once belonged to the marchese.

But he'd miscalculated. He'd never expected this supposed attraction between them would appeal to the press and become front-page news. It would be better to destroy her in full view of the public eye.

Or maybe not.

Perhaps this unexpected twist could work to his advantage. His plan was still in place; it just needed a little fine-tuning. He stepped away from the painting and returned to his desk and a waiting call.

As he picked up the phone, the harsh planes of his face softened.

No one suspected, not even Luke.

He'd fooled them all.

6

Gemma

Rome, Italy

The farmhouse was nearly seven miles outside Rome on the Via Cassia, an ancient Roman road once heavily traveled by everyone wishing to enter or leave the city. Now a much newer highway had diverted all but local traffic, and Adriana had little difficulty locating the unpretentious home. Dwarfed by surrounding ultramodern high-rise apartments, Adriana admired the ageless architectural style of the farmhouse.

The old farmhouses of the region had been built with simplicity and practicality in mind. This one, with outdoor covered stairways, looked as if it had always occupied the hillock on which it sat. It had thick stone walls painted in the sepia color found throughout Rome. Small traditional windows kept the home cool in summer and warm in winter. She glimpsed a thriving vegetable garden off to the right behind a low hedge and heard the unmistakable cluck of chickens. A stand of old olive trees likely provided the inhabitants with all their olive oil.

Approaching the front door, she sniffed the delightful scent of orange and lemon trees from a nearby orchard. Adriana thought of her villa in the Tuscan hills and how long it had been since she'd been able to get there for a relaxing visit.

The midmorning sun was warm and delicious. She reached up and removed her raffia hat with its beautiful hand-embroidered ribbons woven through the crown. She shook her head and felt her hair swish around her face. Raising her hand to knock, she wondered if the trip here would answer any of her questions. Was she wasting valuable time? Was she being foolish? Besides wanting to wipe that arrogant smile off Thorne Weston's face, was there really anything to be gained by trying to locate a woman who had known Adriana's dead husband a lifetime ago?

She knocked and almost immediately the door opened. Before she could speak, something shot out of the house, a blur of speed and energy. It collided with her bare legs; she lost her footing and fell to her knees.

"Bella! Bella!" the old woman at the door cried. She was clearly agitated as she continued to call, "Bella, Bella, Bella." Shoulders hunched with age, she moved stiffly toward Adriana. Her gray hair was pulled into a simple bun and she wore a soft navy dress. Because of the woman's stoop, the hem of her dress nearly touched the tips of her shoes but was shorter in the back, exposing slim ankles in black laced shoes.

Adriana took the hand she extended and got to her feet. As she did, something cold and wet touched her calf. Turning, she saw a beautiful marble-gray whippet sitting on its haunches right behind her.

"Is that how you greet all visitors?" she queried the slender animal. She stooped to retrieve her hat and bag, then turned back to meet the dog's owner.

"I'm so sorry."

"Don't mention it." Adriana accepted the woman's apology and then introduced herself.

"Marchesa Falcone?" Confusion clouded the woman's features. "Falcone?"

Instinctively Adriana reached to steady her, alarmed that she had somehow frightened the old woman.

A younger, heavyset woman hurried from the interior of the house. "What's happened? Who are you?" She threw an arm around the elderly woman and asked, "Are you all right, Mama?"

"*Sì. Sì.*" The old woman's voice was but a whisper. Her free hand clutched the younger woman's arm while the hand grasping the cane trembled. Her pale eyes remained fixed on Adriana.

The younger woman angled her body between Adriana and her mother. "What's going on here?"

"I'm sorry to disturb you. I had just knocked on the door when it opened, and this lovely dog bolted out and knocked me down before I could introduce myself." Adriana smiled reassuringly at both women before continuing, "My name is Adriana Falcone and I'm searching for an old friend of my late husband's. I was hoping she either lived here or someone here might know how I could find her."

"What's her name?"

"Gemma. Gemma Sacco."

The younger woman hesitated, glancing at her mother with a questioning look.

"You have found her," the old woman said. "I am Gemma."

The younger woman wiped her hands on the apron knotted around her waist. "Perhaps you'd best come and have something to drink."

"Yes, that would be lovely." Adriana could hardly contain her excitement as she followed the two women inside.

The interior of the home was much nicer than Adriana had expected, with richly carved wood furniture and rugs in muted jewel colors and several paintings on the walls that she would have enjoyed looking at more closely. A dark walnut dower chest stood against a far wall, looking much like a funeral casket, and it especially piqued Adriana's interest because it was such an unusual piece. Although she would have enjoyed exploring the more formal rooms in the farmhouse, she was led down a short hallway to a lovely blue-and-white kitchen. Sunshine streamed in through a set of half-open doors that opened to a beautiful flower garden.

The younger woman assisted her mother to an upholstered chair in a sunny corner of the large kitchen. "My mother loves to spend the mornings here with me while I prepare the meals for the day. I hope you will excuse this informality, Signora—"

"Marchesa," the elderly woman corrected her. "She is the Marchesa Falcone."

"Marchesa? *The* Marchesa Falcone?" The younger woman blanched and nervously tried to undo her apron. "I am Antonia Mazzini and this is my mother Signora Mazzini. Welcome to our home."

Adriana studied the old woman. Did she know who Julia was? Adriana reminded herself to be patient, not to ask questions yet. "You have a lovely home and I appreciate your hospitality. Please continue with what you were doing."

"I'm preparing an onion tart," Antonia said. "I apologize for Bella greeting you so roughly, but Mama indulges her."

"At my age, I can do what I want," the old woman said.

Signora Mazzini's gaze was fixed on Adriana. Whatever she was thinking was carefully hidden.

Her daughter frowned, confusion flitting across her rather homely face. "Please be seated. Would you care for a glass of wine from our small vineyard?"

"Yes. That would be wonderful." Adriana sat on a cushioned settee across from Signora Mazzini. A basket of peppers, eggplant, arugula and fresh basil stood on a nearby wooden table. As she accepted the glass of red wine, Adriana pointed to the items in the basket and asked, "Is all that from your garden?"

"Yes," Antonia said proudly. "As it did for my mother and father when they bought this property years ago, it provides for much of our needs, as well as gifts for friends and family who insist that our food tastes so much better than theirs."

Adriana sipped her wine. "This is delicious. Are you having some, too?"

"No, not right now." Antonia shook her head at her mother, then said to Adriana, "Mama is only allowed three glasses of wine a day. She must wait until lunch before she has her first." She perched on a small wooden chair next to her mother. "Please, tell us how we can assist you."

Adriana reached into her purse and extracted the picture. She'd looked at the black-and-white photo so often it was committed to memory. In the background was the Trevi Fountain and in the foreground stood a young Piero, breathtakingly handsome with his dark skin, eyes and hair offset by an open-collared white shirt. Two young women stood on either side of him and he had an arm around each of them. One was average height with large eyes and long glossy black hair. The other was lushly beautiful. Her light-colored hair appeared wild and untamed, framing her face in a sensuous cloud. Her eyes were fastened on Piero, and she was smiling at him.

Although Piero had an arm around each of them, his position with the light-haired woman bespoke intimacy. Her body curved into his like a lover's and a hand was touching his cheek. Her face appeared alight with shared pleasures.

Adriana knew that at least one of the people in the photo was dead. What had happened to the others? This was the only lead she had to Thorne's mysterious "Julia." But so many years had passed. Was this old woman really one of the young, carefree women in the photo?

Adriana held it out to the younger woman, who glanced briefly at it. She reached toward a small table beside her mother's chair and picked up a pair of wire-rimmed glasses. "You'll need to put these on, Mama." She waited a moment while her mother put on the glasses and then gave her the photo.

The old woman's hands, knotty with arthritis, shook as she looked at the photo, but Adriana wasn't sure if it was because of what she was seeing or simply because she was old and infirm. Signora Mazzini sighed and then turned the photo over. She squinted, evidently unable to read the faint writing on the back.

"The names on the back are Gemma Sacco and Julia." Adriana watched intently for some sign of recognition. Italian people did not need words to express themselves; gestures and facial expressions spoke volumes. But not in this case. "I am trying to find Julia. Do you know where she is?"

The room was quiet, the only sound the soft panting of the dog, Bella, who had positioned herself next to Adriana's chair. Adriana held her breath, wondering if the older woman had even heard her.

Finally the woman's lips moved and Adriana strained to hear. "No," was all she said.

Adriana hid her disappointment. "Can you tell me when you saw her last? Does she have any relatives in the area? Someone I could contact to find her?"

With a last glance at the photo, Signora Mazzini handed the photo to her daughter and spoke too quietly and rapidly to her for Adriana to catch it. But whatever it was, it wasn't good, for Antonia said, "My mother cannot help you any further, Marchesa." Quickly she stood up and returned the photo to Adriana. "She is very tired now and must rest."

Adriana was disappointed to come so far and

learn so little. She extracted a small card from her purse and handed it to Antonia. "Please call me if your mother remembers anything more, would you? Either about my late husband, Piero, or the woman, Julia. I would be most appreciative."

"My mother says she does not know this other woman, Julia."

Adriana wondered what it was about Julia that made everyone who had ever met her forget her as if she had never existed. "Perhaps after she thinks about it, she'll recall something."

Adriana bade a formal goodbye, stopping to pet the dog, who seemed quite taken with her and would even have even followed her to her car if Antonia had not called the dog back to the farmhouse.

On an otherwise fruitless trip, she'd made at least one friend.

7

The Bodyguard
Genoa

Nico was late. When Adriana had contacted the P.I. again before leaving Rome, he had agreed to meet her at the La Parladora Café. Adriana ordered another coffee and tried to relax. But she couldn't stop thinking about her meeting with Signora Mazzini. There had to be a way to persuade her to reveal what she knew about Julia. A waiter brought her coffee and Adriana took a sip.

At last Nico arrived. Several women in the neighborhood café called out greetings to him, which he acknowledged with a perfunctory nod. He obviously hadn't shaved in several days, and the stubble combined with longish black hair in need of a trim and dark silver-rimmed glasses gave him a rough, even dangerous aura. It took him only a second to locate Adriana and he approached with all the grace of a predatory animal. Although dressed in slacks and a knit shirt, he was far from domesticated.

He smiled as he pulled out a chair and sat opposite her. "A good flight, I presume?" He signaled the waitress for coffee. When she placed it before him, he added cream and sugar and stirred slowly, watching Adriana as he did so. "What's troubling you? The trip was not a success?"

"Yes and no. You were right—she is Gemma Sacco, but she says she doesn't know Julia. I think she does know her, or did, but I didn't want to press her to tell me about her. Whenever I try to find out anything more about her, everyone has a convenient lapse of memory. I just don't understand it."

"Would you like me to spend more time investigating? Perhaps some more information about the family? About the husband? It shouldn't be too difficult. They've lived in the same area for years. Although, as I've warned you before, whenever one asks too many questions about events or people during the war years, there is often resistance to revealing any information. There may be more to Julia's story than we suspect."

"Are you referring to the fact she was in love with my husband?"

"Who was married to another woman at that time."

It was difficult for Adriana to acknowledge Piero's infidelity to his first wife, so she said nothing.

"Are you prepared to admit he cheated on his first wife?" Nico asked.

"Not Piero. He wouldn't be unfaithful."

"Your husband was hot-blooded and married to a sickly woman, almost an invalid, I understand." Nico shrugged, as though that settled the matter.

"So you think this woman was a lover?"

A thick eyebrow arched and his lips quirked in a knowing smile. "You've seen the photo."

"Lover," Adriana conceded.

He raised his coffee cup to his lips. "My specialty is cheating spouses. I'm seldom wrong."

"I find this all very hard to believe. Piero never mentioned another woman, except Luisa, his first wife."

Nico set down his coffee cup. "Men are much better at keeping secrets than women. He probably figured she had nothing to do with you. I'd be willing to bet you didn't tell Piero about every guy you ever kissed. Some affairs are not just about sex, they're also affairs of the heart and, in my experience, when the heart's involved, the affair becomes very special. And very private."

Adriana curled her fingers around the still-warm cup. "My husband was a very complex man. I thought I knew him well, but there were times when I did feel there was a part of him that remained off-limits." She raised her eyes to meet Nico's calm gaze. "My husband was much older than me. Perhaps Julia is best left a part of my husband's past, but I do know that he would want me to reclaim his ring. And to do that I need to learn who Julia was. Even if I find out something that hurts me."

Nico was silent for several moments. Then he said, "You say this Thorne Weston has a ring that belonged to your late husband. Can you tell me when your husband lost it?"

"He didn't lose it. It was stolen."

"Did he tell you so?"

"No. He always said it just disappeared—sometime around 1967 when Luisa, his first wife, was ill and dying. He never found it, although he always missed it and continued to look for it right up until he died. But Thorne Weston has it now, and the only way he could have it is if the ring had been stolen."

"Then perhaps we need to learn more about what was happening at the time your husband lost it. Would you like me to see what I can find out?"

"Yes."

Adriana did not tell Nico there was a connection between Thorne Weston and the woman in the photo, this Julia. Perhaps Nico already suspected as much, but she did not want to distract him. First she needed to know who Julia was. Then she'd concentrate on Julia's connection to Thorne Weston. "Right now I have another difficulty that perhaps you can help me with."

He flashed her a quick, surprised smile. "Certainly."

She hesitated, uncertain how he would interpret her request. "I've been invited to a cocktail party. As a matter of fact, it's due to begin in half an hour. I hadn't intended to go, but since I've returned earlier than expected, there is no way I can avoid it. Especially since it's being held at the Falcone family palazzo and hosted by a cousin of my late husband's, Donatella, and her husband, Emilio, who heads the Falcone Line operations. They live in another wing of the palazzo and I can't arrive and not attend. But neither do I want to answer their questions about where I've been. Sometimes the responsibilities that go with being a Falcone are overwhelming."

"I get it." Nico smiled. "You need an escort."

"I need protection from their prying questions," she said with a laugh. "Are you available?"

"At your service, Marchesa."

He stood up and she saw the outline of a gun under his jacket. "Do you *always* carry a gun?"

"That's what I do, Marchesa." He straightened, dark eyes no longer so warm and relaxed. "In my profession, one never knows when it will come in handy."

"Yes, but—"

"Look, Marchesa, I'm not a baby-sitter. Tonight, consider me your bodyguard."

When they arrived at the palazzo, Emilio and Donatella stood by the saloon doors.

"Emilio, I'd like you to meet my friend, Nico Lintner," Adriana said. "Nico, this is Emilio Donato and his wife, Donatella."

Nico inclined his head. "A pleasure to meet you, Signore Donato. Signora Donato."

"This is a surprise," Emilio said. He was dressed in an immaculate navy suit, and with his iron-gray beard, mustache and tinted glasses, he looked every inch the head of finance for the Falcone Line. "Carla sent your regrets," he went on, clearly undecided whether or not Adriana was still considered an official guest.

"My schedule changed." Adriana smiled. "As usual, Donatella has outdone herself. The food looks fabulous and we're famished. You'll excuse us?"

Adriana linked her arm with Nico's and drew him toward a small buffet on a nearby table.

"Correct me if I'm wrong, but you *do* live here, don't you? This *is* your palazzo, is it not?" said Nico, studying the antipasto selection. "Why are you treated like a guest in your own home?"

Adriana lifted a glass of red wine from the tray of a passing waiter and murmured a quiet greeting to him. She waited until he had moved away before answering. "I'm the interloper. They've all lived here most of their lives and I'm a relative newcomer. They're in denial and like to keep me in check by continuing to treat me like the young American bride who married a man old enough to be her father. They all thought I wouldn't last a year!''

Her smile was bittersweet. ''I inherited all this when Piero died and they're Piero's family. I have my own apartments here and we're all able to live fairly independently. Out of respect for my late husband, I've learned to pick my battles. So far I've kept them in the boardroom. Emilio and Donatella enjoy entertaining at the palazzo and remember when an invitation is declined or ignored. Since I've arrived back earlier than I expected, showing up for their cocktail party will keep the peace.''

''It's a tough way to live.''

Adriana fingered the hand-painted silk scarf she'd knotted loosely around her neck to add a touch of elegance to her simple black dress. ''It's what my husband would have wanted me to do.''

''Sounds like you're doing penance, rather than living.''

''How I live is my business,'' Adriana snapped. ''I didn't ask you for advice on how I lead my life, only to be my escort tonight.''

Immediately Adriana regretted her sharp words. Nico didn't deserve them. ''Forgive me, Nico. I...I'm not quite myself tonight.''

Nico shook his head. ''You needn't apologize, Marchesa. I took no offense.''

Adriana smiled gratefully and might have said

more, but Donatella, who had been moving from guest to guest, chose that moment to approach.

"Why haven't we met your young man before this, Adriana?" she asked. "I don't recall meeting you before, Signore Lintner, either here at the palazzo or the Falcone offices. How long have you known Adriana?"

Without missing a beat, Adriana interjected, "Long enough, Donatella. And since this is Nico's first visit here, perhaps it's best if we don't frighten him away with too many questions."

Nico smiled and answered quietly, "I don't frighten easily."

Donatella laughed. "There. You see, Adriana? Your young man is not as secretive as you are."

"Secretive?" Adriana mentally chastised herself. The scene she'd hoped to avoid by bringing Nico was about to happen, anyway. "I have many friends and acquaintances, as I know you understand, Donatella, and with both our busy schedules it's simply impossible for either you or me to keep each other informed of every detail of our lives. Since you've now met Nico, surely you don't consider him a secret any longer."

"I'm delighted to have the privilege of being here tonight, Signora Donato." Nico selected an eggplant appetizer from a passing waiter. "And to meet such a charming and beautiful hostess. Adriana assured me I was in for a treat and she was certainly right."

"Really?" The frown lines on Donatella's forehead nearly disappeared. "I'm happy Adriana was able to cut her trip short. Where did you say you'd gone, Adriana?"

Adriana was sipping a dry Ligurian white wine and suddenly wished for something sweeter. "To Rome, and it was just the usual business, Donatella, a travel agency and a new ad agency I wanted to visit. But it was necessary, since I'll be returning to the States soon."

Emilio disengaged himself from a nearby group and joined them. His arm slid around Adriana's waist and she resisted the urge to move away. "Our guests are especially pleased that you're here tonight." He nodded in the direction of several of the men on the Falcone board of directors and Adriana understood his meaning. Everyone was always so much more comfortable when she did as expected. "Of course, there was some concern when I mentioned you'd been away, and no one knew where you'd gone. Really, my dear, you can't forget—"

"I *never* forget, Emilio." She removed his hand from her waist and stepped away. "But I cannot live in a cage."

Emilio glanced at his wife. "We will discuss this subject later, Adriana."

"The subject is closed, Emilio." Adriana linked her arm through Nico's. "Come, Nico. Let me show you the gardens."

The cobbled terrace was weathered with age and softly lit with torches around the perimeter. Pots of flowers decorated the balustrades. "Isn't this terrace lovely? I've always enjoyed coming here at night. There's even a quarter moon tonight. Can you see the gardens below? Mostly we have some fruit trees and the cook keeps a wonderful kitchen garden. Can you smell the basil and parsley?"

"They're very protective of you, aren't they?"

Adriana sighed. Salvaging the evening seemed an impossibility. "Donatella was Piero's closest relative, even though she's a distant cousin. She was engaged to Piero's older brother, who died during the war, and Piero left no children, only me, his 'child bride.' We've all been through so much with Piero's passing that I really don't want to confront them. Donatella is childless and she thrives on the responsibility of running the palazzo, while Emilio worries that the same thing that happened to Piero will happen to me."

"And you don't think so?"

"You know about my husband?"

"All Italy does. For that matter, the whole world knows he was kidnapped. Even though you paid the ransom, his life wasn't spared."

"So you tell me. What good did it do to do as the kidnappers asked?"

"Perhaps it was the delay in paying them?"

"We can stand here and play 'what ifs' forever.

You've met Emilio. He thought it was a bluff. For years he's handled the company's financial affairs and he didn't want to strip the company of so much money. He said Piero wouldn't approve. So I had to sell what I could, jewelry and some stocks, and so forth. Unfortunately it took time, but I *did* pay the ransom.''

She leaned on a balustrade and a breeze from the distant bay ruffled her hair, blowing strands into her face, which she brushed away. ''Did you know Piero fought them? His body was a mass of bruises and some broken bones.''

Beside her, Nico sucked in his breath.

''I am careful, as all women today need to be. But I cannot, I will not, let them wrap me in cotton and become less than I am. Less than Piero would want me to be.'' She turned abruptly, walking swiftly toward a set of stairs leading to the garden. ''Come. I want to show you something.''

Flickering torches provided enough light to see the walkway winding through the carefully laid-out gardens. The evening was mild and fragrant with the scents of flowers and herbs. The breeze stirred tree limbs and their faint rustling was soothing. Adriana stopped beside an ancient olive tree, which stood alone in a distant section of the grounds. Its spreading branches were dark outlines against the night sky.

''This tree is at least a hundred years old,'' she

said. "Imagine what it's endured to still stand on this plot of ground. I found this place shortly after I married Piero and have always come here when I feel at my lowest. It seems to give me strength. One day, I climbed the tree and sat on one of these branches and found something. Look."

Adriana stepped closer so Nico could follow her finger as she pointed to a spot high up on the trunk. "There. Initials carved into the tree. A *P* and a *J* inside a heart." She looked at him expectantly, wondering if he would make the same connection she had made.

He paused, as if sorting his thoughts. "Piero and…Julia?"

"I never knew what the initials meant until Thorne Weston mentioned the name Julia to me. I still didn't make the connection until one day last week. It just seemed to fit. But who was she? Why didn't Piero ever mention her to me?"

She stood in the shadows and watched Nico reach into his pocket and pull out a silver cigarette case. A lighter flared and smoke curled about his head. "I'll do what I can," he said. "But if the answer is here at the palazzo, you may be the only one who can solve this puzzle."

"Perhaps," Adriana said. She moved away from the tree. "We'd better go back." As they walked side by side up the walkway, she said, "Thanks for listening to me this evening. I thought I'd come back from Rome with all the answers. Instead, I've been left with many more questions.''

Pausing at the end of the walkway, she was reluctant to move the few remaining feet to the stairs leading up to the terrace—and back to a roomful of people she no longer wanted to see. She tried unsuccessfully to stifle a yawn.

''I think you also need some sleep. It's been a busy few weeks for you,'' Nico said, stubbing out his cigarette in a nearby urn.

''Yes, I guess so.'' The quiet of the garden had relaxed her, and she realized she was indeed tired. ''If you don't mind, I think—''

''Look out!'' Nico shoved her against the stone wall supporting the terrace above them with enough force to knock the breath from her. Stunned, Adriana felt the ground beneath her feet reverberate when a heavy clay pot crashed on the exact spot where she had just been standing.

''Stay here. Don't move,'' he whispered, then slipped into the darkness. Seconds later she glimpsed him on the stairs, using the shadows to reach the terrace.

Adriana stared at what remained of one of the heavy clay pots that had lined the terrace railing. She paled, realizing that Nico had saved her life, or at the very least, spared her grave injury.

She stepped away from the wall, then noticed that a shard of clay had nicked her leg below the knee.

Blood trickled from a small cut. Hurrying up the stairs, she searched for Nico, hoping he had a handkerchief she could use.

"I told you to wait," Nico said when she found him at the top of the stairs.

She ignored the reprimand. "Did you see anyone? What made the pot fall?"

"I don't know, Marchesa, and no, I saw no one." He noticed the cut on her leg. "You're hurt." He knelt, reaching inside his jacket and pressing a linen handkerchief to her calf.

"It's nothing. Are *you* all right?"

"I'm fine." He stood up. "That should get you past the welcoming committee inside. But you'd better put some antiseptic on the wound as soon as you can."

Adriana touched Nico's arm. "Thank you, Nico. You saved my life when that pot fell off the balustrade."

"That pot didn't fall by itself." His eyes searched hers. "Who wants you dead, Marchesa?"

8

The Ride

Bloodied hands pounded on the inside of an automobile trunk. A hoarse voice, nearly a whisper, called her name, his tone honey soft, like a caress. "Adriana carissima..."

Adriana's eyes snapped open. Caught between the dream and reality, she was disoriented. The tangled bedding was suffocating and she quickly tossed it off. Struggling upright, she felt the coolness of the room penetrate her silk nightgown and shivered.

This time his voice had sounded so real, so close.

Knowing how impossible the idea was, she took several deep breaths. When she'd finally seen a doctor a year ago about the dreams, breathing exercises had been suggested to slow her rapidly beating heart. Yet the compulsion to cast her gaze about the room, seeking the familiar face and form of the man she had so loved, remained.

Whenever she began to think she had finally accepted Piero's death and moved on with her life, the dream returned.

To prove her a liar.

Or to warn her?

The thought sprang from some subconscious well and she shuddered at the implication. She pulled the bedding back up around her sore shoulders, recalling the force of Nico's shove, the crash of the urn and the cut on her leg.

Was Nico right? Was she in danger? Was that why the dream had come back after so many months? Was that why Piero had called out to her?

Ridiculous.

Reaching for a soft blue robe on a chair beside the bed, Adriana stood up and pulled it on. She belted it securely over her nightgown, then opened the drapes and looked outside. The sun was up and she could see part of the garden below; everything appeared in pristine condition. On the terrace, there was no break in the line of pots. Another had replaced the one that had fallen, and Adriana couldn't detect the new from the old.

It was as if the accident had never happened.

She and Nico had said good-night to Emilio and Donatella without mentioning the incident. Nico had left, but not before urging her to be careful. He had promised to look into matters in Rome and contact her when he returned. Adriana had gone to the kitchen to speak with one of the staff and then gone directly to her apartment and bed, expecting to sleep without waking until at least noon.

Instead, she'd been haunted by the dream.

When she glanced at herself in the bathroom mirror, she looked as if she hadn't gone to bed. Her face was wan and there were shadows under her eyes. Instead of thirty-three, she thought she looked closer to forty. She would have to apply extra makeup to conceal the effects of her restless night.

Wandering into her tiny kitchen, she made a pot of coffee. While she waited for it to finish perking, she made some toast and filled a small glass with orange juice. When the coffee was ready, she poured herself a cup and placed everything on a tray, which she carried to a table near the windows in her bedroom. She preferred to eat breakfast here in her apartment, alone with her thoughts and view of Genoa.

Although it was Saturday, Adriana had work with her, which she would attend to at her desk in the small alcove off the sitting room. Sipping her coffee, she flipped through her Daytimer, rereading some of her comments and considering the necessary follow-ups. When she picked up her gold pen, she noticed her nails and made a notation to schedule a manicure appointment. She could see several employees working energetically in the kitchen garden beds, and it made her think of Antonia Mazzini. Would the woman call? Or would Nico succeed in learning something more about the family that could lead her to Julia?

Her thoughts were interrupted by a knock on her apartment door. She'd left orders not to be disturbed and was surprised. The household staff usually obeyed her requests without fail. She rose and was crossing the sitting room when the door swung open.

It was Emilio, and she could see he was furious. His face was flushed and he was waving a crumpled sheet of paper in her face.

"You and your secrets!" he shouted. "Why didn't you tell me?"

"Emilio, whatever is the matter? Is it the urn? I asked Giorgio to see that the pot was replaced and the broken one removed. I didn't want you to worry unnecessarily."

"You wouldn't listen to me, would you?" he continued as if she hadn't spoken. "You insist on having your own way. Progress, bah! You will be the ruin of the Falcone company—and this family!"

Abruptly he paused, his chest heaving. He swiped a hand across his forehead, which was beaded with perspiration. He looked at the paper clenched in his hand, then placed it on a console table and used both hands to smooth out the wrinkles. Adriana recognized it as a fax and wondered who had sent it.

"What is it, Emilio?" Her alarm increased. Was something seriously wrong? "Have you been to the office this morning?"

"Yes, I have been to the office." He glared at her. "Otherwise I would not have learned this secret you've obviously been keeping from me. *Dio mio.*"

Adriana was about to invoke divine help herself. "And exactly what did you learn this morning, Emilio? Enlighten me," she said, holding out her hand for the paper that evidently held the key to his theatrics.

"This!" He thrust the paper at her but didn't wait for her to read it. "See!"

He jabbed at the paper with his finger, nearly knocking it from Adriana's hand.

"It says the shipyard that is building Falcone ships is kaput! Bankrupt! Everything is stopped! No ships, no money. You've cost us a fortune!"

Stunned, Adriana sat down on an overstuffed sofa. Her hand shook as she deciphered the fax. Although Emilio continued to shout, she ignored him. She skimmed the text, took a deep breath and then reread it. This time she did so very slowly, taking time to digest the full implications of what she was reading and to consider its ramifications, as well as possible solutions. Finally she stood up, folding the fax and putting it in the pocket of her robe.

"I'd heard a rumor about this, Emilio, but when I tried to have it checked out, I couldn't substantiate it. A mistake, I see now."

"You call losing millions of dollars a *mistake?*"

"What you fail to realize, Emilio, is that the

money is not lost yet. The ship is still there, and one way or another, it's going to get built. You can count on that.''

She turned and started toward the bedroom, untying her robe as she walked. "Make sure the money for the next payment on this ship is available immediately. I may need it sooner than we planned.''

"Don't walk away from me!'' Emilio shouted. "Where are you going?''

Without turning back around, she said, "I'm going to Bremerhaven to get back my ship.''

Hamburg, Germany

Thorne hated going through immigration and customs. It seemed a waste of valuable time, and on this unexpected trip there was no time to waste. He had needed to act quickly and decisively. Nevada had quickly determined that an American Airlines flight leaving MIA in two hours would get him to London faster than his own plane, which had just gone into the hangar for some routine maintenance. His housekeeper had packed a bag for him, and it had been waiting for him at the airport.

Arriving earlier that day in London, he'd met with company attorneys and then caught a British Airways flight to Hamburg. Now all he needed to do was pick up a car, get to the hotel and sleep a few hours before driving to Bremerhaven first thing in the morning. His attorneys were working through the night to draft proposals and would likely fly in to join him in a day or so, depending on the outcome of his preliminary meeting in the morning with the shipyard. Thank God it was late at night. With only a garment bag and nothing to declare, he was waved through customs and immediately veered toward the rental-car counter.

The woman standing alone at the rental counter wore jeans and a T-shirt that clung in all the right places. Blond hair peeked out from beneath a sports cap, and Thorne figured the jolt to his senses was worth the equivalent of several cups of coffee. As he reached the counter, he took one last look and wondered if the front matched the back.

The clerk instructed the woman on how to pick up her car. Accepting the set of keys, the woman turned away and Thorne shrugged. *Why be disappointed? Her face probably doesn't match her body, anyway.* With a lopsided grin, he said to the waiting clerk, "Weston. You've a Mercedes reserved for me."

Flipping through some papers, the clerk asked, "Is that *W-e-s-t-o-n?*"

"Yes." Out of the corner of his eye, he noticed the woman stop and begin to turn around. Maybe he would have his curiosity satisfied, after all.

"I'm sorry, sir, but the car you reserved is no longer available. I can substitute—"

"I don't want a substitute," he enunciated slowly. "I want the car I requested. A Mercedes."

"I don't have one available. As a matter of fact, I only have one car currently in stock. When you weren't here by 9:00 p.m., we took the hold off the car. I can call other rental agencies if you like."

Thorne didn't need this complication. Considering his options, he glanced over, suddenly aware that the woman had not moved away but was watching them.

It was *her.*

He muttered an obscenity.

No, wait. The eyes were the wrong color. Adriana Falcone's eyes were blue, not green. So this couldn't be her, and yet—

"Mr. Weston, would you like me to start calling?" The clerk reached for a telephone and waited for his answer. Not taking his eyes from the stunning woman, he said, "No, don't bother. I'll take what you have."

He turned to the clerk. "Tell me—did that woman get *my* Mercedes?"

He didn't know why he asked. The clerk only confirmed what he already knew.

Running a hand through his dark hair, Thorne stared at the registration card in front of him. Would he even fit in the one and only car available, a tiny subcompact? Shoehorned into the car, he imagined the miserable late-night drive to Hamburg.

"Mr. Weston."

He might not have recognized the woman, but he did recognize the voice. The marchesa had returned to the counter. "So, it *is* you, after all," he said, studying her face. "The green contacts had me fooled."

"The change of eye color makes me less recognizable and life a little easier, especially when I travel." She glanced beyond him to the patient clerk holding the keys to his tiny rental car. "If I'm not mistaken, I believe I rented the car you had reserved, a large-size Mercedes? If you're going in my direction, I can give you a lift."

"Hamburg?"

"Yes. I'm staying at the Vier Jahreszeiten Hotel."

"Must be fate." He reached down and picked up his leather garment bag. Glancing at the clerk, he said, "I won't need that car, after all." To the marchesa, he said, "Let's go."

He followed her through the terminal and to the car-pickup area, matching his longer stride to hers. When they reached the car, she popped open the trunk and quickly placed her bag inside, refusing his offer to help with a quick shake of her head. Although Thorne would have preferred to drive, he didn't offer and instead opened the door and climbed into the passenger seat. She removed her cap, allowing her hair to fall in a pale cloud around her face. He didn't speak until she had started the car and pulled into traffic.

"I'm surprised to see you here, especially at this time of night." Surely she knew about the bankruptcy. Or did she? "Are you in Hamburg for any particular reason?" he asked.

"Actually, Mr. Weston—"

"Call me Thorne."

She hesitated and Thorne sensed her reluctance. She wanted to maintain her distance and thought the more formal style of address would protect her. It wouldn't, he thought, with a wry twist of his mouth.

"I assume you're here for the same reason I am, Thorne." She glanced at him as if something in his expression or body language would confirm her suspicion. "To check on the construction of a ship."

"I come here periodically." Thorne probed, "It's a coincidence that we both arrived tonight, isn't it?"

"I had a few days free in my schedule," she said, flipping on the turn signal to change lanes.

"You've been a busy lady." He thought about the havoc she had created in his life.

"I have, haven't I?" she said, slowing for a red light. "Has the press made your life uncomfortable?"

"Colored contacts may be a good idea, after all," Thorne admitted, thinking of the press who dogged his every move in Miami. "My love life has also suffered."

"Because of the interview?"

"Hasn't it affected you, too?" asked Thorne, detecting the interest in her voice. "Surely there's a man in your life who dislikes the press implying that I'm a rival for your affections."

"I don't date," she said softly. "If I did, your girlfriends would have nothing to fear from me."

"Because I'm not your type?" He grinned. "I've found that a little time and attention quickly changes any woman's mind."

As she pulled the car into the hotel entrance, the lights illuminated the interior of the car. Thorne felt a stab of satisfaction at the sight of her flushed face.

She stopped the car and hotel valets immediately appeared, opening doors and assisting with luggage. Thorne stepped from the car and waited for her to join him at the entrance.

As she walked toward him, Thorne thought he'd never seen a more beautiful woman. As his hand cupped her elbow, he heard a voice shout, "Marchesa!"

Startled, Thorne looked up and a flash exploded in his face. Adriana involuntarily moved closer to him and he put his arm around her, pulling her against him. Ducking his head and shielding her face against his chest, he hustled her into the hotel.

In the lobby, Thorne held her in his arms for several seconds longer. Taking a deep breath, he registered the feel of her body against his. Outside, he saw several valets chasing a fleet-footed photographer. He felt her plant hands on his chest and push away from him. When he looked down into her eyes, he caught a fleeting impression of confusion.

"When this picture hits the tabloids, Marchesa," he warned, "it's going to be harder to convince those 'girlfriends' of mine that you're not interested in me."

Early the next morning, Thorne stood in front of the concierge at the Vier Jahreszeiten Hotel. "I left word with the clerk when I arrived last night that I needed a Mercedes this morning."

"*Ja*, Herr Weston." The concierge glanced at a nearby clock. "But your car has not been delivered. I'm sure it will be here no later than 9:00 a.m."

Thorne knew the man had no doubt called upon his many contacts to facilitate this request, and he tried not to show his annoyance at the delay. Although he'd had room service early that morning in his suite, he considered having another cup of coffee to kill time. He was still deciding when he saw Adriana Falcone.

This time there was no mistaking her. Her eyes matched the stylish blue suit she wore, the skirt short enough to cause several men in the lobby to stop and watch as she crossed to the registration counter. She handed the clerk a package and, with a glance at her watch, moved away from the counter.

Thorne stepped directly in front of her, blocking her path to the doors leading outside. "*Guten Tag*, Marchesa."

He conceded points to her when she showed no surprise at seeing him. Every gleaming pale gold strand of hair on her head was in place. Her makeup was so subtle he wasn't even sure she was wearing any, and her jewelry—chunky gold bracelet and matching earrings—were large enough to be noticed but small enough not to detract from the overall impression of polished perfection.

"Good morning." She smiled, removed a valet stub from the elegant briefcase she carried and waited for him to step aside. "I've a busy day ahead, as I'm sure you do, too."

"Yes, but there's been a delay with my car." Thorne glanced at the stub in her hand. "If you're headed for the shipyard, can you give me a lift?"

"I'm sorry, but that's not possible," she said. "I'm sure your car will be along soon. Have a nice day."

Stepping around him, she headed for the exit doors and left him standing in the center of the elegant lobby. If she wasn't going to the shipyard, where was she going?

The concierge hurried up to him. "Herr Weston, my assistant informs me that your car was canceled several hours ago."

"Canceled? I didn't cancel the car!"

"*Nein,* Herr Weston. It was your wife." The concierge paused. "Frau Weston telephoned earlier this morning and said you would not need the car, after all."

"Frau Weston?" Suddenly Thorne Weston understood why the marchesa had not given him a ride—and exactly where she was headed.

9

Devil's Triangle
Bremerhaven, Germany

Adriana's morning glimpse of Bremerhaven, a city on the Elbe River, reinforced the seriousness of her mission. Nothing was more important to the Falcone Line than a successful conclusion to her trip.

Commerce happened in Hamburg, but all aspects of shipbuilding happened in Bremerhaven. Wet docks. Dry docks. Repairs and overhauls. But especially, new shipbuilding. The scale was immense, with hotel-size floating palaces being built; everywhere Adriana looked there were huge facilities to accomplish all the many phases of construction. It was here that the M.S. *Castello* had been built to her specifications. Now the sister ship was nearly completed—but construction was halted because of the just-announced bankruptcy.

She'd committed a fortune so far, and additional payments were scheduled for each building phase.

Plus, she had an option for a third ship, which she intended to exercise at the appropriate time. Now her ship was in immediate jeopardy, and if she didn't resolve this situation to her advantage, it could ultimately jeopardize the entire Falcone Line fleet.

Parking the car outside the main offices of the shipyard, Adriana adjusted the shoulder strap on her briefcase. She saw her partially constructed ship on a distant dry dock, and she was anxious to see how far work had progressed since her last visit.

The basic design was the same as the M.S. *Castello* and had long since been worked out on computers, which had taken into consideration the capabilities of this particular shipyard. The basic anatomy of the ship comprised about thirty steel sections, each weighing approximately four hundred tons; these were all put into place according to a timetable. Adriana knew exactly when each piece was to be hoisted or fitted in place, and she was integrally involved in establishing a distinctive decorating theme for this particular ship, the M.S. *Pisano*. Steel, piping and cable were relatively the same, but paint colors, fabrics and other decorating materials varied with each ship.

When Adriana entered the building and stepped into the reception area, a shipyard representative immediately greeted her by name and led her down a hallway to the office of the vice president of shipyard operations, Herr Wilhem Stierhofer. He rose from his desk when she entered and extended a hand in greeting.

"It's nice to see you again, Wilhem," said Adriana, ignoring his gesture that she be seated. She preferred to stand. "I'd expected to meet with the company president this morning. I'm glad you'll be joining us. As you can imagine, I have a great many questions."

"Unfortunately Herr Schellin is preparing for an important meeting, Marchesa Falcone. He's requested that the company's financial officer and attorney join us, instead. But first, I'm sure you're anxious to see your ship. Shall we visit the dry dock first?"

Adriana didn't budge. "I really must insist on seeing Herr Schellin. How long is his meeting expected to last?"

"I—I'm really not sure. I'll leave a message with my secretary that you wish to see him. Perhaps he can see you later in the day." He smiled, his bald pate shiny with perspiration. "Shall we go? The others are waiting."

Since inspecting her ship was also a priority, Adriana agreed. But there was no way she was leaving the shipyard without speaking with the top decision maker.

Hours later Adriana was frustrated and losing her patience.

Her meeting with Wilhem had been moved to a larger conference room, and they'd been joined by one of the company's financial officers and an attorney. They'd spent several hours detailing the complicated situation that had led to their filing for bankruptcy and discussing possible scenarios for their future.

"Gentlemen, what you're telling me is that my ship has sailed into a devil's triangle. The millions I've given you in good faith to begin the next phase of building no longer exist. As of this moment, you can't give me any solution for resolving this situation."

The financial officer reached for a stack of papers, but Adriana had seen enough. "No, I don't want to see charts and graphs." Elbows on the table, she pushed the papers away. "I want to see the cabin units brought onboard my ship. I want to see the M.S. *Pisano* ready for floating out in three months."

She stood up, scooped up some papers and stuffed them in her briefcase. "So far, gentlemen, I've done things your way. Now I'm going to do them *my* way."

Seconds later she was marching down the corridor with a stream of company representatives trailing behind her. She'd spent enough time in the offices to know exactly where she was going. She didn't even glance at the several assistants and secretaries sitting outside the president's office. She simply put one Ferragamo pump in front of the other without breaking stride as she twisted the doorknob to the president's office and walked in.

And found Thorne Weston standing where she should have been.

The company president and several members of the company's board of directors were seated throughout the room, and they were all listening to Thorne. He stopped in midsentence when she entered.

"I hope you don't mind if I join you, gentlemen." She stood in the doorway and her gaze traveled to each one of the men with the exception of Weston. He was the last person she cared to see at the moment. "Evidently whatever Mr. Weston has to say is so vitally important that none of you has time for anything—or anyone—else. Now I'm curious, too, as to what could be so terribly important to all of you."

Adriana used the awkward moment after her little speech to sit down in one of the Danish-designed chairs. She placed her briefcase beside the chair, sat back and slowly crossed her legs. Every man in the room watched as she did so—as she'd known they would. She hadn't worn an especially short skirt that day without knowing exactly what she was doing.

Looking directly at Thorne, she said, "You were saying?"

"I was saying that it's time to conclude this meet-

ing for today. My attorneys will arrive tomorrow
and we can sit down and discuss my proposal in
greater depth,'' he said to the others in the room.
Uncrossing his arms, he strolled toward her. ''That
is, Marchesa, if we have your permission to adjourn?''

''Actually, no.'' Tapping the fingers of one hand
on the arm of her chair, she held his gaze. ''I'd like
you to brief me on your proposal.''

''As you wish.''

A half smile appeared on his handsome face, and
Adriana belatedly wondered if she'd reacted exactly
as he'd hoped she would.

''What I'm proposing, Marchesa, is to buy an interest in this shipyard and take over.'' The half smile
became a full-fledged grin. ''Immediately.''

She was out of her chair before he had finished
speaking. ''Absolutely not!'' She strode over to the
shipyard president. ''Herr Schellin, I can make you
a better offer than Mr. Weston.''

Dressed impeccably in a pin-striped suit, Herr
Schellin looked strained. ''We are faced with difficult choices, Marchesa Falcone, as I'm sure you're
aware. We're all trying to find solutions to solve
everyone's difficulties. The shipyard has signed a
letter of intent with Mr. Weston.'' He stood up and
touched her arm lightly, guiding her toward the
door, then he lowered his voice and said, ''I'm
meeting with Mr. Weston and his attorneys tomor-

row morning to outline the status of construction in the shipyard and discuss the fine points of our preliminary agreement. If you'll call me later tomorrow, I'll have more specific information."

"Do anything with Mr. Weston and you'll have an even bigger problem on your hands. Me." She pulled a cell phone from a pocket of her briefcase and started punching in numbers. "You can expect me to sit in on any meetings you have with Mr. Weston tomorrow, Herr Schellin. I'll be here, along with my attorneys."

By the time she reached her Mercedes, Adriana had placed two calls to Italy. She was glad she had a powerful car. She wanted to put as much distance between herself and Thorne Weston as physically possible.

Hamburg

Room service had come and gone with Thorne's dinner. Too keyed up to sleep, he'd finally bundled his notes and papers together and headed for the hotel bar. He'd found a secluded table, ordered a martini and spread out his papers. The pianist played soothing background music and he decided he'd made a good choice. A drink or two, and then perhaps he could finally conquer the difference in time zones and get some sleep. He'd need his wits about him in the morning.

Savoring an olive, he glanced up and saw Adriana Falcone coming through the lobby dressed in what looked like jogging clothes, a sweatband around her head. She wasn't walking through the lobby, she was charging.

Still riled up. She's going to be even madder tomorrow.

He could hardly wait.

Then she saw him and he groaned. She came straight at him, her Reeboks eating up the distance separating them. She slid into the empty chair across from him, glanced at the papers on the table and scowled.

"Trouble sleeping?" he asked.

"You're not going to get away with this."

"Don't bet on it."

"No?"

Her chest heaved and he couldn't help noticing her small rounded breasts outlined by the damp T-shirt. He fought the urge to let his gaze linger and explore. The picture of her standing at the rental-car counter flashed through his mind, and his body reminded him forcefully of her effect on him. He sucked in his breath, willing all such thoughts into cold storage.

"No." He twirled the stem of his martini glass. "Would you like something to drink? Since you are inclined to visit with me, there's actually something I'd like to discuss with you."

"Scotch. Straight up," she said to a hovering cocktail waitress. "And a separate check, please."

He waited while the waitress served her drink and she signed the tab with a barely readable scrawled signature. He made a mental note of her room number and then wished he hadn't. The instant she sat back he said, "Sell me your ships."

She took a healthy slug of the whiskey. "Say that again. I must have misunderstood you."

"Sell me your ships."

The glass hit the table with a thud, amber liquid sloshing over the rim. "I'll see you in hell first."

She jumped out of the chair, but this time Thorne was ready for her. She'd taken only two steps before he grabbed her, spun her around and propelled her against the wall. Propping his arms on either side of her and using his body to hold her against the wall, he spoke quietly and forcefully. "Think about it, Marchesa. No more problems, no more headaches. Enough money to do whatever in the world a beautiful woman like you wishes to do. Name your price, and we'll settle things between us right now."

Her chest heaved with exertion and agitation. "We'll settle nothing!" she snapped. "Now let me go."

"I'll be generous." He watched her eyes turn from blue ice to blue fire and increased the pressure of his body against her.

"I pass." Her face colored, but she continued to glare at him and added, "On everything."

Adriana waited for the valet to bring her car. A breakfast meeting with a squadron of Falcone company attorneys had left her on edge. Although a lot had been discussed, it was pointless to speculate too much until Thorne Weston divulged exactly what he intended.

The valet pulled her Mercedes to a stop in front just as Thorne Weston strode out of the hotel. He was surrounded by a group of men dressed in sober dark suits and carrying attaché cases. Wearing casual slacks, knit shirt and sport jacket, he should have looked out of place amidst all the suits, but he didn't. His air of authority was apparent even to the two valets, who immediately snapped to attention, one instantly leaving to retrieve his car. Glancing around, he caught her watching him.

Turning abruptly away, she almost bumped into the valet, who smiled delightedly at the money she shoved into his hand, forgetting all about getting change. Adriana took a deep breath as the solid door shut her into the cocoonlike sanctuary of the automobile. She fastened the seat belt, adjusting the straps to minimize wrinkling her understated black suit.

The passenger door opened and Thorne Weston

levered himself into the seat beside her. "My car is too crowded," he said.

"Don't make this a habit." Adriana flexed her fingers on the steering wheel and kept her voice neutral. "Fasten your seat belt."

"Giving orders this morning?" he asked, one dark eyebrow lifting in surprise. "You shouldn't feel so confident today."

"I won't discuss business with you without my attorneys present."

"Unless we're discussing the sale of your ships to me, Marchesa, there's no other business to discuss."

"That's where you're wrong, Thorne Weston," she said, shifting the car into Drive and hitting the gas.

Adriana pulled out of the hotel parking lot and into traffic swiftly and smoothly. Obeying the fifty-kilometer speed limit while in the city, Adriana was relieved to reach the autobahn, where she immediately moved into the left lane and watched the speedometer climb to two hundred and sixty kilometers within seconds. Slower cars traveled in the right-hand lanes, leaving the left clear for more powerful cars like the one she was driving. Pulling up behind a slightly slower car, she blinked the headlights for it to get out of her way.

"Your middle name isn't Andretti, is it?"

He'd been strangely quiet while she drove and now she knew why. "You aren't afraid of a little speed, are you?"

"Not if *I'm* driving." He shook his head. "But I've never seen a woman drive the way you do. We're going over a hundred and fifty miles an hour. How did you learn to handle a car as powerful as this one?"

Glancing at him and seeing that his question was serious, she decided to answer him. "I took a course in defensive evasive driving. It's usually offered to chauffeurs and bodyguards, but I like to drive my own car and thought it would be a good idea if I took the course, too."

"You mean, the course offers to protect people from kidnappers and killers?"

"Yes."

He whistled, low and soft. "Do you seriously think you need it?"

She shrugged. "Who knows? I certainly know from experience that such a thing can happen."

"Your husband?"

"Yes," she said, remembering all the reasons she loved Piero. And all the reasons this man could never compare to him. "My husband, Marchese Piero Falcone."

He hesitated, as if choosing his words carefully. "It's been eight years," he said.

"Seven."

He looked away from her and a sweep of dark lashes hid his eyes. "You still miss him?"

"Every second of every day," she whispered softly, more to herself than to anyone else and not even caring whether he heard her reply or not.

But he did.

"Don't you think he'd have liked you to live without worrying about your safety?" Thorne paused, watching her reactions to his question. When she didn't answer, he continued, "Why not put such worries behind you? Accept my offer to buy your ships."

"Do you want to continue riding in this car?" she snapped.

He sighed. "Something tells me you're going to issue another order, and one I won't like."

"Probably not, but if you want to get to Bremerhaven in this car, you'd better pay attention." She took her eyes off the road and looked directly at him. "Don't mention my ships. They're not for sale. Not any of them. And if they were, you'd be the last man on earth that I'd sell them to."

His expression was impassive. "Well, that's pretty clear."

"Good, I'm glad you think so." They were almost at their destination. Adriana felt relieved.

She'd survived thirty minutes with Thorne Weston; only ten more to go.

"How'd you get that cut on your leg?"

The short suit skirt stopped several inches above her knees but was hiked even higher as she sat behind the wheel. Even though she wore panty hose, the flesh tones did not entirely conceal the gash on her calf—although, for Thorne Weston to notice, it meant that he had to have been giving her a very thorough inspection.

"I don't see that it concerns you."

"I suppose not. Did it happen when you were out jogging?" he persisted. "I didn't notice a rip or tear in your sweatpants last night."

"That's because it didn't happen last night. I repeat, it really doesn't concern you."

"Does it hurt?" He reached down suddenly and touched the cut with his finger, glancing up at her as he did so. Despite herself, she flinched. "I thought so. You'd better see a doctor."

"I'll do no such thing. It's just a cut. It will heal itself."

He shook his head. "It looks like it might be infected. You could get blood poisoning if you don't take care of it."

"That's impossible. I put some antiseptic on it."

But had she? Adriana couldn't remember. Nico had told her about putting antiseptic on the cut, but she'd been very tired that night. She'd made arrangements to have the mess cleaned up and, after a hasty shower, gone straight to bed. Then the next morning had turned chaotic with Emilio's unexpected news.

"How did it happen?"

His tone was quiet, but there was a steely undercurrent that suggested the question was actually a polite demand. Exasperated, Adriana said, "If you must know, a pot—actually, a large urn filled with plants—fell from the terrace of my home. A piece of the broken pottery hit my leg."

"All the more reason to have your leg looked at. Dirt is always a culprit." Shifting in the seat and stretching his long legs, he frowned. "Do urns fall from your terrace often?"

"No. It was an accident."

"Things are always breaking around you. Champagne bottles, pots." His fingers drummed on the armrest. "Either you're accident prone or you lead a very complicated life."

"You don't know me well enough to say something like that." She turned toward him so swiftly that a lock of her hair swirled around a cheek. For some unholy reason, he seemed fascinated by it. His eyes never left her face as she tucked the errant strands behind an ear. "What about you? How did you get that tiny scar near your right eyebrow?"

His tone turned icy. "I fell."

"Sounds to me like *you're* accident prone." She slowed for the Bremerhaven exit. "Or you lead a very complicated life."

"Touché." His lips quirked in a rueful smile. "Perhaps I just hate seeing the perfection of a great pair of legs marred by an ugly cut."

"Then I suggest you worry about other things for the rest of today."

"I intend to." He straightened as they approached the shipyard offices. He'd popped open his seat belt before Adriana pulled into a parking space and turned off the engine. Unclipping her own belt, she started to open the door. Instead of getting out of the car, Thorne Weston reached across, clasped her upper arm and turned her to face him. "If you don't like what I have to say today, just remember I've given you an out. Think it over carefully. My offer to buy all your ships—including the one under construction—stands."

"You always have an agenda, don't you?" He radiated an energy that both fascinated and repelled her.

"You didn't want a ride this morning, did you? You want what you've always wanted from me— the Falcone ships." She knocked his hand away and opened the car door. "Well, you're not going to like

what I have to say today either, Mr. Weston. The
answer to your offer is unequivocally no.''

She got out, slamming the door behind her and
not waiting to see if he followed her or not. In the
distance, she saw the Mercedes with his attorneys
turn into the parking lot.

She didn't kid herself as she climbed the steps to
the office. She'd need more than a fast car to keep
one step ahead of Thorne Weston.

10

Cats and Men
Bremerhaven

Her feet were killing her.

In order to assess the exact status of each ship under construction or repair, Adriana and about a dozen men had literally traipsed the length and breadth of the huge shipyard and explored the cavernous shells of steel. Although there had been several suggestions that she wait in the comfortable offices, Adriana had insisted on her inclusion. On several occasions when she'd lagged behind or had trouble keeping up, she'd caught Thorne Weston watching her and each time his *why don't you quit?* expression had made her even more determined not to falter.

But now, after walking miles, she wasn't sure she would make it up the last set of steps. Even more troubling was the throbbing in her calf; she hated the thought that Thorne Weston might be right about the cut on her leg. Besides all the walking, she'd managed to avoid him, always making sure that some of the other men were between them. The shipyard officials, sensing the coolness between the Blue Ribbon Cruises team and hers, managed to keep between the two groups.

Now everyone returned to the shipyard conference room, where a late lunch had been set out. Adriana, using the excuse that she wanted to retrieve something from her car, parted company with the group. The short flight of stairs to the offices looked more like Mount Everest; she wasn't sure she would make it up without help. Halfway to her car, she kicked off her heels. The pain was excruciating. Reaching out, she steadied herself on a nearby truck. Her outrageously expensive medium-size heels on the pavement seemed like instruments of torture, and she groaned aloud at the thought of having to put them back on. She wiggled her toes, hoping to regain some feeling. She wanted to examine her leg, too, but that would have to wait.

"You shouldn't have done that to yourself!" The outraged bark came from about ten or fifteen feet behind her.

Adriana closed her eyes, her hands pressed on the dusty truck. "Go away," she said. But so far Thorne Weston hadn't done anything she'd told him to. She doubted this time would be the exception. "And quit sneaking up on me!"

"Sneaking!"

She opened her eyes and pushed away from the truck. She turned, all her weight on her feet now, and winced.

"That does it." Bending, Thorne Weston picked up her shoes and then, before she could protest, scooped her up in his arms. "You should thank me for sneaking up on you, Marchesa, or did you plan to spend the rest of the day propped against that truck?"

"Put me down!" She squirmed, trying to get free. His arms merely tightened around her. "You'll be sorry!"

"I'm already sorry." His face darkened, his eyes fathomless black pools. "Give me your keys."

"No."

"Yes."

"You can't make me." Adriana clutched her shoulder bag to her chest.

Jaw clenched, he carried her effortlessly the short distance to her car, then carefully set her down on the passenger side. Using his hips and legs, he pinned her to the car and prevented her from putting her full weight on her aching feet. The intimacy of the act startled her. Then he gripped her leather bag. Their gazes locked, she held on as tightly as possible, but one by one, he pried her fingers away.

When he had the purse in his possession, there was no mistaking the look of triumph that flashed briefly in his eyes. Angrily Adriana watched while he extracted the keys and snapped her purse shut. He used the remote to unlock the doors, then, scooping Adriana into his arms again, opened the passenger door and thrust her inside.

"Don't *ever* tell me I can't have something," he said. He used his body to still her struggles, then pulled the seat belt across her lap and breasts, and finally snapped the seat belt in place. He leaned over her and warned, "It just makes me want it more."

Picking up her shoes where he'd dropped them beside the car, Thorne tossed them onto the floor at her feet. He shut the passenger door and walked around the front of the car, all the while watching her, daring her to try to get away.

Dazed and confused, Adriana had difficulty breathing. Thorne Weston was getting under her skin, reminding her in the most elemental manner that she was a woman who needed a man. For too long she had denied the need, pretended it didn't exist. Now, it seemed, she was paying the price. When he'd buckled her into the seat, a red-hot haze of shimmering sexuality had enveloped her, short-circuiting all her normal safeguards, all rational thinking.

Near the left fender, he suddenly looked away, and the spell was broken. He'd been distracted by someone or something. Drawing a shaky breath, Adriana acknowledged her weakness. Thorne Weston was dangerously attractive—and she was far too vulnerable.

Luigi Gallo, an attorney from the law firm representing the Falcone Line, hurried toward Thorne. There was a brief conversation, and Luigi glanced at her. Apparently satisfied, he turned and headed back to the shipyard office.

Seconds later Thorne sat in the driver's seat beside her and started the engine. She tensed, disturbed all over again by his nearness.

"I expected you to honk the horn," he said, shifting the car into gear and backing out of the parking space. "Although Luigi hardly seemed inclined to mount a rescue attempt. He's not the type. Aren't you afraid that I'm abducting you?"

"It did occur to me," she lied, mortified by her real thoughts. "I decided that if you were leaving, there really wasn't a necessity for me to remain, either. We are returning to the hotel, aren't we?"

There was no way she could reveal to him how he made her feel. Once she arrived at the hotel, she would be safe. She need never see him alone again.

She simply needed to survive the next forty-five minutes.

"Okay, we're agreed." Thorne strode down the hotel hallway carrying her in his arms. "I don't like it, and you don't like it. So shut up and get out your room key."

"I could have walked."

"The key," he said. He was definitely going to have to spend more time in the gym. Carrying Adriana Falcone through the hotel lobby, into the elevator and down an endless carpeted hallway had taxed him in more ways than one. "You would have fallen flat on your face if I hadn't caught you in the lobby. You should be thanking me, instead of complaining. Now get that key in the lock before I collapse with the both of us."

As she inserted the plastic key in the lock, he noticed her hand tremble. Had he frightened her? He hadn't meant to, but the anger gnawing at his gut wouldn't go away. He was angry at himself for feeling so protective of her, and so attracted to her. He should have left her alone in the parking lot. Let her crawl back to the building if necessary. Instead, he'd acted like a lovesick cowboy. Scooping her up, he'd actually enjoyed the feel of her in his arms, liked having her helpless and dependent on him. His second mistake had been propping her against the car and using his hips to hold her in place. It had been all he could do not to make love to her right there in the parking lot, pressed against the car. Like a flash fire, desire had erupted, threatening to consume him. Sheer willpower had made him stop.

When he lowered her onto the queen-size bed in the luxurious suite, Thorne scowled at her, trying to ignore her tumbled disarray. Her blond hair was tousled, her face flushed, her large cobalt-blue eyes confused and questioning, and her black suit skirt had hiked up to tantalizing heights.

"Get some rest and, for God's sake, stay off those feet. You look exhausted." He crossed to the window and pulled the curtains partly closed to eliminate some of the late-afternoon sunshine streaming through the window. It was time for his next strategic move, but he needed her rested and conducive to his proposal. "There are some things I'd like to discuss with you when you're feeling rested. Perhaps if I call…"

Unwittingly his gaze strayed back to the bed.

Either way he was damned.

Propped on one elbow to watch him, her suit jacket gaped just enough to allow a glimpse of one tantalizing breast. She'd drawn her legs up slightly, which only accentuated their beautiful shape.

She literally took his breath away.

And then he noticed what she'd been trying to hide by drawing up her legs.

"What the hell—"

In two strides, he was back beside the bed. "Why didn't you say something? That cut needs a doctor's attention."

She didn't say anything, which he took as an acknowledgment that he might be right, after all. Picking up the telephone, he dialed the hotel's general manager and made arrangements for a doctor to come immediately to the suite.

"Strip," he ordered, slamming down the phone.

"I beg your pardon." He didn't know how it was possible, but her blue eyes seemed even bluer. Maybe it was the contrast with her increasingly pale face.

"You heard me, Marchesa." Palms on the bed, he leaned over her. "Strip. Take off the panty hose. The doctor's on his way and he'll want to treat that cut. So you have two choices—take them off yourself, or I will."

Everything with her was a battle.

"You'll have to leave," she said.

"No way."

"I'm not taking *anything* off until you're out of here!"

Her eyes never left his. He felt as if he was looking into a blue laser beam, one that was trying to search out all his secrets, probe all his weaknesses. *It will never happen.* He sent the silent message to her and saw her eyes widen slightly with understanding.

You'll never beat me.

In the boardroom...or in the bedroom.

She gasped. It was if he'd spoken the words aloud. Maybe there was something to telepathy, after all.

"All right. Turn your back," she said at last. He

detected her effort to make herself sound tough and in-charge. She failed miserably.

"And if I don't?" He couldn't resist the taunt.

"Then I'll call security and have you thrown out." Her tone sounded less breathy and stronger. "So, *honey,* make my day."

He laughed, then straightened and turned his back, a grin on his face he couldn't erase. He suddenly understood why some men were such avid hunters. There was a thrill to the chase.

And an even greater thrill when the quarry continued to elude capture.

Arms crossed, he listened to the slight rustle behind him. Then his active imagination filled in what he couldn't see.

"Ouch!"

He started to turn.

"Don't you dare! Stay put!"

"What's the matter? Are you all right?"

"Yes, it's…just that the hose was stuck to the cut. I had to yank it…and it hurt."

"Are you done yet?"

The mattress creaked, bedding rustled, and her breathing was more audible. "Yes, but it's bleeding…"

He was halfway to the bathroom for a clean washcloth when he heard the knock at the door. He hesitated for a fraction of a second and then veered for the suite door. Opening it, he found the hotel manager, who introduced the man with him as a highly regarded doctor. He'd come directly from a nearby hospital as a personal favor.

A few succinct sentences and Thorne had filled in the doctor, who immediately went into the bedroom. Thorne started to follow him in when he heard Adriana whisper something. The doctor immediately looked over at Thorne. "Sir, if you would be kind enough to wait outside? My patient would like some privacy."

Friend? Lover? Husband? Thorne read the questions in the doctor's eyes and shook his head. He was none of them. There was no logical reason for him to remain, yet he had an irrational urge to shove the stout doctor out of the way and storm to her bedside. The only way he knew she'd be all right was if he was there beside her.

Instead, he returned to the sitting room, murmured his thanks to the hotel manager and took the next elevator back to the lobby. His behavior bordered on the ridiculous. He acted as if he was the only one who could care for her properly while at the same time he was plotting to bring the world she knew crashing down around her.

She had to survive without him.

The decision made, he pushed open the hotel doors and waited for the valet to get a limo. He had arrangements to conclude and needed to return immediately to Bremerhaven.

Adriana Falcone safely tucked away in her hotel room was a move he had not anticipated.

He intended to use it to his advantage.

Hamburg

"We've been screwed," Adriana said.

The schnitzel no longer looked appetizing. She put down her fork and studied the men seated at the dining table with her. Mario Gavino, who was in his mid-fifties and looked it, was an operations vice president. Renzo Marossa was the other attorney who, along with Luigi Gallo, belonged to the law firm representing the Falcone business interests. Renzo was so formal and correct that Adriana sometimes wondered if he slept in his business suit. Tonight the three men looked angry and glum as they finished recounting what had occurred after her departure from the shipyard.

"He's got the money to pull it off," said Renzo, the youngest of the men. "His reputation in the industry is that he's a man who doesn't take no for an answer and always gets what he wants. Looks like he's going to pull this one off, too."

"He has the advantage of knowing his ship will be completed on time," Luigi commented, reaching for his beer. "Our problem is that our ship is still in limbo."

"Limbo?" Seething, Adriana couldn't remember ever being more upset. "We're at his mercy—and rest assured his ship will be the first vessel to float out. I venture a guess that we'll hear excuse after excuse why work on the *Pisano* hasn't continued. He's got our cruise line exactly where he wants us— no longer threatening his expansion plans."

"I'm not so sure." Luigi sipped his beer, the eyes behind his wire-rimmed glasses thoughtful. "Sure, our cruise ships would fill an upscale niche he hasn't yet covered, but he has the resources to acquire anything he wants. He has other cruise-line competitors—why single out the Falcone Line? What makes us so special?"

All three men automatically looked at Adriana.

The ring around his neck and the name Julia are the key to why the Falcone Line is on his agenda, Adriana thought. If she could only discover the identity of Julia, she'd be able to turn a disadvantage to an advantage.

"Gentlemen, I don't know why Thorne Weston covets our cruise line, but I assure you I intend to find out."

While the waiter removed their dinner dishes and brought coffee for Adriana and schnapps for the men, Adriana began to calm down. She still felt a bit dopey from the painkiller the doctor had given her, though it was wearing off and her leg was beginning to throb. The doctor had cleaned the cut and also written a prescription for an antibiotic, which he'd had filled for her and delivered to her suite. Before taking a short nap, she had telephoned her legal team with instructions. Later, Luigi's telephone call with news regarding the conclusion of the shipyard meeting had awakened her.

Dressing in a pair of loose black crepe lounging pants to cover her bandaged leg, Adriana had teamed the pants with a blue cashmere sweater set and slipped into cushioned sandals that felt more like slippers. The men were already seated at a quiet corner table when she arrived.

She'd been astonished to learn Thorne Weston had returned to Bremerhaven. If she hadn't known otherwise, she would have also accused him of being responsible for her cut leg. He'd certainly used her injury to his advantage and, as if to ensure his success, thrown in a little charm and sexiness. Her own plan was not meeting with success; perhaps she should learn to play this game of his but with her own rules.

Signing the bill, Adriana stifled a yawn. "I'm going to excuse myself. It's been a long day for us all."

"I'll take you back to your suite, Marchesa."

Luigi tossed his linen napkin on the table and shoved his chair back. Anticipating her refusal, he added, "I insist."

Smiling, Adriana linked her arm through his. Her leg ached and she was grateful for his considerate offer. Renzo and Mario trailed behind as they all acknowledged the quiet *guten Abend* of the staff.

They headed for the elevators and were halfway through the lobby when the hotel doors burst open and a laughing group entered. Although several women were in the group, Adriana spotted Thorne Weston and some of the men who worked with or for him in the group, too. Beside her, Luigi muttered, "Uh-oh."

"Stay close to me," she said. "I do *not* want that man anywhere near me tonight." Her hand tightened on Luigi's arm and she tried walking faster. Renzo and Mario closed around her, trying to shield her from the other party's sight. Hurrying toward the elevator, Mario punched the up button. Watching the lighted floors above the elevator doors, Adriana waited for them to open. The loud laughter had ceased abruptly, but Adriana did not glance back to discover why.

The elevator doors finally opened. Two women stepped off and Adriana stepped forward, grateful for the hand that held the door open.

"Hey, what are you doing?" she heard Luigi shout.

Adriana was in the elevator now, and she turned just in time to see Luigi's startled expression and Thorne Weston barring his way into the elevator.

"Sorry, gentlemen," Thorne said, "but this elevator is filled."

Panicking, Adriana stumbled toward the panel to hit the open-door button, but it was too late. The doors slid shut and the elevator began its climb. Adriana and Thorne Weston were the only people on it.

"Why did you do that?" she asked, trying unsuccessfully to keep the uneasiness from her tone.

"I told you earlier today that Luigi didn't seem to be the rescue type." Thorne moved closer to her, and she stepped away, only to have his arm curl around her waist and pull her against his hard body. "As usual, I was right."

"Stop this elevator. I want to get off."

"Your room or mine?"

Twisting, she glared at him. "Mine. I want to get off on *my* floor. *Alone.*"

"You wouldn't get five feet." He shook his head. "What were you doing downstairs? The doctor ordered you to stay off your feet until he sees you in the morning."

"How did you know?"

"You didn't think I'd leave and then forget about you?" His hand tightened at her waist. "Don't you ever follow orders?"

"Not from you I don't." She tugged at his hand. "Let go of me."

"Relax," he said, "and lean against me. Don't pretend you're not in pain—I can see it in your eyes."

"You're the pain," she accused. "Now let me go."

"Don't be difficult, Marchesa." The elevator doors opened on eight—*his* floor—and Adriana pushed against him and instantly regretted the action. His arm tightened like an iron band and she heard him inhale sharply.

"Very well." His voice sounded ragged. "You win."

Reaching across her, he punched the number five—*her* floor. "Get your key out."

She opened her mouth, but took one look at his face and forgot what she was going to say. There wasn't any point, anyway. He'd made up his mind. She resigned herself to her fate.

She fumbled for and found the key she'd slipped in the pocket of her pants, and when the doors opened at her floor, permitted herself to be unceremoniously scooped up into his arms once again.

He seemed to cover the distance from the elevator

to her door in seconds, allowing her to lean slightly out of his embrace to put the card key in the door and twist the knob. He kicked the door open and, as he had earlier in the day, went directly to the bedroom and deposited her on the bed.

"I need to talk to you," he said, then strode toward the door. "Just not tonight."

She heard the door shut and knew she should have felt a sense of relief.

She didn't.

Coconut Grove, Florida

Nevada stepped out of the shower and toweled herself off. The mirror above the vanity had steamed up from the shower, but not enough to totally obliterate the reflection of her showgirl figure. It simply reinforced what the bathroom scales had already confirmed. Her body was still perfect. For the past ten years, her weight had remained unchanged, not a pound less or a pound more. Every once in a while, she wondered what would happen if the scales said otherwise. But it was a trail of thought she was reluctant to follow. An old boyfriend had once ventured his opinion by saying, "Control your weight, control your world."

Tonight the knowledge she retained that control was a comfort after an incredibly hectic few days.

She'd flown to L.A. to address a convention of travel agents and taken the red-eye back. Clothing tumbled out of several suitcases scattered about her bedroom. Fortunately the cosmetics bag on the counter didn't need unpacking. She'd long ago decided to buy two of everything, so her travel bag only needed replenishing.

Tossing the towel, Nevada pulled on a pair of panties and a favorite T-shirt, which on her tall frame barely covered her hips. Originally hot pink, the shirt was now faded and the imprinted Blue Ribbon Cruises barely discernible. Tropical foliage outside her Coconut Grove two-bedroom cottage gave her the privacy to walk around nude, but since the day she'd discovered two neighborhood teenage boys peeking through her windows, she'd made it a practice always to be at least partially clothed.

The house was an impulse, but one she'd never regretted. She'd discovered it by accident. She'd been out riding her Harley through the Grove one Sunday, noticed the Open House sign and followed the unpaved lane to this cottage and bought it that afternoon. When she had the time, Nevada liked going to flea markets and finding something new. Although she could afford anything she wanted, the house with its eclectic, comfortable furnishings was where she felt the happiest.

Professionally she was often labeled a ''tough,

sexy broad" who wore power suits with matching handmade shoes and purses. She had her hair and nails done regularly. Women who met her were intimidated; men wanted to take her to bed.

Her simple tastes and personal life-style didn't jibe with the Nevada Sinclair people thought they knew. This cottage was her secret place; everyone thought she lived in the fancy condo with its doorman and guarded entrance.

Spacious and sleek with decorator furnishings of leather and chrome, the condo was her official address, but she spent very little time there. Occasionally she used it for business entertainment, but lately she stopped there only to pick up her mail and make sure the answering machine was forwarding her calls to the cottage. Over the past several years, Nevada had shaped the cottage into a place that suited her—a place where she could be herself and not worry about what anyone else thought or felt.

It was good to be home.

While she decided whether or not to go out for dinner, she hit the play button on the answering machine. She'd no doubt hear how Thorne was making out in Germany.

Sprawling on the bed, she stared at the ceiling as she listened to the messages that had accumulated over the past few days. A couple of men she'd occasionally dated, her secretary about a meeting the next morning, and the ship captain she'd had a drink with while spending a few days onboard one of the vessels on a special-incentive cruise. A tiny smile played around her wide mobile lips as she thought about the evening, then disappeared when the last message played. There wasn't one from Thorne.

Disappointed, she got up off the bed and wandered into the kitchen, where she stepped out into her tiny yard with its flagstone patio. Returning to the kitchen, she came back out with an open tin of gourmet cat food and a bottle of beer. She placed the tin near the back steps, then, sitting down, took a swig of beer and waited for Brady to put in an appearance.

Black and bushy, the old tom hung around enough that Nevada's neighbors considered him her cat. But Nevada knew otherwise. Brady was the one who controlled the relationship, coming and going as he pleased and remaining a strictly outdoor animal. Sometimes Brady would allow her to pet him, but only after his belly was full.

Soon she saw a movement in one of the hibiscus bushes. She didn't move, just sat on the steps in her panties and T-shirt, holding the bottle of beer, long bare legs extended. Brady sauntered across the tiny lawn, bushy tail dragging, black coat badly in need of brushing and yellow eyes belligerent as if to ask, *Where the hell have you been?*

"Mind your manners," she whispered. He stopped and looked her over carefully, then pretended he'd just spotted the food. With bored indifference, he crouched by the tin and started to wolf down the food.

"Hey," she said. "Just remember to say thanks before you leave, would you?"

When he finished, licking the tin spotlessly clean, Brady strolled closer to her and flopped just short of reaching distance. Like a certain man she knew.

"Why do you have to be so difficult? Why do I have to come to *you?*"

Again, Nevada thought of Thorne and wondered if he'd call that night or the next day. Cats and men. She sure knew how to pick 'em.

11
_____

Joint Venture

Bremerhaven

Adriana studied the men seated around the teak conference table and made a daring decision. There was no doubt that Thorne held the upper hand. Her own offer was not in the same league as his. The money he was prepared to put into the shipyard was more than she had, and everyone at the table seemed to know it. But her desire and willingness to gamble with them on the shipyard's success had carried weight with the men at the table, enough to make them reluctant to immediately commit to Thorne Weston's proposal.

If nothing else, she had succeeded in delaying a decision.

Thorne's amiable smile had long since vanished from his handsome face. His mouth was tight and his forehead creased. It was about time he learned everything wasn't always so easy. His team at the

table took their cue from him and were more subdued.

"Gentlemen," she said as she rose from the
leather conference chair, "if you would give Mr.
Weston and me a few minutes alone, I think we can
conclude this meeting to everyone's satisfaction."
When Thorne started to object, she cut him off.
"Grab a cup of coffee, everyone, and let the two of
us discuss what's best for our respective cruise
lines."

Beside her, Renzo look questioningly at Adriana.
"Do you want me to stay?"

Since Thorne's men were already leaving the
room, Adriana knew it would be perceived as a sign
of weakness if she asked a member of her team to
remain. She shook her head. "Go ahead, Renzo. Just
don't go too far."

Adriana stood near her swivel chair. In front of
her on the mahogany table was a paper tablet filled
with her notes. She placed her gold pen neatly beside it, took a tiny sip of water from her glass, set
it back down and moved quickly to join Thorne.

Exchanging pleasant small talk with the various
shipping executives as they filed out of the room,
she was particularly attentive to Herr Stierhofer and
Herr Schellin. When the last man was through the
door, Thorne pulled it shut and Adriana heard the
lock click.

She stiffened with resolve. He knew exactly how

to make her absolutely furious, but she was determined not to lose control. If she let him get to her, she knew he'd win.

"You're bluffing." Like bullets, he spit out the accusation.

Adriana pushed a chair away from the table and sat down. "Prove it," she said, deliberately crossing her legs.

She saw his jaw clench as he fought to maintain eye contact. When his gaze wavered and dropped to the bandage on her leg, Adriana knew the battle had shifted in her favor. Confidently she baited him further by swinging her leg back and forth and waited for him to meet her eyes again.

As if reaching a decision, his shoulders squared and he moved several steps closer, stopping within touching distance of her chair. His gaze traveled slowly up her legs and lingered on the area where her short suit skirt barely covered her thighs, then it hovered on her clasped hands and whitened knuckles. She might as well have been wearing only her lacy bra and panties the way his gaze succeeded in strip-searching her.

Bracing himself against the conference table, he crossed his arms. Everything about him seemed larger than life and intimidating. He crossed his arms and Adriana noted how big and capable his hands appeared.

He wasn't wearing Piero's ring and hadn't since their first meeting.

She wanted to ask why he didn't have the ring on, but first she had another matter to settle. Realizing Thorne wasn't going to take a seat, she stood up and faced him.

Thorne reached across the table to where he'd been sitting and picked up a packet of materials. "This is a financial profile of the Falcone Line— and you." He slammed the papers on the table, the sound like a shot. "You don't have the money to buy your way into this deal."

"Who says?" Adriana had a sinking feeling in the pit of her stomach. "A bunch of papers proves nothing."

"Look at them." Picking them up again, he shoved them at her.

Reluctantly Adriana accepted them. As he continued to glare at her, she riffled through them and the sinking feeling turned into a sick feeling. The report was too thorough; it hid nothing, not even the fact that Adriana feared not having enough money to build the second ship. "So what if a little of this is correct?" she challenged. "Business is great. These past few months have been extremely profitable and successful. Even if some of the information in this report should be true, it will be outdated."

"The point, Marchesa, is that today you can't compete with me at this table. You've used that sexy-as-hell body of yours to charm and mislead these men, but the truth is that no amount of batting those baby blues is going to change anything. I've got the money to buy a majority interest in this shipyard—and you don't.''

"Now who's bluffing?"

"That report is not a bluff."

"How can you be sure?" She tossed the papers back on the table. "I hope you didn't pay too much for that information. It's just about worthless."

"I knew you'd once been a model in the States." He crossed his arms again, which only made him seem to loom larger over her. "I didn't know you were also an actress. In this case, not good enough."

She shrugged. "Good enough, I'd say, to throw you a curveball today."

The fingers of one hand flexed. His face was dark with fury, and Adriana didn't doubt he wanted to wring her neck with his bare hands.

"Let me remind you that I'm still, figuratively speaking, at bat. And my batting average is very high." He grinned. "You'd better take your best pitch."

"I have the money. It's just a matter of a phone call to Emilio Donato, head of Falcone finances, and the money will be here. I want to be your partner and in this ownership. Name your price."

"My price, Marchesa, is what I've always

wanted.'' Leaning closer, he radiated intensity. ''Your ships. Sell them to me.''

''You're crazy.'' She started toward the locked door.

''Come back here,'' he said with such authority that Adriana stopped, took a deep breath and turned to face him.

He muttered what sounded to Adriana like an especially foul swearword.

''I'm going to say this once, and only once. I'm investing 200 million dollars in this shipyard. The deal is going to happen, and when it does, I'm going to make absolutely certain that your new ship is the last ship on the completion schedule.'' He leaned forward so that his eyes were level with hers. ''Do not for an instant question whether or not I can make this happen. I can.''

He was silent for a moment, as if to let his words sink in. ''If you want the construction of the *Pisano* finished, there's only one way it's going to work. And you're not going to like it.''

''Try me.''

''I'll allow you to participate with me when I form a new ownership structure of the shipyard, along with the current owners. The ships will be finished on schedule, and we'll buy time for the shipyard to remedy the factors that brought about this financial crisis. If you want in on this venture, I don't want cash.''

"What do you want?"

He made her wait for his answer. "I want collateral."

"Collateral?"

"A fifty percent interest in the M.S. *Pisano*."

Hitting him wasn't an option, but it was an instinctive reaction to his smug proposition. "That's unacceptable," she said, wanting to scream, *No, No, No.* But her mind reasoned, *Wait a second. Maybe you can salvage something here.*

"I can put up property. There's the villa in Tusc—"

"Read my lips, Marchesa." He leaned so close Adriana could see herself reflected in the black pupils of his eyes. "The M.S. *Pisano,* and only the *Pisano.*"

Pressing her lips together, Adriana looked at a distant point beyond Thorne Weston's shoulder. She needed to overcome her volatile emotions and maintain focus. Taking a deep breath, she couldn't resist asking, "Why? Why the *Pisano?*"

"One—she's already here at the shipyard. Two—she's your newest and best ship."

"You only want the best, isn't that right?" Adriana searched his face, trying to weigh the controlled expression and coolly calculating eyes against her gut instincts. She knew she couldn't trust Thorne Weston, but she wasn't in a position not to trust him. She needed her ship completed on time, and Thorne

Weston was offering her a way to salvage a potentially disastrous situation.

"The *Pisano* would be completed on schedule? I have your assurance?"

"Certainly."

"How much of an equity interest would you give the Falcone company in the shipyard? What are your projections as to future profitability?"

"We can hammer out the fine print with our attorneys. Is it a deal?"

"There's a large payment due in several months on the *Pisano*. As a fifty percent owner, I'd expect you to ante up your half." Privately Adriana had been concerned about the availability of funds for this payment. "When the shipyard is profitable and my ship's completed, I want a clause that I can sell out and get back your interest in the *Pisano*."

"Agreed."

Reluctantly, but feeling it was her best option, Adriana nodded. "Deal."

"Good." He stood, extending his hand.

What had she just done? She'd intended to make a deal but hadn't expected to risk so much. When she clasped his hand, she shivered. His strong capable hand engulfed her smaller one; his fingers tightened a fraction on hers and his thumb suggestively caressed her wrist.

"Let's have dinner tonight."

She frowned. "I don't feel like celebrating."

"Celebrating? Hardly." A dark eyebrow quirked as if he found her suggestion amusing. "We have business details to wrap up. Let's do it over dinner. Now, let's tell everyone our news."

As she watched him move toward the door, she knew that her future held more battles—and no guarantee they would end as favorably. He had resources greater than hers and she needed her own leverage.

And more than ever she needed to know his relationship with Julia. And exactly how he'd acquired Piero's ring.

Miami

Luke knocked on the open office door and was about to turn away when he spied a set of legs sticking out from the side of the desk.

"What the hell are you up to now?" he asked, stepping into the messy office and peering behind the desk. "Oh, my, this is interesting." He chuckled at the outraged squawk that followed. Nevada's delectable rear end was high in the air while the rest of her was flattened under her desk. Luke enjoyed the moment. Nevada Sinclair had one of the best asses he'd ever seen and her legs were to die for. For as long as it lasted, he was determined to enjoy the view.

When she started backing out, muttering some

words he really didn't want to hear, Luke stepped back out of her way. As soon as she was clear of the desk, she reared up, still on her knees. "I dropped an earring, you pervert!"

He held up his hands. "Hey, I came by on business. Can I help it if my timing was perfect?"

Bracing a hand on the desk, she stood up. In her heels, she was as tall as Luke. "You're pathetic. Did you break up with another one of your string of wanna-be wives? You know, a steady relationship might eliminate the need to ogle every woman you see." She tilted her head and clipped the earring in her hand to her earlobe. "Not to mention the strain on your eyes."

"You've been writing too many publicity releases. You're starting to believe your own hype." He looked her up and down and whistled, low and wolfish. "Besides, you know you eat it up. The day guys stop looking you'll enter a convent."

"Listen to you." She sat down in her desk chair. "Underneath this disguise, I'm just an old-fashioned girl who'd rather be home baking pies and sewing curtains than taking the red-eye three times a week."

Laughing, he sat down in the chair opposite her desk. He draped his arms across the low back and stretched out his legs. "I'm leaving for San Juan later today. I heard you'd just gotten back from L.A.

and wanted to touch base with you before I left. Got
a few minutes?"

"Not really. I'm due at a new incentive-group
meeting in a few minutes. Can we make it fast?"
Nevada reached for a cookie tin on her desk and
popped the lid. A delicious odor filled the room.
"Want one? I need an opinion."

Luke remembered he hadn't eaten lunch. He
reached for a cookie and took a bite. "Mmm. This
is delicious. What kind is it?"

"Chocolate-chip rum coconut."

"Rum?"

"Just a drop or two," said Nevada. "Meyer's.
That dark Caribbean kind you like so much."

"Great." The more he chewed, the more he loved
it. "We should offer these on our ships. Can you
get the recipe from whoever gave them to you?"

"Yeah, I guess I can do that." Nevada grinned.
"It's my recipe."

"Right, Nevada. The last place I picture you is in
a kitchen." He reached for another cookie but Nevada slapped his hand away and moved the tin out
of his reach. "Though a few minutes ago, I confess,
I easily envisioned you in a bedroom."

"That does it." She slammed a drawer shut and
stood up. "I'm going to my meeting."

"Okay, okay. I'm feeling punchy today. Too
much travel, not enough R&R." He waited until she
slowly sat back down and stopped glaring at him.

"Just wanted to know if you'd heard from Thorne. I got a garbled voice message—he's somehow acquired an interest in the Falcone ship under construction at the Bremerhaven shipyard. Did he tell you more about it?"

"No." Nevada's smile disappeared.

Luke wondered if he'd just made a serious faux pas.

"It was late when I got home last night. I missed his call," she explained.

"Well, that's it, then." Luke stood up and tried to lighten the mood. "Hey, when I get back from this trip, if that cookie baker is single, how about an introduction? If she looks as good as she bakes, I could be very interested."

Nevada gave him a look that would have cut most guys off at the knees. "Sorry, she's very picky. Besides, you're not her type."

Straightening his silk tie, Luke feigned outrage. "What? A handsome, never-married, charming— not to mention rich—bachelor is not her type? What's wrong with me?"

"Start with self-centered, egotistical and…and… clueless!"

"Clueless?" He followed her out the door and watched as she headed down the hallway without even a "See ya." He wasn't in the least clueless. Thorne had acquired an interest in the Falcone ship.

And Luke knew Nevada was wondering the same thing that he was.

Had Thorne also acquired the marchesa?

Hamburg

It should have been a perfect meal.

White asparagus, peeled and poached in its own juice, and served in small casserole dishes. New Malta potatoes with drawn butter. Farmer's-style boiled ham and sliced Westphalian ham. A great bottle of white wine.

It should have been perfect, Adriana thought, but it wasn't.

"Why did you ask me when we're having the next board of directors' meeting?" Adriana asked, stabbing a tender piece of asparagus.

"It seems to me like an entirely reasonable expectation," Thorne said, his expression watchful. "As the holder of an ownership interest in a Falcone ship, don't you think I'm entitled to attend?"

"Isn't a fifty percent interest in one of my ships enough to satisfy you?" she asked, trying to ignore the way her body tingled under his scrutiny. "Or is this just the beginning of your interference in my company?"

"Marchesa, let's not discuss ships, yours or mine. Tonight I'm only interested in you."

In the candlelight Thorne's dark eyes gleamed in

a way that made Adriana feel like part of the main course. Her breath caught and held. He wasn't above using physical attraction to distract her from paying attention to business.

"Tell me why you insist that my attorneys include decision-making rights in the agreement regarding the *Pisano*," she said. "I've put up an interest in the ship as collateral, but I certainly didn't intend for you to participate with me in the ongoing construction and decision-making process regarding the ship."

"I thought your guys would have explained the details to you." Thorne looked up, a thick slice of ham on his fork. "They returned to the hotel in plenty of time to brief you before we met tonight."

"I was out." Adriana toyed with another piece of asparagus, normally a culinary treat, and anticipated his next question.

"Where were you?" He watched her fiddle with the asparagus. His voice dropped, seductively soft. "You were late for our dinner date, too. Why?"

"You know, Weston—"

"Thorne."

"Look, would you quit sounding like the Grand Inquisitor? Where I was this afternoon is none of your business."

"It is when it ruins our dinner."

"My dinner was ruined the instant I learned you intended to meddle with my ship. I'm doing just fine without your personal involvement.'' She believed in being direct. ''I'm not as obtuse as you imply. I do understand that your temporarily taking ownership of the shipyard with your millions of dollars and your excellent credit line will allow the shipyard the necessary time to restructure and become profitable again. This partnership between you and me, with the shipyard owners, will allow construction on all vessels, especially ours, to continue as planned.'' Taking a sip of the excellent wine, she asked, ''How am I doing?''

''You're doing just fine, Marchesa.'' He speared a new potato. ''Please continue.''

''I also understand that my participation in this partnership gives me the assurance I need that the *Pisano* will be ready as scheduled. What I fail to understand is why you now insist on not only controlling the shipyard affairs but interfering in the finishing phases of my ship.''

''It's a lawyer thing. Yours and mine agreed that it's best if I protect my interests.''

''I don't really have a choice, do I?'' A waiter hovered nearby and Adriana placed her silver on the plate to indicate she was finished. Almost instantly, her plate was whisked away. ''Ever since I decided to position a ship in Miami, I feel as if you've become my personal nemesis. Why? Why do you want not just the *Pisano*, but all the Falcone ships?''

''I think I've made myself very clear. I have an

interest in acquiring your cruise line. This shouldn't
come as a shock to you. Everyone expands by buying older ships from more successful lines, or buying out an entire line, or absorbing it into their system as a separate division.''

''Is that what you want to do? Continue to operate
the Falcone Line as a separate entity? Not change
anything? I'm not, mind you, even remotely entertaining such a possibility. I'm just curious about
your motives.''

''My motives?'' He sat back while a waiter
cleared the remaining dishes, then ordered coffee
and brandy for them both. ''The version for public
consumption is that I have money to invest and I
choose to do so by expanding my existing company.
The Falcone Line offers an older, more affluent upscale market, and acquiring your cruise line would
allow me to broaden my demographic base.''

''And the personal reason?'' Adriana held her
breath and waited for his answer.

''Shall we say my personal reason is…private.''

''You're not going to tell me?'' Adriana looked
appalled. ''You want to know all about my personal
business—you've even *hired* someone to look into
all my financial affairs—and you have the utter audacity to tell me your reasons for harassing me and
my company are *private?*''

He looked at his wristwatch. ''Now who's being

obtuse? Surely you understand the word *private,* Marchesa.''

"Yes, I do. I also understand the name 'Julia.' And since you're wearing a ring around your neck that belonged to my husband, I also understand the word *thief.*"

For a big man, he moved fast. Adriana barely had time to blink before he had moved from the cushioned banquette opposite her to the banquette beside her, pushing his way in and forcing her to slide to her left to accommodate him.

His voice was low and silky soft. "Are you taunting me, Marchesa?"

"Isn't that what you've been doing to me ever since we met? When you flaunted my husband's ring in my face back in Miami, wasn't that what you were doing to me? Telling me that I'd better watch out because you were going to make my life miserable?"

He had her back against the wall at her side. He radiated an intense energy, normally enough to have frightened her. But she was as angry as he and not about to back down, even when cornered. "You're used to always getting everything you want, aren't you? Well, you'd better realize once and for all that this time you won't get what you're after."

"Oh, really?" He grasped her chin, holding it with a thumb and forefinger and shoved his face right in front of her. "What if I'm not after any of the things you think I want? What if I want something entirely different?'' He gave her a second or two to understand his meaning. He waited until he saw the recognition dawn in her eyes and said, ''What if what I want is *you?*''

Her heart missed a beat. Even the suggestion that he was staking a claim on her frightened her. There was no room in her life for a man, much less a man like Thorne Weston who would take far more than she was willing to give. Her voice was a mere whisper as she said, ''You can't just take anything you want.''

''Shall we see what I can take?'' he asked.

''You can take only what I'm willing to give.''

''It's a mistake to challenge me, Marchesa,'' Thorne said. His hand settled on the curve of her neck and he could feel her racing pulse. It was a dead giveaway.

In the candlelight her skin was luminous. She looked like an angel—and made him feel like the devil. Her lips parted and it was all the invitation he needed. His mouth came down on hers. She fought him, as he knew she would.

Nothing was ever easy with Adriana Falcone.

She didn't stand a chance against him and he didn't know any other way to demonstrate that any attempts on her part to stand up to him were doomed to failure. She stopped struggling, but he felt her passive resistance. He tempered the ferocity of his kiss with a fierce effort of will. His hand rested on the curve of her neck and, as he struggled to bring his spontaneous desire for her under control, he wasn't sure if the racing pulse beneath his fingertips belonged to her or to him.

With each breath, her breasts rose and fell against his chest, heightening his acute awareness of her body. As the fog of desire lifted, he became aware of her own hand gripping his jacket lapel, her ragged breathing. Somehow one of her legs had slipped between his, and again he wanted to cover her, not just with his lips, but with his body.

The clatter of plates and silverware somewhere nearby broke through the burning hot haze of desire that had overcome him. His breathing ragged, hers shallow and breathless. His body was marble-hard against her softness.

Pulling slightly away, Thorne gazed into her passion-glazed eyes. "It would seem, Marchesa," he whispered, "you're willing to give more than I expected."

Her hand, which had been gripping his lapel, began caressing his chest. He sucked in a breath, the sensation of her touching him so intimately robbing him of all caution. Only when her hand fastened on the ring, hung from the chain around his neck and hidden beneath his shirt, did he realize he'd been duped. Big-time.

He looked into eyes that no longer seemed to belong to an angel. Although clouded with desire, her eyes were also bold and calculating.

"I've just realized that I've been using entirely the wrong approach, Thorne." Her hand tightened possessively on the ring, holding a handful of his pristine white dress shirt along with the heirloom. "I might have to take what I want."

12

In the small salon on the main floor of the palazzo that served as her private study, Donatella sat at her elegant French secretary desk, taking care of some paperwork. She had chosen to do this while waiting for the luncheon guests to arrive. About to jot a notation in her desk calendar, she noticed the day's date.

La disgrazia. Bad luck.

The uneasiness she'd experienced all morning crystallized. It was a Friday and the seventeenth. The seventeenth, whether a Tuesday or Friday, was considered an unlucky day. Almost involuntarily, Donatella softly repeated the familiar saying: "On Friday and on Tuesday, neither marry nor embark."

She glanced at her watch, wondering if there was time to stop Emilio from bringing Adriana and their guests to the palazzo. There were too many changes taking place and she'd felt off balance for some time. Lately she tried to identify when this feeling had first surfaced and decided it had started when Adriana had succeeded in convincing Emilio and the others to expand the Falcone Line into the Port of Miami. Donatella had been right to oppose this idea, as evidenced later by the American television people who invaded the palazzo like a swarm of conquering invaders.

Donatella shuddered at the remembrance. The palazzo had just returned to a comfortable routine when Emilio had informed her that Adriana was returning with another group, including an important American. He'd been adamant about lunching at the palazzo and Donatella had had no choice but to agree.

Even if there was time to catch Emilio, she knew he did not share her superstitions, many taught to her by her mother at a very early age. He would laugh at her suggestion to cancel the luncheon.

Opening the desk drawer, Donatella removed a small jewelry box. Inside nestled a charm engraved with the number thirteen, considered lucky. She'd seen the charm the previous week in an exclusive jewelry store the family favored and impulsively purchased it. Running a fingertip over the raised numerals, she decided not only to keep the charm but return to the shop and choose a gold chain for it.

Perhaps if she kept it on her person, the feelings

of foreboding plaguing her would vanish as suddenly as they had appeared. Slipping the charm into her dress pocket, Donatella went to greet her guests.

Thorne had waited a long time for this day.

The board of directors' meeting at the Falcone shipping offices in Genoa had gone exactly as he wished. Now he and his London attorneys, William Lamont and Paul Edwards, were about to sit down for a celebratory late luncheon at the Falcones' elegant palazzo. The others had preceded him to a smaller salon off the foyer, but Thorne lingered behind.

The grandeur of the palazzo exceeded his imaginings. The foyer he stood in was the size of a ballroom. The walls, especially those lining the staircase and the gallery above him, were hung with paintings in heavy ornate gilt frames, each stacked one upon the other. Velvet drapes softened arched windows two and three stories high. Besides artwork, there was a fortune in antique furniture and Roman statuary.

An enormous marble staircase led upstairs to a gallery and beyond. Thorne wondered where the marchesa's rooms were located. She had preceded him in a separate car and quickly disappeared somewhere in the vast home. Ever since their dinner date, she had been cool and distant, treating him like a stranger. Her greeting in the Falcone boardroom had been restrained, to say the least.

But today something besides the marchesa held his attention. The portrait hanging above a magnificent carved library table. Thorne's footsteps echoed on the mosaic-tiled floor as he crossed the room and stood before the painting. The identity of the couple was no mystery.

The Marchese Piero Falcone and his bride, Adriana.

Like something out of a fairy tale, Adriana was depicted seated on a thronelike chair. She was a vision of cream and gold except for her startling blue eyes. Piero stood beside her. Although it had been years since their one and only meeting, Thorne had no difficulty recognizing him. The marchese's hair, unlike the ink black of Thorne's memory, was laced with silver and his handsome face bore a few more wrinkles. One tanned hand was resting on his wife's shoulder, as if declaring ownership to one and all. Whether accurate or not, the artist had captured a look in the dark eyes of both regal contentment, as well as challenge.

She belongs to me. I dare you to take her from me.

Thorne sucked in his breath. A shiver raced down his spine at his eerie awareness of the dead man's thoughts. He chalked it up to the animosity he'd carried for nearly a lifetime.

He hated Piero Falcone. It was a hatred beyond comparison, beyond any other reasonable concept. He had long since given up trying to understand the intense feelings he'd harbored since the boyhood vow he'd made as he crouched beside the lifeless body of his sister. In the years since, the only way he'd ever been able to make any sense of his hatred had been when he'd first come across the word that seemed to best explain why he'd been so driven.

Vendetta.

It was ironic that the Italian concept of avenging a loved one's death came the closest to explaining the *why* of his own intent.

The sound of a woman's footsteps indicated that his time alone had ended. Masking the feelings the portrait had brought to the surface, Thorne turned, a smile hovering on his lips. Emilio Donato's wife, Donatella, was observing him from a few feet away.

"When you like, Signore Weston, please join us in the salon." She nodded toward an adjacent room. "We'll eat when Adriana is here, which should be momentarily." Thorne wondered briefly if the woman was ill. Her face was very pale and her mouth seemed clamped in a grimace of pain. He was about to inquire if she was feeling all right when she turned abruptly and hurried away. With a shrug, Thorne glanced back at the painting, wanting one last look before joining the others.

"That's not for sale, Mr. Weston," Adriana said from behind him.

"That's fine with me, Marchesa." He squared his shoulders and turned. "I have absolutely no interest in acquiring it."

He held her gaze, wondering if she fully understood his meaning. When her cheeks flushed, he knew she had. There was a distinct difference between acquiring and sampling. He wouldn't allow the marchesa to think he could be diverted by a few searing kisses in a restaurant.

She walked toward him. "Until now you've seemed bent on possessing everything with the Falcone name attached to it." She stared at him, her blue eyes shuttered and unreadable. "You can't imagine how skeptical I am to hear you've finally lost interest."

His smile turned wolfish. "I did get what I came for," he reminded her.

"Half ownership of the M.S. *Pisano*? In exchange I got a percentage in the shipyard." She reached his side and looped her arm through his. They were in the salon doorway when she added, "Along with a little...physical intimacy thrown in to seal the deal?" With a squeeze of his arm and a lighthearted laugh, she disengaged herself. "At the time, I recall thinking that with a smoother approach you might have gotten a lot more."

As she walked off and joined a nearby group,

Emilio Donato and several Falcone board members immediately surrounded him.

Gotten a lot more.

The words hummed through his body for the next hour. Fiercely he tried willing them away, only to have them bob to the surface whenever he caught a hint of her flowery scent, heard her soft tones in a sea of other voices or saw her moving gracefully around the room. Once she even brushed against him, her hand touching his waist with the heat of a burning brand.

Lunch in the formal dining room with its beautiful frescoed ceiling and elegant furniture took the edge off his appetite. Despite his growing impatience to conclude this final formality and head home to Miami, he enjoyed the Genoese specialties of minestrone with a floating island of basil pesto, a delicious pastry vegetable tart filled with artichokes melted into a creamy mixture and followed by green salad tossed at the table with salt, balsamic vinegar and Ligurian olive oil.

Throughout the meal, he wished more than once that Adriana was seated at the far end of the table, instead of across from him. She distracted him with her explanations about each dish, and he found it impossible to ignore her. He was conscious of every bite she took, how little she ate, and every word she spoke to anyone other than himself. He had an irrational urge to fire his two London attorneys—they seemed much too attentive to her.

When Donatella Donato, at the far end of the table, began asking him about Miami, he welcomed her questions. When she later invited him on a tour of the palazzo, he accepted. Now it was he who wanted to keep distance between himself and the marchesa.

But since he wanted to know as much as possible about the family, a personally conducted tour of the palazzo might be quite instructive. While the others adjourned to the terrace for coffee, drinks and dessert, Thorne accompanied Donatella through salons, two ballrooms—one small and one large—several small courtyards and a guest apartment.

There was an overwhelming sense of family history. He found it difficult to grasp the concept of generations of a family dynasty living and dying within these walls—if not for the portraits. The walls seemed alive with the presence of long-dead men and women dressed in stiff court clothes and solemn expressions. Thorne rubbed his neck on more than one occasion, so strong was the feeling of being watched.

"Do you feel it?"

So Donatella *had* noticed him rubbing his neck. Although he judged her to be in her sixties, she carried her age well, climbing the steps with the agility of a mountain goat. He had had to increase his pace to keep up with her often as she led him from room to room.

"I don't know how you manage to live here," he admitted, "It must be like living in a fishbowl, with all these dead ancestors seeming to watch one's every move."

"They aren't watching," she said, her eyes such a deep dark brown that it was like looking at a solid brown wall. "Just reminding us of obligations and responsibilities."

"If they could speak, I imagine they would have a lot of secrets to tell."

"You're mistaken, Signore Weston," she said. "The Falcone men and women take their secrets to the grave."

Later, sipping a glass of local white wine on the terrace overlooking the bay, Thorne mentally reviewed his agenda. He'd succeeded in acquiring partial ownership of a Falcone ship. Soon it would be time to put his next ball into play.

"Enjoying the view?"

He hadn't been aware of Adriana's approach, but just hearing her voice made his heart stutter. He had definitely, he conceded, underestimated his opponent.

"It's beautiful," Thorne said. "I've been to Genoa on several occasions, but I usually stay on the ship when we're in port. I've never really seen the harbor from this vantage point.''

She turned, leaning both elbows on the balustrade behind her and tilted her head back. The afternoon sunlight caught her hair and made it gleam with white-gold highlights. ''I'm not surprised. Throughout Genoese history, pirate rivals have come by sea.''

He laughed. ''So now I'm a pirate?''

''Aren't you?'' Her blue eyes took on the color of the distant sea.

He shrugged, thinking of all that he wanted to plunder. ''Certainly more civilized.''

''Really? I have difficulty thinking of you as civilized since your behavior around me has been rather *un*civilized.'' A frown marred the perfection of her brow. ''Why have you treated me so differently? Why am I the exception?''

He took a sip of wine and decided to answer questions with some of his own. ''Are you this audacious because you're on familiar ground? Do you feel more secure here? Is that why you've turned into a tease this afternoon?''

''Here in Genoa we've historically defended ourselves from invading pirates.'' She gestured toward the bay with a hand. ''I see no reason to deviate from that now.''

''Then what did you mean when you said I could've gotten a lot more?'' A breeze ruffled her hair and his hand itched to smooth it back in place. But he knew how dangerous touching her could be...and how difficult it was to stop. More than once his plans regarding the Falcones had nearly been compromised because of his weakness for the marchesa.

"It was meant as advice, based purely upon my own limited experience with you." She raised a hand to capture the errant strands of hair, neatly tucking them behind an ear. The motion accentuated the curve of her breasts beneath the silk sweater. "Your technique could—how shall I say it?—use some refinement."

The devilish glint in her eyes indicated he was definitely under attack. He stepped in front of her to block her body from the view of the others scattered around the terrace and braced a hand on the railing, his hand brushing her arm.

"But surely you'll agree that such barbaric behavior suits a pirate like me?"

"Only in wartime," she conceded, and then quickly qualified. "Skirmishes don't count."

"Everything counts." Regretfully, Thorne removed his hand and stepped away from her. He was finding her nearly impossible to resist.

She straightened and stepped closer. "So far you're losing. I suggest you send for reinforcements."

"Don't worry, Marchesa." He drained his wineglass. "The battle hasn't even begun yet."

Adriana watched Thorne walk away and wondered what it was about him that made her feel so alive. It had been so long since she'd felt like flirting with anyone, much less the devastatingly attractive owner of a rival cruise line.

Even now she could hardly bear to take her eyes off him. She wanted to commit him to memory. Long and lean with just enough muscle in all the right places to make her want to touch and taste, to feel and be felt. Eyes that hinted at secrets yet to be discovered, hands that promised, a mouth that teased and probed.

She should thank the man. He thought he'd taken something away, but she knew he'd left something behind. He'd given her back her *feelings*. She was ready to embrace life.

She was relieved that Thorne Weston was returning to the States. He didn't want anything she was willing to give. He only wanted what he couldn't have.

And she had yet to discover what she wanted from *him*. She only knew that he made her pulse pound and her breath catch in her throat.

And left her with only one certainty. She couldn't trust him.

* * *

Donatella stood at the arched window in her study, the one room in the palazzo where she felt safest. Minutes before, she had said polite goodbyes to Emilio's business associates, including Signore Weston, and hurried to this sanctuary. She needed to think, and this was the best place to do so; she needed to examine the premise and decide on a course of action.

She watched as Signore Weston and the other two men climbed into Emilio's Mercedes to be driven to the airport. She stood in the window for long minutes after the car had pulled away and Emilio and the others had stepped back inside the palazzo, all the while clenching the charm in her pocket.

Minutes later, the front door opened again and Adriana stepped outside. She had changed into snug leather pants, boots and a jersey that left little to the imagination, and carried a helmet in her hand. Donatella briefly wondered where she was going and made a mental note to inform Emilio that Adriana continued to put herself at risk.

Donatella pulled the lucky-thirteen charm from her pocket and stared at it, trying to focus. The thought in her head was crystal clear but so absurd, so far-fetched, that she knew Emilio would think she was crazy if she put it into words. But as ludicrous as the idea seemed, Donatella recognized the truth radiating from her superstitious heart.

Her fears had taken form and substance.

The past had returned to haunt her.

Despite her precautions, it had been, after all, a day of bad luck.

"Imbecille! Cretino!"

The one-way street was narrow, winding and hazardous, but the roar of the scooter was unmistakable. The diversion was a welcome distraction. Thorne had been trying to erase Adriana Falcone from his mind. The world was filled with beautiful women, and he was in the enviable position of having many of them at his beck and call. A night of exhausted lovemaking in another woman's bed would relegate the marchesa to obscurity and allow him to focus on the task at hand.

William Lamont, one of his London attorneys and seated beside the driver, peered out the car window in an effort to see what had provoked the driver's response. "It's some lunatic on a bright yellow scooter. She's trying to pass us!"

"Che cafone!"

"What a jerk," whispered Paul Edwards, translating the driver's Italian. Seated on Throne's left, Paul was not only an attorney but married to an Italian, and his knowledge of the Italian language had been especially valuable to Thorne recently. He glanced over his shoulder and amended, "But a drop-dead gorgeous jerk."

Suddenly the chauffeur hit the brakes, tossing his

passengers forward, seat belts straining. The scooter shot past in a blur, horn blasting.

"She drives like a maniac!" said William, looking distinctly rattled.

His interest piqued, Thorne leaned forward to catch a glimpse of the woman. The yellow scooter and helmet were hard to miss, the woman encased in formfitting leather and a jersey even harder to ignore.

Thorne tapped the driver's shoulder. "Don't let her get away. Catch up to her."

Paul repeated Thorne's instructions and pulled some lira from his pocket to reinforce the command. Minutes later the road widened and an intersection ahead prevented the daredevil on the scooter from winding through the traffic. Squeezing into an opening, Thorne's driver nosed alongside the scooter. Thorne already had his window down when the woman glanced in their direction and smiled.

Flipping up her visor, she grinned at the astonishment on all their faces.

"Jesus H. Christ," muttered William.

"Shit," said Paul.

The driver's voice wobbled, "The marchesa!"

Thorne heard it all and saw it all but said nothing. For that split second in time, his eyes locked with hers.

"*Arrivederci*, gentlemen," she called. With a mock salute, flip of the visor and roar of the motor, the scooter blasted away from the car, zipped through the busy intersection amidst a squeal of brakes and honking horns.

Thorne hit a button and his window closed. He sat back and thought about the portrait in the palazzo. As if Piero Falcone stood before him in the flesh, Thorne issued his own challenge.

I'm taking her away from you.

She belonged to you once, but now she's mine.

13

Margaritas and Mango Bread

Miami

Reclining on a lounge chair on the aft deck of the
Lady Julia II, Thorne's luxury yacht, Nevada sipped
a margarita and studied the star-studded sky.

The trip to Key West had been a spur-of-the-
moment idea. Thorne had arrived back from Germany and Italy several days before. As soon as he
entered the Blue Ribbon Cruises building, she had
been notified via the office grapevine, rather than a
direct summons from Thorne. Cutting short a staff
meeting, Nevada had hurried to his office to welcome him home.

Thorne seemed tired, tense and irritable. His kiss
was perfunctory. When she mentioned she had kept
the weekend free, he had given her a strange look,
which, at the time, she had ignored.

"You and Luke round up some fun people and
let's take the *Lady Julia II* to the Keys this weekend," he suggested, dashing her plans.

All week Nevada had been looking forward to his homecoming. Her plans had been limited to just the two of them. Lazy mornings in bed, a leisurely breakfast on the patio reading the Sunday paper, a walk on the beach. She had spent an entire evening going through her recipe books planning to cook the perfect meal for him. Instead, they had dined the previous evening with eight others at a Fort Lauderdale restaurant and then all boarded this rich man's dream-yacht for a moonlight cruise to Key West.

The eight other people in the party consisted of Luke and Jill, his date; two men from the company's ad agency and their wives; and Mark Graham, the vice president of the company's sales department, and his live-in girlfriend, Sophia.

Separate staterooms had been Nevada's first clue.

"I've given you your favorite stateroom." Hand at her waist as they boarded the yacht, Thorne had casually informed Nevada of the sleeping arrangements. "I'm so jet-lagged, I may sleep the entire weekend."

A quick peck on her cheek and Thorne had disappeared shortly after the yacht was under way and his guests were settled. With a staff of six in attendance Nevada seemed to be the only one who missed him. Although she knew this was not a trip to flaunt the intimate nature of their relationship, she

had found herself wishing she hadn't been so insis-
tent about keeping it private.

The next morning, Nevada had awakened and
learned the yacht had dropped anchor off Key West.
After a day of fishing and diving in the blue waters,
everyone had changed and left in small motorboats
for an evening in Key West beginning with watching the sunset from Mallory Square. Nevada had
begged off. Her excuse had been a tough week and
a good book, but in reality she worried that maintaining the pretense of uninvolvement with Thorne
would prove even more difficult after a few drinks
in one of the local bars.

Space, Nevada thought for the umpteenth time
since Thorne's arrival home. *Give the man some
space.* Over the years there had been times when
she had needed the same from Thorne.

The solitude helped her focus. With only two
members of the crew onboard, she had been nearly
alone. After a brief workout in the gym, she'd showered and changed into a silk caftan. Wandering into
the elegantly appointed kitchen, she had puttered
with a recipe for mango bread. The result was now
in the oven.

The stars, lights from shore and moonlight shimmering on the tropical waters were relaxing and
soothing. The sound of a motorboat approaching and
laughter roused her. Within minutes she identified
the voices as those of Thorne and Luke and Luke's

date, Jill, as they returned to the yacht. Nevada glanced at her watch. Damn. She wasn't in the mood for company.

The deck was dark and she remained quiet, hoping to slip away before anyone noticed her. For a few minutes, the yacht was quiet and then Nevada heard the three of them in the lounge behind her. She picked up her empty margarita glass and was just contemplating a quick rush for a set of stairs nearby when the door behind her opened.

"Hiding from us, are you?"

"Go away, Luke. I'm communing with nature and you'll spoil the mood."

"Yeah, right. You know you can't live without me."

"Wanna bet?"

"Sure."

He settled on the lounge chair beside her. Other than the quiet murmur of voices and soft music from the lounge, it was so utterly still on deck that Nevada could hear Luke breathe. She stole a glance at him. He looked very relaxed in khaki shorts, tropical-print shirt and Top-Siders.

"Well, do I pass inspection?" he asked. "I realize you don't get to see my legs too often so go ahead. Indulge yourself. It feels good."

"You're drunk."

"I am not. I've just got a nice buzz going, and sitting here with you feels good." He stretched out a hand and found hers, fingers linking. "You okay?"

"I'm fine," she lied. "But what about you? Your girlfriend seems the jealous type."

He shrugged. "Jill's not my girlfriend. Just another pretty face."

"Surely there was something about her that attracted you?"

"Besides the obvious?" He paused and she could feel his eyes on her. "Of course, she doesn't hold a candle to you. You've got cleavage with a capital *C*."

"Men." She tried to disengage his hand but failed. "Aren't you ever interested in anything else?"

"I guess that's the problem lately, Nevada." He drank from a beer bottle. "Faces and bodies blur. And say what you like about breast-fixated men, but most of the women I meet are interested in the M-word. Money. Whatever happened to the notion of a good, old-fashioned girl?"

"Oh, they're around, buster. You're obviously just looking in the wrong places."

"Or most of the good women are already taken." His thumb caressed her palm. "You are taken, aren't you, Nevada?"

Like the moon, Luke's question hovered over them. For the merest flicker of an instant, Nevada felt her heart miss a beat. But she was, above all, a practical woman. "I *knew* it. You have had too much to drink!"

She jerked her hand from his grasp and leaped out of the lounge chair. "Excuse me. I've got something in the oven."

Luke sat upright. "The oven? Are you preg—"

"You idiot." Nevada didn't know whether to laugh or cry. "The *kitchen* oven."

"Whew, for a minute there…" He collapsed back on the lounge chair, digesting the information. "Hey!"

Turning away, Nevada hesitated. "What now?"

"You can cook?"

The note of incredulity in his voice was like a blast of arctic air. She'd had enough. Heading for a circular staircase, she didn't bother to lower her voice. "Don't panic, Luke. It's only a TV dinner."

After ten minutes of observing Jill's breasts, Thorne was just about convinced they were fake. And, if he wasn't careful, in a few minutes he knew he'd soon find out. So far, Thorne had kept his cool around the aggressive redhead. But with each drink, keeping his cool was becoming more and more difficult, especially when the lady in question, Luke's date, was about to pounce on him.

"Where did Luke disappear to?" Thorne looked around for his friend, wondering how he'd been left alone with this woman. She gave new meaning to the word *predator*. If Luke didn't show up soon, he was going to be the meal.

"Mmm, what does it matter? Isn't this cozy—just the two of us?" She inched closer to him on the banquette, her bare leg plastered to his and her torso twisted to reveal what she obviously considered a prize set of breasts. Her drink sloshed over the rim of her glass and she giggled. Dipping a finger into the wine, she popped the finger into her mouth and sucked. Beneath lashes caked with mascara, her gaze was bold and direct.

"I'm got some business to discuss with Luke. I'll find him and send him in here later," Thorne said, standing up abruptly.

She stared at his crotch and then arched a finely penciled brow. "I didn't scare you off, did I?"

"Nothing scares me off," snapped Thorne, angry at himself and at her. "Luke's my friend. I don't poach."

"Or stray?"

He smiled. This was one savvy babe. She had somehow managed to ask a question even he didn't dare ask himself. He put an end to any further discussion. "Good night, Jill."

Grabbing another bottle of beer from the bar, he headed outside, shutting the door on her quiet laughter.

"She's on the prowl," Thorne said. The deck was

shadowed and quiet. "Hiding out here won't help you, Luke. She'll find you."

"The hell she will." Luke's voice drifted out from the region of a set of lounge chairs. "The next guy she meets up with will get pulled into her stateroom. My money's on that blond steward of yours."

Thorne walked over to Luke, eyed the adjacent chair but leaned against the railing, instead. "Why did you invite her?"

"Exactly the question I've asked myself since noon today." Luke sighed and gazed up at the sky. "Do you ever wonder what our lives would have been like if it weren't for Blue Ribbon Cruises? If I hadn't bumped into you that day at the pier, I probably would have crashed in some hotel on the beach for a week or so, done some surfing and then hired on to another yacht bound for God-knows-where. By now I might have been living in a beach shack with a bare-breasted woman and a couple of kids."

Thorne studied his friend, trying to measure how serious the question really was. With only a slight hesitation, he cleared his throat and said, "You know I couldn't have done it without you, don't you, Luke?"

"Sure you could've, Thorne. You're so driven, so much more focused that I ever will be. But thanks for saying it." He sat up, feet on the deck and arms gripping the lounge chair. "We've climbed the mountain, Thorne. Don't you ever ask yourself what's next?"

"You know what's next, Luke. Expansion. More ships to be built, more ports as destinations, more itineraries."

"What about marriage and children? Settling down?"

"What's gotten into you? You've been almost engaged more times that I can count. And every time you chickened out. A little late for regrets, isn't it?"

"No regrets about not marrying any of the women in my past, Thorne. Just wondering if I'll ever meet a woman I would *like* to settle down with." He stood up, running a hand through his wavy hair. "Not to mention a little tired of dates like the one this weekend. Even screwing my brains out gets old after a while."

"I think, Luke, that what you need is a change of scenery." Thorne mulled over an idea before asking, "How about a trip to Italy? On company business, of course."

"Italy? What have we got going on there?"

"The Falcone Line's company headquarters is in Genoa, as you know. I'd just like you to keep an eye on things there for a while."

"Things?" Luke lowered his voice. "Are you talking business? Or are we talking about the marchesa? Is she getting to you, Thorne?"

"Of course not." Leave it to Luke to see through

him right away. He knew from the grin on Luke's face that he didn't believe his denial for a minute. "It's just that she's...unpredictable."

Luke laughed. "You mean she doesn't do what you tell her to do."

"Well, that's a given. No, I mean she takes risks. She's an accident waiting to happen, and I don't want any complications messing up this deal."

"I'll have to check my schedule to see when I can go, okay?"

"Call my secretary on Monday and let her know." He finished his beer. "Have you seen Nevada around? She hasn't been acting like her usual self on this trip. Or is it just my imagination?"

"It's hard to tell," Luke admitted. "She's pretty good at hiding her feelings. I was actually relieved to see Jill making a play for you, but I suppose Nevada might have had different feelings on the matter."

Thorne turned, leaning over the railing and listening to the gentle slap-slap of water against the yacht's hull. "Do you think I take Nevada for granted?"

"That's between you and Nevada. I do think she's loyal to you, regardless of any personal understanding you two have."

"Did you know about that ship's captain last year?"

"You mean her 'summer fling'?"

Thorne chuckled, although at the time he'd been mildly irritated. "Was that what she called it?"

"You were pretty tied up at the time with that television actress."

"I guess she was *my* summer fling."

"All in all, makes for a pretty complicated relationship, doesn't it?"

"Did you know I asked Nevada to marry me once? It was years ago, when I brought her back with me from Las Vegas. We lived together for a few months. Of course, I was never at home. It was the early days of Blue Ribbon Cruises and I worked around the clock. One day, I came home and she'd moved out. Said she'd rather work for me than live with me. Figured she'd see more of me that way. Guess she was right. We never really broke it off. We're like a couple who are separated but still like each other and occasionally sleep together."

"Life is never simple." Luke yawned and got to his feet. "I'm turning in. See you in the morning."

"Good night." Thorne watched Luke walk away. He would miss him while he was in Italy, but he had no choice. Luke was one of the few men he trusted.

"Nevada's in the galley," Luke called from the lounge doorway. "Marry her, Thorne, or cut her loose."

Thorne went looking for Nevada. He found her bending over and peering into the oven. The well-lit galley allowed Thorne a more than adequate look at the body outlined beneath the sheer summer caftan. He watched as she placed the pan on the stovetop and raised an arm to wipe some moisture from her forehead. Tendrils of seal-brown hair curled around the nape of her neck, and Thorne remembered all the times he'd nuzzled her neck while fondling her generous breasts.

All the times Nevada had welcomed his touch.

All the times he'd stroked and teased her to the point of no return.

He knew Nevada could put out the fire that had been in his belly for more than a week.

"Thorne." Her dark brown eyes flared with surprise and her lush mouth split into a welcoming smile. "I thought you were in the lounge with Luke and Jill."

"I was." His gaze stripped her bare and he knew letting her go would be difficult. "I was on my way to bed."

Nevada removed the oven mitts and her smile vanished. Moving as only she could—a showgirl walk, head high, shoulders back, breasts jiggling—she reached him in three steps and entwined her arms around his neck. Her face was almost level with his, her hips nearly touching him. Her gaze was unwavering and direct. "I'll come with you," she said.

He placed his hands lightly on her hips and then

moved them slowly upward, as if committing the contours of her body to memory. The long waist, slim shoulders and toned arms. With an ache in his groin but a greater ache in his heart, he gently disengaged her arms. "Not tonight, Nevada."

"There's someone else?"

He shook his head. "No one."

But they both knew he was lying.

In the dead of the night, the tears came, gushing uncontrollably. Nevada lay in bed, her back to the cabin wall and her face pressed into a down-filled pillow to muffle her sobs. Even the soothing rocking motion of the yacht failed to ease the despair that had seeped into her soul.

It had been hours since the rest of Thorne's guests had returned to the yacht and gone to bed. Thorne's cabin was on another level and she wondered if he was asleep—and if he was alone. She'd have had to be blind to miss the way Luke's girlfriend had flirted with Thorne.

It seemed to Nevada she'd spent a lifetime searching for a love that continued to elude her. Was she truly unlovable, as her mother had so often told her? Nevada's mother, a petite blonde, had joked with family and friends that Nevada was a changeling; someone had swapped babies in the hospital and given her a basketball player's daughter, instead of

her own. A gawky, gangling daughter like Nevada
could never really have come out of her body.

Not that it mattered any longer, Nevada knew. By
the time she was making enough money as a Vegas
showgirl to support them both, the first stages of
Alzheimer's had already set in, and when Thorne
stepped in to pick up the hospital expenses, her
mother had ceased to even know she had a daughter,
much less one who didn't resemble her in the
slightest.

Nevada's mother had never married, and if she
knew who had fathered her daughter, she never
mentioned it. Thorne had been the first person Nevada had ever leaned on for support, and over the
years Thorne had helped her to become a confident
woman.

But she still had a way to go, she realized, swip-
ing at the tears staining her face and staring at the
ceiling. Even Thorne had never been able to rid her
of the black hole in her center. She shifted, trying
to get comfortable, and thought about getting up and
splashing cold water on her face.

The light tap on her door startled her. The knob
turned and someone opened the unlocked door,
stepped quietly inside and pushed the door shut.

Luke.

"Are you all right?" he whispered.

His body was a dark shape moving slowly toward
her as his eyes adjusted to the dimness.

"What are you doing here?" Nevada whispered back. The lump in her throat made her voice sound more like a croak.

"I heard you crying."

"But your cabin is—"

"Jill's in that cabin," he said, sitting on the edge of the bed. "My stuff's down here. I wanted some space."

Nevada digested his explanation and said softly, "I didn't think anyone would hear me."

"My bed's on the other side of the wall. I wasn't asleep." His hand reached out, patting the bed until his hand connected with her arm. "Do you want to talk about it?"

"I've been dumped. Do you know a cure?" she said, unable to suppress her misery. "Is it wrong to want to share my life with someone who loves me as much as I love him? Someone who'll fill the empty space in my bed and hold me at night?"

"Nothing wrong with that, and nothing's wrong with you." Luke lay down on the bed, his head resting on the pillow beside her. "Okay, the space is filled. Now let's deal with the holding part."

He turned and Nevada felt his breath on her face.

"Come on, turn toward the wall and let's snuggle spoon-fashion," he said gently. "Tomorrow everything will look different to you."

Nevada turned, wriggling her hips into the hollow his curved body formed. Her back nestled against his chest and his arms looped around her, one hand slipping beneath her pillow to link up with the arm draped over her. Nevada exhaled, comforted by the press of Luke's big body, the lulling motion of the ship as it rode the night waves and his steady breathing. Gradually the tension left her and she felt drowsy.

She squirmed, one final adjustment before drifting off to sleep, and felt the instant response against her fanny. Her eyes flew open. Pretending to ignore Luke's reaction was impossible.

"Damn." The arms banded around her tightened. Nevada lay still, breath suspended.

"This isn't going to work." His tone was deep and husky. "Besides this sheet, what else is between us?"

"What are you wearing?" she asked.

"Boxers." He hesitated. "Please don't tell me you don't have a stitch of clothes on."

"I always sleep in the nude."

He groaned. "This definitely isn't going to work."

He moved his hand at the same moment Nevada shifted away from him. As she did so, Luke's hand brushed against her breast. In a fraction of an instant, she knew he'd discovered her hard peaked nipple and instinctively arched, aching for his touch. His hand cupped her breast, thumb skimming her sensitized nipple.

Luke swore, his breath hot against her cheek. "Tell me to leave. *Now.*"

Caught in an explosion of heated blood and flowing juices, Nevada twisted in Luke's arms, her mouth seeking his. The sheet twisted down around her waist and her bare breasts pressed against his broad naked chest. His mouth covered hers and his hands pulled her tightly against him. His tongue plunged into her open mouth, and body and mind merged with one overwhelming need.

When Luke lifted his mouth, Nevada tangled her hands in his hair. "Stay," she urged, pulling his head down. "Chase away the shadows."

Luke answered by taking her to a place where the light was white-hot and dazzling.

14

The Sitter

Genoa

Adriana had been back in Genoa for more than a week and was just starting to feel as if she was getting caught up at the office.

"I don't know what I'd do without you, Carla. Provisioning and purchasing equipment for the new ship is a job in itself, never mind all the details relating to the rest of the fleet."

Sitting in a chair on the other side of Adriana's desk, Carla looked up from her steno pad. "The decorator called about the Fisher Island condo in Miami. Have you had a chance to look at the swatches she sent?"

"No." Adriana shook her head and gestured toward the stack of paperwork on the right-hand side of her desk. "I suppose it's somewhere in all of this. And it's just my personal mail. At least, I've finally waded through almost everything in my in-box."

"I should warn you that today's mail hasn't arrived yet, so enjoy the empty box while it lasts."

"You sure know how to make a person's day," said Adriana with a grimace. "Were you able to reach Nico for me?"

Carla shook her head. "No, and believe me, I tried. All I get is his answering machine. Where does he go? It's as if he disappears off the face of the earth. One minute he's here and the next, poof, he's gone."

Adriana wondered if Nico was in Rome. On the day Thorne Weston left Genoa, she had found a message from the P.I. and hurried off for an impromptu meeting with him. Once again, they had met at a small café and Nico had briefed her on his progress. He was still doing a background check, but so far had only turned up that the Sacco/Mazzini family had lived in the house since the war, that it was paid for and the family was more prosperous than they appeared. Money was not a problem, but Nico did not yet know its source. Nico had encouraged her to continue her search of the Falcone family archives. Often, he said, they were the best source of information.

Carla snapped her steno pad shut. "I searched everywhere yesterday for an address or alternative number. You originally gave me his name and number on a slip of paper. I didn't ask where you got it. Perhaps Emilio?"

"No," Adriana said without elaborating. "But I'm sure I'll hear from him. Is there anything else?"

"Well—" Carla cleared her throat and refused to meet Adriana's eyes "—actually there is one other small matter."

Adriana put down her pen and leaned forward. "Most people like to save the best news for last, but you always do just the reverse."

Carla stood up, clutching her steno pad to her chest and looking as if she was going to dash for the door at any second. Adriana suppressed a smile at Carla's standard manner of handling unpleasant tasks.

"I can take it, Carla," she reassured her assistant. "Drop your bombshell and leave."

Taking a deep breath, Carla spit out her news. "We had a fax this morning from Mr. Weston. As the new co-owner of the M.S. *Pisano*, he wants a representative in Genoa. Luke Benedict will be arriving to serve as a liaison between Blue Ribbon Cruises and the Falcone Line. He'd like you to arrange for him to have an office here."

Carla turned and had almost reached the door when Adriana's small desk calendar hit the wall to her left. Carla stopped, flipped open the steno pad and stood poised to write.

"Tell Mr. Weston," Adriana enunciated in a clipped, measured tone, "that Luke Benedict can stay home. I do not, repeat, do *not* need a baby-sitter.''

Luke stepped into Thorne's office just in time to dodge a flying missile. Stooping, he picked up the wad of paper. ''What's this?'' he asked, grinning. ''Good news?''

''Just the marchesa,'' Thorne said with a ferocious scowl, ''informing me that you can stay home. She doesn't need a *baby-sitter*.''

''Good.'' Luke was relieved, his mind immediately conjuring up a vision of Nevada. ''I've got lots to do here.''

''Forget it,'' Thorne snapped. ''You're going. What the marchesa needs is a good overhaul. She's entirely too accustomed to getting her own way.''

''I can see you two are well matched,'' Luke said with a shrug. ''Are you sure this trip is necessary?''

Thorne came around his desk and leaned against it, crossing his arms. ''There's no telling what she'll do if left to her own devices. If you're there keeping an eye on her, Luke, I'll know the situation is under control.''

''I've got work here that—''

''You were supposed to go on vacation next month, anyway. Now's the time to see just how good those people you've been training for the past several years are. Besides, we've got faxes, E-mail and cell phones. There's not much that can't be accomplished from Genoa as easily as if you were down the hall in your office."

"Any idea how long this is going to take?" Luke walked to the window and stared out. He wanted to spend time with Nevada, and sooner rather than later.

"No, not yet." Thorne joined him at the window and rested a hand on Luke's shoulder as they stood almost shoulder to shoulder. "I may need you in Bremerhaven later on, too. Better pack for a long stay."

"I've got an appointment in Genoa for a crash course in Italian. I've picked up some from guys on the ships, but they only talk about soccer and *amore.*"

"Love?" One dark brow angled upward. "I guess I should mention one more thing." Thorne cleared his throat, "Don't mix business with, um, pleasure."

Luke's smile faded. "Wouldn't think of it, boss." *Is Thorne aware of my interest in Nevada?* he wondered. "I'll take good care of her."

For you.

An hour later Luke punched the down button for the elevator and glanced at his watch. He was cutting it short, as usual, and leaving himself little time to pack before he had to catch the first leg of his flight to Italy later that night. He had a housekeeper, Mrs. Gomez, who came in five days a week whether he was in or out of town. She made sure his Key

Biscayne condo was always immaculate and his things just where he wanted them. But he had always preferred to do his own packing. Even Mrs. Gomez could not meet his strict standards in this department. It was a habit he had acquired from his father, a Marine Corps captain who had treated his family like recruits.

Luke heard the elevator stop and waited impatiently for the doors to open. When they did, he was face-to-face with Nevada. His mouth pursed and he whistled, low and appreciatively. It was an automatic reflex at the sight of such striking beauty. Her red figure-hugging suit was enough to bring any man to his knees, and Luke was no exception.

Like a gauche schoolboy, he simply gaped.

"Down, boy," she said, stepping off the elevator. "Going somewhere?"

"Italy. I'm on my way to the airport." *And maybe just in time.*

She brushed past him. "Have a good trip."

"Hey, not so fast." Luke snagged her arm and spun her around. "Aren't you going to miss me?"

Whenever Luke stood toe-to-toe with Nevada, he was usually glad he was six-two because the extra few inches were about all the defense he could ever muster around her. With his hand banded around her upper arm, he held her and tried to block out the pressure of her breasts against his forearm. She took a deep breath and her breasts pushed against him.

He took a step back, hoping she hadn't felt his physical response to her nearness.

He noticed how her brown eyes were flecked with gold. Eyes of a lioness, he thought, aware suddenly of a predatory gleam in them.

"Miss you? Maybe." She moved closer, ignoring the looks and giggles from several passing secretaries. Luke felt hot, whether with desire or embarrassment, he couldn't be sure. "But thank you for restoring my confidence. I was beginning to think I'd lost the ability to turn a man on."

His blood was on fire, but a part of his brain remained detached and focused. He pulled Nevada into a nearby empty office, kicked the door shut and glared at her.

"You damn well know you could bring a cadaver back to life if you wanted to."

"How about I concentrate on you, Luke?"

She didn't bother to conceal the hitch in her voice or the sudden sheen of tears in her eyes. Stripped of her usual bravado, she might as well have been naked. "Would that work?"

"As you've learned, I'm not immune, either, Nevada." Removing a linen handkerchief from his pocket, he gently wiped a tear that had fallen down her cheek. "You don't realize how special you really are, do you?"

"Not special enough, Luke." She raised her eyes.

He sighed, wishing he could help her. "He's just one man, Nevada."

"But he's the one I wanted." She took the handkerchief from him and blotted her face. "Thanks for the shoulder to cry on."

She belonged to Thorne, he reminded himself, but couldn't bear to relinquish her entirely. "I'll call you from Italy. How's that? You can help me from feeling too lonely—especially since I don't speak the language."

"That would be nice, Luke." She placed a hand on his lapel. "How will you amuse yourself in Italy?"

Surprised at how much he liked her hand resting on his chest and aware that one of his was lightly touching the curve of her hip, Luke grinned. "I thought I'd visit the Riviera."

"Gambling? You?"

Luke pretended to look affronted. "Perhaps. I'm usually lucky at the tables."

"That is, if you ever reach Italy," she teased with a light laugh.

The sparkle was back in her eyes and Luke knew she would be all right.

"Distracted by a beautiful woman is the best excuse for missing a flight." Bending over, he brushed her still-damp cheek with his lips. "By the way, that mango bread of yours was delicious. I raided the yacht galley early yesterday morning and couldn't stop eating it.''

Her eyes narrowed. "How did you know I baked it?"

"Simple deduction. The cook didn't know how it appeared in his galley. That left only you, especially since the cook said there were no TV dinners on board—and never would be as long as he worked on the yacht."

He glanced at his watch and moved toward the door. With a hand on the doorknob, he risked upsetting her with a nagging question. "Thorne had some of that bread for breakfast, too, and enjoyed it as much as I did. Why didn't you tell him you'd baked it?"

A look of immense sadness appeared on her lovely features. "He never asked."

Parking the car beside the entrance to the Staglieno Cemetery, Adriana hesitated before turning off the ignition. Many of the mausoleums, funeral vaults and statuary within the cemetery had been created in the past several centuries by leading sculptors, and their ornate and detailed work made the cemetery a tourist attraction. But the fancy spires and elaborate structures always made Adriana uneasy.

After a few moments she turned off the ignition and climbed out of the car, wondering what had prompted this desire to visit Piero's grave site. During the first year following Piero's death, Adriana had come here frequently. But her visits had gradually diminished as she had taken on more responsibility within the company. The last time she'd visited was several months before, just before her trip to Miami. She had wanted to tell Piero about her plans for opening a Falcone Line office in Miami.

But today she didn't want his blessing. Today she wanted his forgiveness.

She desired another man.

Following the path, she tried to ignore the marble angels and gargoyles who seemed to mock her passing. Piero was dead. She was young. She was a woman with a healthy sexual appetite. Then why did she feel so unfaithful?

She was a little out of breath when she reached the Falcone burial section, which was comprised of several elaborate mausoleums built early in the nineteenth century and the more recent family vault. She had insisted on a separate grave and a simple marble headstone for Piero. His father and brother were buried nearby.

Adriana had brought a small bucket to the grave, and she removed a brush from it to sweep the headstone. Then she swept dead leaves from the area and generally tidied up. Caretakers maintained the grave, but she liked to perform her own small rituals. Finally she took a soft cloth and began to polish the headstone, rubbing the cloth gently over the smooth marble, paying particular attention to the engraved letters. All the while she talked softly, communing with the husband she had loved and lost.

At last she pressed her lips to the marble and waited for the strong connection to her husband she always felt when she visited his grave, but today there was nothing, no answer from him to any of her questions. All she heard were voices farther down the hillside and the chatter of birds in some nearby trees.

Puzzled, she stood, dusting off bits of grass from her dress. Today she felt oddly detached from her late husband. The memories were distant and, although wonderful, no longer painful. She also felt strangely relieved, as if a weight had been lifted from her shoulders.

She looked at the other graves. There was Piero's father, Vincenzo, and his older brother, Stephano, who had died during the war and whom Donatella had once been engaged to. There were fresh flowers on his grave and she wondered if they were from Donatella.

Passing the vault, Adriana paused, studying the names. Piero's mother was buried here, rather than beside her husband. Land was precious and stacking bodies or ashes was a practical solution. Adriana touched the names, recognizing some from the pictures scattered throughout the palazzo. She knew where Piero's first wife, Luisa, was, but she'd always been a little reluctant to go near this particular section. It was because she'd felt so incredibly fortunate to have Piero for a husband and didn't want to remind herself that he had first belonged to another woman whom, if not for poor health, he would have remained married to.

She no longer felt reluctant and, kneeling, found Luisa's resting spot. Reaching for her cloth, she cleaned the plate until she could easily read the inscription.

Marchesa Luisa Elena Sacco Falcone
1921-1968
Wife to
Marchese Piero Antonio Falcone

It took a full minute for the words to register. Sacco. *Sacco?* Adriana scrambled to her feet. Luisa *Sacco?* How could it be? Was Gemma her sister? And if so, what was Signora Mazzini hiding? And again, who was Julia and what was she to the Falcone family?

Adriana turned and walked slowly to her car. She had gotten an answer, after all.

Just not the one she expected.

When she arrived at the palazzo, she went immediately to the archive room. The door was locked. Adriana tried again. Surely she was mistaken. The door was never locked. But it refused to budge.

Had Donatella locked the door to prevent her from entering? Why did she seem so opposed to Adriana's search? Was it simply because she considered all of the palazzo, including the archives, her domain? Donatella and Emilio were out of town for several days, so those questions would have to wait.

Out of respect for Piero, Adriana had permitted Donatella to maintain control of the running of the palazzo. Adriana had many other duties to keep her busy and conceded that Donatella certainly ran the Falcone home smoothly and with little cause for complaint. But if Donatella had deliberately locked the door, Adriana intended to find out why.

Several hours later, Adriana switched on a lamp in her sitting room and looked longingly at the down-filled cushions on her couches. After obtaining a spare key to the archives from the housekeeper, she'd spent hours searching for information about Luisa and Julia. She had located some journals from before the war kept by her husband, but oddly there was no mention of his first wife. It was almost as if she had never existed.

Stifling a yawn, she sat down at her desk, soothed by the sight of the distant lights of the city. As she snapped open her briefcase, she pondered the coincidence of Luisa and Gemma sharing the same last name. She'd left a message for Nico—perhaps he could find the link. Scooping a pile of personal correspondence from her briefcase, she stacked it on her desk.

Instead of sorting the mail as Carla had advised, Adriana just took the first letter from the top and worked her way down. She was halfway through when she found the thick manila envelope. The handwriting was in block letters and there was no return address. Slitting it open, Adriana pulled a sheaf of what appeared to be pages from a handwritten journal, ragged on one edge as if ripped from the binding.

Adriana glanced at the first few sentences. The handwriting was delicate and, although faint, legible. Her hand began to tremble as she read on.

15

Julia

Rome, 1942

My life changed irrevocably one afternoon in 1942 when I assumed another woman's identity...

"Forget your past, forget your name," he had whispered, handing her the forged documents. "Think only in Italian. Act and speak only as the Marchesa Luisa Falcone would."

Seated in a small trattoria off the Via Venetto, Julia thought it seemed like years rather than months since she had accepted the papers and assumed another woman's identity.

The deception had begun when Julia, only nineteen, arrived in Italy for a holiday. Although no one believed the Germans would ever actually occupy Rome, assuming another woman's identity for one summer had seemed to Julia nothing more than an exciting adventure. Julia had been eager not only to visit her best friend, Gemma Sacco, but to spend the summer working at the Sacco family's newspaper as a reporter. No one had counted on Julia enjoying the role so much that she delayed her return to the States.

Posing as the Saccos' oldest daughter, Luisa, for the summer had seemed a lark at first. Married to a Genovese marchese and shipping heir, Luisa had spent very little time in Rome since her marriage five years earlier. Her husband, an officer in the Italian army, had been in North Africa for months. Luisa, worried about a favorite aunt who was ill in France, had gone to visit her in the early spring. With the Saccos' full approval, it had been easy for Julia to obtain the proper documentation to pass herself off as a merry marchesa, bored by her husband's absence, who had volunteered to assist the Red Cross and elected to write a newsy social column for her father's newspaper.

It had been just such a function that she'd attended earlier in the afternoon. Luckily she spoke Italian fluently and felt as much at home in Italy as she did in Boston. But assuming another woman's identity—even a woman she knew and resembled in appearance—was a strain. Julia never knew when she would encounter someone who knew Luisa, even though Luisa had not lived in Rome for the past five years. And, unlike Julia, Luisa was shy and quiet, and had cultivated few friends. Julia had to constantly remind herself to be low-key, not to call attention to herself either by her behavior or the way she dressed.

For Julia, nothing could have been more difficult.

Now not even the coffee tasted the same, she thought as she took a sip. The weather, sunny and unseasonably warm for late November, did little to erase the grimness of life.

Julia lit a precious cigarette and leaned back against the straight-backed chair, enjoying the stolen moments of relaxation. Her tawny mane of hair was tamed into a loose chignon at her nape. The pearl earrings and cashmere sweater slung over her shoulders were both items Luisa would have chosen to wear to the afternoon reception, given by the wife of a leading industrialist, Julia had just attended. Like the coffee, a distilled version of the event would appear in Luisa's father's newspaper.

Sometimes Julia wasn't sure if she was more actress than journalist. These days she performed both roles equally well.

Beginning at the age of eight, Julia had spent many holidays and vacations in Italy. Her mother and Signora Sacco were childhood friends, a friendship forged in a Swiss boarding school. Despite Julia's mother's marriage to an American doctor and the *signora's* equally happy marriage to an Italian newspaper publisher, the miles had not severed the close friendship, which had enabled Julia and

Gemma Sacco to be raised almost as sisters. Even the war, which she, like so many others, had thought would never affect Italy, had not deterred her. If anything, the excitement and challenge of being so close to such a world event with the possibility of covering it had merely strengthened her resolve to return.

Exhaling, Julia took note of her fellow restaurant patrons. A well-dressed middle-aged woman with a much younger man. Her lover? Julia wondered. Or son? Then she saw the woman caress the young man's thigh in a most *un*motherly fashion and knew her first guess had been right. The woman was evidently well connected, and from the way she flirted and laughed with her young lover, the war might have been a million miles away.

Not so the two men who were seated at a corner table. Raising her cup of now-tepid coffee, Julia frowned. Although one man looked fairly ordinary, his companion was dressed in ill-fitting clothes and so gaunt-faced he appeared not to have eaten a good meal in some time. His pants in particular attracted Julia's observant eye. They were inches too short. And when he ordered, Julia noted, he simply pointed at the menu. It was then she suspected that the man—and possibly his companion—was an escaped prisoner of war.

As if aware of her intense gaze, the man nervously glanced about; then, seeing her interest, he stiffened. To put him at ease, Julia smiled and resumed drinking her coffee. Casually uncrossing her legs, she picked up her cigarette and took a puff. Ignoring the men, she mentally reviewed her impressions of the afternoon reception.

In a few minutes she planned to return to the newspaper office to type her column, one that had become very popular. Not because the writing was extraordinary, Julia had long since decided, but because for the few brief minutes it took to read it, people were able to forget they were under occupation.

Absorbed in her thoughts, it was only the sudden hush in the trattoria that alerted Julia to the danger.

She turned her head to see two officers in the doorway. One was Italian, but the other was dressed in the distinctive German SS black uniform. As she had, they appeared to have chosen the small restaurant for refreshment, but before seating themselves, the German officer stared arrogantly at the other diners. The Italian officer, carrying a cane and dressed in the light gray flannel uniform with its silver buttons and braid, appeared less threatening. He was also taller and quite handsome.

Almost immediately, the SS officer spotted the two men. Advancing into the room, he halted beside the men's table and demanded, ''Let me see your papers.''

Julia's heart seemed to stop. The man with the ill-fitting clothes seemed immobilized. The other man jerkily rose and began speaking in halting Italian while fumbling in his breast pocket for the requested papers. Apparently panicking, he suddenly shoved the German officer, who stumbled against a nearby table. The Italian officer just leaned on his cane and neither spoke nor interfered. The SS officer sprang to his feet and grabbed the man. During the ensuing scuffle, the other patrons all headed for the exit. Stubbing out her cigarette, Julia collected her purse and approached the other young man, who stood rigidly against the wall. He was so frightened that his freckles stood out in stark relief against his white skin.

Taking his arm, Julia gently tugged him toward the door. "Come with me. Quickly!" she whispered in Italian, not daring to speak English and hoping he understood. Confused, but seeing his chance to escape while his companion kept the German occupied, the man offered no resistance.

Within seconds they were outside on the busy street. Julia linked her arm through his, giving the appearance of two young lovers out for an afternoon walk. She hustled him along as quickly as possible without attracting undue attention. All the while, she strained to hear sounds of pursuit. When she was sure they weren't being followed, Julia steered the man down an alleyway.

Ten anxious minutes later she knocked nervously

on the heavy, hand-carved door of the Convent of the Sacred Heart. When a tiny peephole was uncovered, Julia made the sign of the cross, and the door was immediately opened.

Julia quickly explained to the nun the young man's plight. When the nun gestured him inside, Julia said to him, "You'll be safe now. Soon others will arrange to get you out of Rome."

Shaking his hand, she shrugged off his thanks. His further survival, she knew, depended entirely on the strength of each link in the chain. Already daughters had betrayed fathers, wives their husbands. Yet, daily, strangers risked their lives and the lives of their families to see that prisoners like the young airman, all reached safety.

During the short walk to the convent, Julia had learned that the two men were English airmen, and both were escaped POWs. She intended to hurry back to the trattoria in a effort to find out what had happened to the other man. Within a week after the occupation began, Julia had been devastated by what she saw and heard on the streets. Despite the whispered rumors of what was happening in France, Poland and Germany, who would have imagined Romans—whole families, whole neighborhoods— simply disappearing? One day going about their daily activities, and the next day gone.

It wasn't long before Julia, as Luisa, was approached by a newspaper acquaintance. A young

Italian woman had been taken to German headquarters and her relatives were frantic for news of her. Since Julia had recently mentioned a German officer in one of her columns, she had been asked if she could learn anything more about the missing woman.

Her attempt to help the woman failed, but it did put Julia in touch with a special group of people whose main purpose was to furnish the Allies with military intelligence. Although she readily realized the danger, there had been no question about her commitment. No risk was too great if she could make a difference in the war's outcome.

Resister. Spy. Antifascist. Double agent. People all around Julia were dying for a lot less than any of the labels the Germans liked to brand Rome's various citizens with.

There was no doubt in Julia's mind what her fate would be if it was discovered that she was an American.

16

The Spy

Genoa

"**H**e's here!"

"Ask Nico to come in, Carla." Shaking her head at Carla's unrestrained adoration, Adriana added, "And please try to keep your hands off him."

"Oh, I had something more specific in mind," said Carla with a saucy wink.

"I bet you did." Adriana felt a twinge of envy. For some reason, she now realized, she had simply assumed that with Piero dead the sexual side of her life had died with him. The thought of being intimate with anyone else had always seemed...unnatural.

Now her state of celibacy seemed peculiar.

But what could she do about it? An affair with the only man she had the least interest in sleeping with was too risky to even contemplate. Besides, she had yet to learn Julia's identity.

As Nico entered the room, Adriana got up and came around her desk to greet him.

Nico seldom smiled, Adriana realized as she led him to an arrangement of leather couches in a corner of her office. He was always so solemn, as if he carried the weight of the world on his shoulders. He settled on a couch facing her, but didn't sit back as she did. "You're well?" he asked. "No more accidents?"

"No, nothing." She smiled. "I can't wait to hear. Did you learn anything about who sent me Julia's journal?"

Seated on the edge of the couch, he seemed ready to spring at the slightest provocation, and his deep brown eyes fastened on her in a disconcerting manner. It made her so uneasy that she blurted, "Is the news bad?"

He shook his head and a lock of silky blue-black hair swung forward over his brow. "About the only fact I've been able to verify is that Gemma Sacco Mazzini, the old woman you met briefly, was indeed your late husband's sister-in-law." Thoughtfully he added, "I don't know why she didn't tell you. For that matter, other than acknowledging the connection, Signora Mazzini refuses to discuss the topic. Either with me or with you."

Adriana tapped her fingers on the leather armrest. "Someone sent me those journal pages. Who could it be, Nico, if not her?"

"I have a couple of suspicions but nothing concrete. Although the envelope was postmarked here in Genoa, it could have originated anywhere." He stood up. "I'll keep working on it. Please let me know if you receive any more such letters. I'm going to speak with your assistant on the way out to see if she remembers anything unusual about the mail that day."

"I'm sure Carla will give you her full cooperation," Adriana said with a smile. When he left she picked up the phone and dialed Emilio's private line.

"Emilio," she said when he answered the phone, "I'm going to need twenty million dollars in two weeks to meet the next payment on the *Pisano*. I noticed it's not in my account yet. Have you put the transfer through?"

In the middle of making a notation, Adriana dropped her pen. "What? Is this a joke, Emilio?" She listened for a moment and then interrupted, "I don't care what account you pull the money from. Just make sure I have it."

Adriana replaced the receiver and closed her eyes, trying to get control of her anger. Why was Emilio stalling about the money?

Hearing a light tap at her door, Adriana looked up and saw Luke. She motioned him to come in. Despite herself, Adriana had grown to like Luke Benedict in the three weeks he'd been in Genoa. Friendly and helpful, he seemed the exact opposite of Thorne Weston. But since he worked for Thorne, Adriana didn't trust him.

"Luke, how was your trip to Milan?"

"Wonderful," he said, grinning. "But if I buy one more suit or shirt, I'll have to purchase another set of luggage, too, just to carry it all back home." He sat down in the chair opposite her desk. "From now on it's museums and exploring the Italian Riviera for me."

"I may have to visit Rome on some personal business," Adriana said. "If you're still here when I go, perhaps you'd like to accompany me."

"Sure. I can't think of a prettier tour guide."

Flipping through her desk calendar, Adriana asked, "Have you spoken to your boss lately? We've got a ship payment due soon and I've placed several calls to him in the past few days, but I can't seem to connect with him."

Luke flushed. "He's tough to catch, but I assume you left messages with his assistants? He's usually pretty good about returning calls, although it sometimes takes a few days. Plus, there's the time difference. Is there anything I can help you with?"

Adriana studied Luke thoughtfully, wondering if he was being truthful with her or if this was just a stall tactic originating with Thorne Weston. "You can tell him I'm planning to inspect my ship the week after next. I'm counting on his payment to ensure that the ship progresses according to schedule. You can assure him that I won't rely on phone calls—I'll show up in his Miami office to collect it personally.''

"I'll be happy to relay your message to him, Marchesa,'' said Luke, the twinkle in his blue-gray eyes fading. "Will you also check your calendar to see when you're free for that sight-seeing tour you promised me?''

"How much of Genoa have you seen?" Adriana sat back in her chair and, removing her reading glasses, made a conscious effort to relax her body. She was too uptight; too focused on business and not taking time for herself. "We can start by exploring the Piazza San Matteo and the Piazza De Ferrari. The finest collection of paintings and sculptures in northern Italy are found in the palaces, museums and churches in their vicinity. Afterwards I'm sure you'll be able to find your way around.''

"I usually can.''

"So I've noticed, Mr. Benedict.'' He'd spent time in the sun over the weekend and his handsome face was tanned and relaxed. He wore his clothes to perfection. The suit was fitted to show off his broad shoulders, lean torso and long muscular legs. A cuff with monogrammed initials peeped discreetly the required distance from beneath his suit sleeve. The tie, Adriana decided, must be one of the handmade Italian silks he'd purchased on his trip. The vivid blues and yellows of the tie contrasted nicely with his blue-gray eyes and sandy hair. Perhaps an evening with a man who asked nothing from her was just what she needed. "If you're free, why don't we make it tomorrow night?"

"That's a date, Marchesa." He rose in one lithe movement from the chair. "That is, if that terrific-looking guy who was here just before me doesn't mind."

"Nico?" Adriana laughed at the suggestion. "He has nothing to say about how I spend my time—or with whom."

Adriana watched Luke stride from her office. An evening out the next day, instead of working either at the office or at home, was appealing, and some of the tension bothering her earlier seemed to have disappeared.

She had the impression that Luke Benedict was closer than most people to Thorne Weston. Perhaps he knew something about Julia. Tomorrow was not just about sight-seeing. Tomorrow night was still business.

Luke returned to his hotel to call Thorne. He didn't trust the phone at the Falcone Line and had gotten into the habit of calling Thorne immediately after leaving the office each afternoon. Considering Thorne's busy schedule, Luke had been surprised when he nearly always reached him. On several occasions, in fact, it had almost seemed as if Thorne had been anticipating his call.

"She wants to know why you aren't returning her calls," Luke said without even prefacing his remarks with a hello or, as he was beginning to feel comfortable saying, *Ciao.* "Why don't you?"

The silence on the other end of the line was indicative of Thorne's displeasure with Luke's question. "I'll call her when I have something to say to her, not when *she* wants to talk to me."

"Well, my friend, I hate to disillusion you, but if you don't call her, she's likely to lay siege to your office, so you'd better be prepared for the consequences." Luke carried the phone to the hotel-room window and looked outside at the activity on the bay as he spoke. "She plans to go to Bremerhaven the week after next to check on her ship. Is it on schedule? If not, you can expect a visit from her."

"Just keep her in Genoa, Luke. I don't want her in Bremerhaven. If necessary, go yourself. What else have you learned?"

"Well, she's pretty chummy with some guy named Nico."

"*How* chummy?"

"I honestly don't know and she isn't saying." Luke turned from the window and paced back to the bed. "He reminds me of a predator—big, powerful and very savvy. But rather than hunting the marchesa, he seems more like…I don't know, a protector, if that makes sense to you."

"Luke, just tell me one thing," Thorne demanded in a curt, authoritative tone Luke seldom heard. "Is he sleeping with her?"

"How the hell should I know? Maybe he is and maybe he isn't," Luke answered hotly. "I don't know what goes on in her bedroom." *That's your department.*

Thorne took a deep breath, clearly audible on the transatlantic line. "Let me tell you again, Luke. I want to know everything the Marchesa Falcone does. Not only at the office, but her private life, as well. Including, more specifically, her bedroom."

"Damn, Thorne!" Luke snapped. *Isn't Nevada enough for you?* "I'm an operations vice president, not a spy."

"You work for me. I'm asking you to do a job, Luke. If you can't do what I ask, I'll get someone who will."

Luke's knuckles whitened on the telephone receiver. "In that case, you'll be pleased to hear that I'm making progress. Tomorrow night, the marchesa and I have a date."

When he heard the sharp intake of breath on the other end of the line, Luke's mouth twisted in an altogether unpleasant smile. "I should be able to be more explicit about the one area that interests you the most—her bedroom."

* * *

"Make a wish," Adriana urged.

About to toss a coin into the Piazza de Ferrari fountain, Luke was prompted by Adriana's sheer delight in the event to suggest, "You have to make a wish, too."

"Oh, but tossing a coin is simply to insure that you'll come back to Genoa someday."

"But if you toss one with me—" Luke gazed down at her upturned face and thought he'd never seen her look so beautiful "—it will ensure that we come back here—together."

She stared at him and he knew the instant she made her decision. "All right." She accepted a coin from him, shut her eyes and said, "On the count of three. One—two—three!"

Both coins flew through the air and plunked into the fountain at the same time. With a whoop, Adriana grabbed Luke's arm, her face alight with pleasure. "I've never done that before. Not even in Rome. What fun. Especially if my wish comes true."

She was enchanting, Luke thought, and he understood completely Thorne's attraction to her. The evening had begun with a short set of instructions from Adriana on scooters, and then he'd followed her through a rabbit warren of streets until they had finally stopped at a small café nearby.

"Wish or no wish, I certainly hope we repeat this evening again soon." Luke had not decided how much he would relate to Thorne. "Dinner was delicious. Are you sure you wouldn't like to have an aperitif? Or a cappuccino?"

"No," she said.

Amazing what a change of clothes could do, Luke thought. Instead of a designer suit, she had changed into formfitting jeans, knit shirt and flats. The private, self-contained businesswoman had vanished and a delightful fun-loving woman had appeared in her place.

"Like Cinderella, my coach is turning into a pumpkin soon. I can't pretend a briefcase of papers to review isn't waiting for me in my apartment."

"Do you do anything besides work?" he asked, turning away from the fountain and crossing the piazza toward the café where they'd parked their scooters. "Hobbies? Men?"

"No to everything, Luke." She skirted a young couple who were kissing, oblivious to the world around them. "I enjoy going to my villa in Tuscany, but I don't get there often. Especially with the new ships going into service it has been even more difficult to break away."

"Surely you go shopping? That list you gave me for Milan wasn't a figment of my imagination."

"Once, possibly twice a year, I do shop, Luke. But it's just something I have to do, not necessarily something I *like* to do."

Her lips were perfectly shaped, Luke decided as

he listened to her. He loved the way her mouth formed each word, revealing at times perfect white teeth. He wondered if Thorne had ever kissed her. She was certainly kissable, the kind of woman a man would have to be of dubious gender not to want to take to bed. But as carefree and natural as she had been the entire evening with him, the marchesa had subtly conveyed to him that she was not for the taking. Like a beautiful piece of art for viewing only.

"You told me you like to surf. Do you like any other water sports?"

"Yeah, I like sitting on the beach and watching all the pretty girls go by," he teased. "I usually go scuba diving or snorkeling when I'm at home. Often with Thorne. He has a beautiful yacht he likes to take out on the weekends when he has time."

"He still hasn't called."

"No?"

"No."

They were steps away from the parked scooters, but she stopped so suddenly that a teenager following too closely behind bumped into her. Luke reached out to steady her. The marchesa looked up at him, and the effect of her magnificent blue eyes trained solely on him was devastating.

"Do you mind if I ask you a rather personal question, Luke?" She lightly touched his forearm and at his raised eyebrow said, "Don't panic, Luke, I'm just exercising some feminine wiles and I'm a bit rusty.''

"I don't know about the rusty part. Everything about you seems to be working just fine." Luke tried to ignore his hammering heart. "What do you want to know?"

She hesitated for a second, then asked, "Have you ever heard Thorne mention a woman named Julia?"

Luke rubbed his chin. "I think a few years ago one of his girlfriends was called Julia."

"No, she wouldn't be his age or younger. Can you think of anyone else?"

"No, not offhand."

"A family friend? A relative? Employee? Someone close to him?"

"No." Bewildered by the question, Luke asked, "Why?"

"Are you sure?" she pressed, ignoring his question and watching him intently.

"Positive."

"I can't tell you why I need to know, just that it's important." The pressure of her fingertips on his arm increased, signaling her tension a second before she asked, "Could you find out for me?"

He groaned. *Not the marchesa, too. What's that called? Oh, yeah, a double agent.*

He was right where he didn't want to be: in the middle.

"Let me think about it, Marchesa," he hedged,

gently sidestepping to disengage her grip. Eager to change the subject, he suggested, "Now how about showing me again how this temperamental scooter starts?"

Luke wasn't at all sure he was the scooter type, after all. He felt more like a linebacker on a tricycle, but it was just the opposite with Adriana Falcone. Even with her helmet on, she was traffic-stopping, perched on the seat, zipping fearlessly around automobiles as if she owned the world.

After determining that he knew exactly how to return to his hotel, Adriana put on her helmet and with a smile and a wave shot into traffic. Luke straddled his scooter long enough to watch her weave in and out, her bright yellow helmet a beacon in the falling dusk.

The smell of the sea, the sound of happy voices speaking in languages he barely understood and the bustle of the popular piazza gave him a good feeling. He had enjoyed his evening, and the scooter wasn't too bad, either, although he much preferred his sporty BMW.

As he was about to turn his scooter toward the hotel, he saw the yellow helmet veer sharply. Eyes narrowing, Luke realized she'd almost been run off the road. A dark sedan had crowded her dangerously against a narrow section of road.

Adrenaline pumping, Luke leaped on his scooter and forced it to its maximum speed, pushing it through traffic and around cars while keeping the marchesa's helmet in sight. After the first bobble, she had adjusted defensively and was trying to out-maneuver the sedan. Although the way the marchesa rode her scooter was enough to inspire a case of road rage, the driver of the dark sedan was pushing it to the extreme.

Brakes squealing and horn blasting, the car had nearly succeeded in forcing Adriana off the road. Only her deft ability to maneuver the scooter had prevented the driver of the car from succeeding. Angling through an opening, Luke pushed the scooter within range close enough to shout, "Marchesa! The alley!"

He didn't know if she heard him above the racket, but when she suddenly swerved into the narrow alley just ahead on her right, Luke gave silent thanks. The sedan braked so abruptly that several cars behind it honked in protest and one driver yelled a curse. Luke barreled through a small open-ing between a shop and the car blocking the traffic lane. Screeching to a halt, he barricaded the alley with his scooter and himself. With a fist, he smashed the hood of the car forcefully enough to cause a dent and yelled, "Want to pick on someone your own size?"

The sedan was several years old, rather battered and nondescript, its windows darkened. Glancing up the alley, he saw the marchesa at the end of it, trapped with nowhere to go. Breathing heavily, Luke paled when he caught the glint of metal through a slightly lowered window.

A gun?

"Need some help?" said a man's voice in accented English.

A black Vespa had burst through the tangle of traffic. Despite the matching black helmet, Luke recognized the distinctive stubble-covered jaw and steel-rimmed dark glasses as belonging to the man he'd seen earlier in the marchesa's office.

"Two are always better than one," Luke said with a nod at the sedan, its engine revving and exhaust pluming up from the rear.

Luke set his kickstand and got off the scooter, walking briskly toward the driver's side of the car. Behind him, the man warned, "No. Come back."

But then with a rubber-burning screech, the car reversed, wedged into traffic and sped away.

Luke turned and saw the black Vespa racing up the alley. He grabbed his own scooter, pushed it aside and followed on foot. When he arrived, the man had the marchesa in his arms.

"Is she all right?" Luke asked.

"A bit shaken but—"

"I'm fine, Luke," she said, pushing away from the man who seemed reluctant to release her. "It was just a scare."

The cute yellow scooter looked ridable, but the

front fender was scraped and bent. "You can't ride that scooter home," Luke protested as she got on.

"Yes, I can." Her blue eyes challenged him to prevent her. "Thank you for helping out. And, Nico, I guess it was lucky you were around tonight, too."

"Guess so." He'd removed his dark glasses and Luke felt a shiver scoot up his spine at the flat, unblinking stare. "I'll ride home with you."

"I'll come, too," Luke volunteered.

"It's not necessary," said the man named Nico without glancing at him.

"Oh, but it is." Luke had been intimidated by the best of men, and he wasn't about to take a back seat to some scruffy character who appeared out of nowhere.

"Fine." Nico's gaze skimmed him assessingly. Luke caught a flicker of grudging approval in his eyes before they shuttered again. "Get your scooter."

With a glance to see that Adriana was managing all right, Luke walked down the alley, the man following beside him on the Vespa.

"Did you see the gun?" asked Luke.

"Yes." The man hesitated, then added, "That was a dangerous and foolish thing you did. You could have been shot."

Luke shrugged. "So could you."

"I'm not a stranger here like you. I know the

customs and I know what to expect. You don't have any idea what's going on here.''

''Would you mind explaining what you just said?'' Luke pivoted, the scooter forgotten. ''Exactly what *is* going on here?''

''Go back to America, Mr. Benedict.'' They both heard the marchesa's scooter coming. ''This isn't any of your business.''

In the darkened alley, Nico's words seemed ominous and threatening. It took only the sight of the shaken marchesa for Luke to make up his mind. ''That's where you're wrong. I'm making it my business.''

''You're making a big mistake.''

Luke started his scooter. ''Don't worry. It won't be the first time.''

They rode in silence all the way to the imposing palazzo the marchesa called home. After once again assuring them that she was fine, she disappeared through the ornate front doors. Ignoring him, Nico rode away immediately.

Luke followed the Vespa's taillights, hoping he could find his way back to the hotel without getting lost.

He now had more questions than ever, but he'd at least had one of them answered. He now knew why the beautiful marchesa was still single.

Dating the marchesa might well be interesting, but it was also dangerous.

* * *

Adriana disliked the bullet-proof Mercedes. It represented everything she hated about her life, everything she hated about the past, and everything she was working so hard to abolish from her life.

The fact that she wasn't succeeding had never been more evident than last night. Nico thought the car had deliberately tried to run her off the road. Adriana was still reluctant to consider that the driver had anything more in mind than to simply scare her. She was, after all, a rather inconsiderate driver herself. There was a chance she had done something to provoke the attack, though she couldn't remember cutting the car off in traffic and she certainly hadn't made any obscene gestures. However inadvertently, she must have done something...

Adriana thanked her driver as she got out of the car and proceeded toward the Falcone Lines offices. Although not totally unexpected, she was still somewhat surprised to see Luke Benedict waiting on the front steps.

"Is that one of your new suits?" she asked in an attempt to avoid the questions she knew were his motivation for this early-morning vigil.

"I'm not here to talk about clothes this morning, Marchesa." He nodded toward the departing car. "I am a little relieved to see you've come in the car. You realize, surely, that riding that scooter of yours is out of the question."

"Look, Luke—" she lowered her voice but moved close enough to Luke that her words carried the weight she intended "—for a while last night, we had a pleasant evening. Nothing more. Certainly not enough that you can dictate to me or, for that matter, worry about me. I appreciate your concern, but I want to assure you that you don't need to worry about me. Ever. I can take care of myself."

"Last night, you could have fooled me."

Stepping around him, she hurried ahead, a distinctive leather briefcase in one hand. Effortlessly Luke caught up with her and matched strides with her all the way to the elevators. She knew he was watching and she tried to suppress her smile.

"Am I forgiven for sounding like just another macho jerk?"

The smile blossomed. "If I'm forgiven for being an ungrateful bitch."

"Truce?"

"Truce."

"In that case..." Luke began as the elevator doors opened and they stepped in. Adriana nodded to several employees before turning to stand by Luke's side. "I want to go to Bremerhaven in your place next week. I've really nothing much to do here. I could be more useful to both you and Thorne if I went, instead of you, next week. Besides," he finally admitted, "I'll worry about you there alone.

You're much safer staying right here. Especially with that tank for a car."

Luke's idea had merit and Adriana wondered why she hadn't thought of it herself. She had more than enough to do and Luke might as well be useful to her. Still she said, "Let me think about it today, all right? I'll let you know tomorrow about my decision."

The elevator stopped on Luke's floor and he stepped out. "There's nothing to think about, Marchesa. It's the best solution."

By the time Adriana reached her office a few minutes later, she felt as if she'd run a gauntlet. Somehow her misadventure of the night before had leaked out and she had to stop more than once to assure employees she was perfectly fine. Nothing to worry about.

Or was there?

That was the real difficulty. She could never be quite sure. On the surface everything could be explained away. But she had lost a husband because no one, particularly her husband, had heeded the signals that he was in danger.

Now that she was so close to achieving his goal, she couldn't afford to risk everything by insisting on doing exactly what she wanted. Someday, and hopefully soon, she would be able to live the life she really wanted.

Setting her briefcase on a corner of her desk, she

smoothed her suit jacket before sitting down. Reaching for a spare set of reading glasses, she skimmed her day's activities and messages. There was always a mountain of work; the load never seemed to lessen. She massaged her temples and sighed.

Suddenly she blinked. A large manila envelope was sticking out from the pile of unopened mail on her desk. Reaching into her desk drawer, she pulled out a pair of thin latex gloves and managed to pull them on her shaking hands.

Gingerly she slit open the large mailing envelope and a sheaf of paper fell out. A quick glance revealed that the penmanship was the same as in the previous set.

She punched a button on her phone and snapped out the instruction, "Carla, hold all calls. Postpone or reschedule whatever meetings or appointments I have for the next few hours. And unless there's a fire, don't interrupt me."

Adriana removed her suit jacket and kicked off her shoes. She carefully picked up the papers and moved toward a couch, where she would be more comfortable. Then she eagerly began to read.

17

Julia

Rome, 1942

Hours later, exhausted and hungry, I trudged
up the steps to the Sacco family home...

The villa was plain and unpretentious, and within
walking distance of the newspaper, which made it
particularly attractive to Signore Sacco. The sepia-
colored stucco exterior and wooden doors worn
smooth in places were indications of the building's
age. When Julia stepped inside, it was like entering
another world.

Whereas the outside was plain, the inside was
lush, with ornate furniture, antique rugs and oil
paintings. Leaving her coat in the vestibule, Julia
began to relax. Finally. For the past couple of hours,
she had been filled with apprehension, especially
when she learned the second airman had been taken
to Gestapo headquarters. She feared for his safety.

And her own.

Hearing voices, Julia walked into the more formal of the family's two parlors. Amidst the handwoven tapestries, several valuable oil paintings in gold leaf, baroque frames and jewel-toned, stuffed and fringed sofas and chairs, stood the cane-carrying Italian officer Julia had seen in the trattoria.

How had he found her? Had one of the links of the chain broken? Was he going to arrest her?

One arm draped across the fireplace mantel, he looked over the heads of Gemma and her mother and directly into Julia's eyes. In that instant Julia knew he was a dangerous opponent. It was absolutely necessary she keep her fear hidden. This man was just the sort who probed for weakness, rooted it out, and then used it to destroy his victim.

Squaring her shoulders, Julia walked into the room feeling much like Daniel entering the lion's den. Whereas Signora Sacco seemed upset—she constantly wrung her hands and her eyes would not meet Julia's—Gemma appeared extremely excited. It was Gemma's almost gleeful eyes that confused Julia.

"So," the officer said, his voice low and deep, "the Marchesa Falcone has returned home at last."

With a slight nod, Julia wished them all a good evening but offered no explanation of where she had been. "I wasn't aware a guest was expected this evening," she murmured, her tone implying that she felt no need to justify her lateness to him. Rather, it was he who owed an explanation. "Unfortunately my father has been delayed at the newspaper office."

"I was under the impression that you rather enjoyed such unexpected events, Marchesa."

He continued to lean against the mantel, perfectly at ease, as if he was lord of the manor. "Where did you get that idea?" she asked.

"Why, this afternoon in the trattoria. Although you must have been surprised when the fight began, you carefully finished your coffee, took a last puff of your cigarette and then calmly left. And not alone, I believe."

He knows.

Feeling as if ice water ran through her veins rather than blood, Julia heard Signora Sacco's muffled moan followed by an almost eerie stillness.

"Your memory is much better than mine, I'm afraid," Julia said with an elegant shrug of her shoulders. "I left along with everyone else. It's wise to avoid trouble whenever possible, isn't it?"

Straightening at last from the mantel, he seemed to tower over her. The silver buttons on his uniform caught and held the light from several small lamps. Dark brown eyes were bold strokes against the canvas of a lean, narrow face. Lines of strain were etched around his dark eyes. It might have been a face like so many others seen on the streets of Rome but for the commanding intensity of his eyes and the granitelike strength of his face. Rather than resting his weight on the cane in his right hand, he merely caressed the smooth worn wood of its handle. With a glance at the Sacco mother and daughter, he ordered, "Leave us, please."

He watched as they hurried out of the room. Gemma glanced back as if trying to communicate something important to Julia.

"We've met before," he announced the moment the door clicked shut. As if hoping to catch her unawares, he seemed to let his gaze devour every nuance of her expression. "Or have you forgotten?"

"I've been away a long time," Julia bluffed, refusing to be intimidated by his threatening expression. "I was very ill last year, and since then, I've had trouble remembering some of the events of my past. The doctors think when the war ends and life returns to normal, perhaps I'll remember."

He countered, keeping his voice neutral. "You seem taller than I remember."

She smiled in response. "I also lost weight. Perhaps that explains it."

"And your hair," he probed. "Wasn't it darker?"

"Is a woman allowed no secrets?"

He walked toward her, limping only slightly, until he was so close she felt his warm breath when he spoke. "As I recall, your eyes were brown. Is there also some womanly way of changing them to hazel?''

''Perhaps you were never allowed this close before? After all, I am a married woman. If my husband were not off fighting to defend Italy from the Allies, he would certainly not approve of this discussion.''

''Is your husband a jealous man? If so, one wonders why he would allow his wife, a marchesa, to roam about the city aiding and abetting the escape of prisoners of war!''

His menacing closeness suddenly felt suffocating. Julia spun away from him, but he reached out and grabbed her arm. Stepping up behind her, his body pressed against hers and she was acutely conscious of his muscular hardness.

''Who *are* you?'' she demanded, glaring at him over her shoulder. ''I'm going to report you to my husband and his superiors. I doubt you'll be wearing that uniform much longer.''

''Perhaps it is time we were introduced properly, Marchesa.'' Tossing his cane onto a nearby plump divan, he turned her in his arms, his hands tight bands on the soft flesh of her upper arms. His body pressed intimately against hers. It was only when his mouth was mere inches from hers that she fully realized his intentions. His kiss, when his mouth settled on hers despite her struggle to prevent it, was possessive and punishing. When he finally lifted his head, Julia wasn't sure if the kiss hadn't ended soon enough—or too soon.

Trembling, she involuntarily leaned against him. The soft flannel of his uniform cushioned her cheek. His hands pressed against the small of her back, pulling her closer. Both curious and fearful of his answer, she asked again, her voice ragged, "Who are you?"

A thumb and forefinger tilted her face so that she was forced to look directly into his eyes. "I'm your husband."

18

Mystery Man

Bremerhaven

Luke picked his way down the corridor on deck number seven of the M.S. *Pisano*, sidestepping boxes, cables, carpet remnants and tools. Several times he stepped into finished staterooms to verify that work had been completed satisfactorily. But as he approached the midsection of the lengthy corridor, Luke swore. Checking his steps, he detoured to a nearby elevator and punched the button for the Lido deck.

Luke located the captain in his office. He was seated at a desk and looked up when Luke entered.

"*Buongiorno*, Captain Robbiti," said Luke, extending his hand. The captain rose, shook his hand and inquired about Luke's trip. After a few moments of pleasantries, Luke revealed the reason for his interruption. "As I walked down deck seven, Captain, I noticed hundreds of stacked life vests blocking the hallway. I recommend they be placed in the cabins where they belong as soon as possible. Right now they're a potential safety hazard. Workmen are doing some welding nearby. One spark from a torch or a cigarette and we've got a major problem.''

''Certainly, Signore Benedict. I'll see that it's taken care of immediately,'' Captain Robbiti said. ''Is there anything else I can assist you with?''

''Everything else seems fine. I understand the owners' sea trials are scheduled soon?''

''I checked with the shipyard management yesterday and it was on next week's schedule. I understand Signore Weston will also accompany the marchesa.''

Luke masked his surprise. ''Who told you Mr. Weston would accompany the ship on the sea trials?''

''Mr. Weston.'' Captain Robbiti returned to his chair and picked up a pen. ''He informed me half an hour ago when I saw him on the bridge.''

Thorne was on the ship? Luke had spoken with Thorne from Genoa three days before and hadn't expected him to arrive in Bremerhaven for another two days. Why had his plans changed?

''Is he still onboard?'' asked Luke.

The captain reached for a walkie-talkie and spoke a few words in Italian. After listening intently for a moment, he clicked it off. ''Signore Weston is on the main deck.''

"*Grazie,* Captain," Luke said and turned toward the door. Hurrying down the corridor, he took the nearest staircase and got off on the main deck. He passed several shipyard workers and two crew members before he saw Thorne standing by the purser's office.

"I didn't realize you were arriving today."

Thorne turned his head and his dark eyes were unreadable. "My plans changed. I left a message for you at the hotel."

Luke shrugged. "I've been here since early this morning."

"I know."

"Still angry about the marchesa?"

"Angry? No. Disappointed? Yes."

"Let's grab a cup of coffee?" Luke suggested, realizing that several crew members and an officer were observing them with interest.

Thorne nodded and beckoned to the purser. "Tell the manager to send coffee and sandwiches to the owner's suite."

Luke followed Thorne up the stairs and down the corridor on the veranda deck to the marchesa's suite overlooking the Lido deck. Thorne opened the door and Luke followed him in.

"I doubt you'll find this comfortable," Luke muttered, his gaze sweeping over the pale peach-and-cream color scheme done in luxurious silk, linen and mohair with accents of gold and crystal. Luke watched as Thorne headed for the bedroom and paused in the doorway. Curious, Luke followed and looked over his shoulder.

The bedroom was feminine and decidedly sensuous. The bed was sumptuous, a combination of blush silk and plump ruffled pillows. A selection of personal photos in gilded bronze frames and Imari porcelain left no doubt in Luke's mind that the entire suite had been designed to the marchesa's exact wishes.

Thorne looked at Luke over his shoulder and said, "You're wrong. I could be very comfortable here."

"With or without the marchesa?"

"Is the marchesa still available?" he asked, a dark brow quirking. "I understand you're irresistible."

The coolness of Thorne's eyes and tone felt like a punch in the gut. Did he know about Nevada? Or was he jealous of his time with Adriana?

"If you're asking about my date with the marchesa, the answer is that she finds me entirely resistible."

"Your date was a disappointment?" Thorne walked to the door and opened it to admit a cabin steward with a tray containing a carafe of coffee and platter of ham and cheese sandwiches.

Luke poured coffee into a mug and helped himself to a ham sandwich. "Not disappointing, but certainly interesting. Dangerous is a better description.''

Thorne sprawled in a chair, a mug of coffee in one hand. ''Dangerous? What are you talking about?''

''Someone tried to hurt her, certainly frighten her and, perhaps, even kill her.''

''You're exaggerating.''

''If you call confronting a car full of armed thugs an exaggeration, then I guess so.''

''Armed?''

''I saw a gun.''

''Why did this happen?''

Luke took a bite of his sandwich and chewed thoughtfully. ''She drives like she owns the road. At first I thought she'd cut someone off in traffic and they were simply angry. Now I think someone was deliberately trying to frighten her and hurt her.''

''Any idea who?''

Luke watched him carefully and debated about whether to say what was really on his mind. ''I wondered if you were responsible.''

Thorne straightened. ''Are you accusing me?''

Luke met his cold stare. ''Just asking.''

''Just asking? After all our years together?''

''You've been secretive from the first about your reasons for wanting to acquire the Falcone Line, and you've made no bones about the fact that you would use whatever means necessary to do so. If you were involved in that incident in Genoa, then I hope to God you only meant to frighten her. If so, you succeeded.''

Thorne exhaled slowly and Luke knew he was trying to keep his temper under control. ''I thought I had your trust.''

''You do.'' Luke shoved his plate away and leaned forward. ''Except when it concerns Adriana Falcone. I don't want to see her hurt.''

''She's going to be, and there's nothing you can do to stop it.'' Thorne stood up and paced the length of the suite. ''I don't know anything about the other night, but I want the Falcone Line and I intend to have it. If you aren't with me, then you're against me.''

Luke met Thorne's angry eyes and didn't flinch. ''I'm with you as long as you play fair, Thorne. If you step over the line, then count me out.''

The suite was so quiet Luke's breathing sounded like bellows. Thorne's mouth was clamped shut, only the slight twitch of a muscle in his jaw revealing his anger. He turned and left the suite. The sharp slam of the door reverberated behind him.

Luke ran a hand through his hair and looked around the suite belonging to a woman he barely knew. What was it about the marchesa that made him feel so protective? Was it because he knew what it felt like to be alone against the world? Or was it the brief flash of fear he'd seen in her eyes that night in the alley before she'd covered it up?

He hoped with all his heart that he would not have to choose between Thorne and the marchesa.

Leaving the suite, Luke decided to call it a day and return to the hotel. He took the stairs, spiraling downward, deck after deck. At deck seven, Luke decided to see if the life vests had been removed and headed down the nearly thousand-foot-long corridor. A hundred feet later he caught the first whiff of smoke. Breaking into a run, he raced down the hallway.

The vests were where he'd last seen them. Only this time smoke curled from the pile, and Luke saw the beginning of flames. Looking around, he ran to the nearest fire station and grabbed an extinguisher. He shouted to two crew members in the distance, alerting them to the fire. When he returned, Luke saw the fire had spread rapidly in the few short moments it had taken for him to grab the extinguisher. Already the smoke was thick and black.

Suddenly there was an explosion of flame shooting upward, licking at the ceiling. Luke aimed the extinguisher, wishing he had time to cover his face. He felt his eyes begin to water and his throat clog. Behind him, he heard the pounding of feet. He held on to the extinguisher even as he felt his head begin to spin, his lungs fill and something excruciatingly hot sear his bare hands.

* * *

Luke came to in a hospital room. He could tell it was because he was hooked up to an IV and a nurse was hovering over him.

"What happened?" he rasped, his throat painfully sore.

"You're a hero," whispered a woman he couldn't see. He tried to turn his head in the direction of her voice, but a sharp pain made him forget the idea. He shut his eyes until the wave of pain receded.

When he opened them again, the nurse had disappeared and Adriana Falcone had taken her place. "What—"

"Don't talk." She came around the side of the bed. "I arrived at the shipyard a few minutes before you sounded the fire alarm. If you hadn't discovered the fire, there wouldn't be an M.S. *Pisano* right now. At the very least, the fire would have set the completion of the ship back months. I can't thank you enough, Luke. You've saved me twice in one week."

Luke tried to sit up and winced. He realized his right hand was bandaged, and he reached up to discover another bandage on his cheek. Again, he attempted to speak.

"Shh. Don't try to talk," cautioned Adriana. "The doctors are trying to determine how much smoke you inhaled. They want to keep you here overnight for observation. You suffered second-degree burns on your hand and forearm. No one's sure how you got the scratch on your cheek.''

Luke mentally replayed the incident and it only raised more questions. ''How did...''

''How did it happen?'' Adriana asked for him. ''I don't know but I intend to find out. The captain told me you had reported the life vests in the corridor and he called the shipyard requesting that workers put them in the cabins. I've got a meeting in the morning to determine why there was a breakdown in communication.''

''What time?'' Luke croaked.

Adriana smiled, softening the worry in her eyes. ''If your doctor releases you in the morning, you're welcome to attend. But *only* if your doctor releases you.''

Luke grabbed her hand in thanks. Somehow he needed to find out how the fire had started. It was the only way he could douse the horrible suspicion growing in his mind. He knew Thorne Weston had vowed to destroy everything associated with the Falcone Line, but would he sabotage a Falcone ship he partially owned?

Luke slumped back on the pillow. Adriana touched his shoulder lightly and whispered a good-bye.

Luke was left alone with only his uneasy thoughts for company.

* * *

Adriana looked up from the videotape and glanced at Luke. Although pale, he looked more refreshed than she did as he sat beside her viewing surveillance tapes taken at the shipyard the day before. They were in a small but comfortable office set aside for their use. So far, the only person entering or leaving the ship that they'd both recognized was Thorne. As much as she knew he wanted to thwart her success, Adriana doubted he would commit arson.

But would he pay someone else to do it for him? The question was uppermost in her mind. Or did his equity interest in her ship preclude him from sabotage?

"I've requested an arson investigation," said Luke.

"You still aren't convinced the fire was an accident?"

"I thought it was strange that all the vests were in the hallway. Normally they're put in the cabins right away. The captain gave the order, the welders were ordered to another area until a crew could be assigned to distribute the vests, and still there was a fire."

"Carelessness?"

"Possibly. But I want to be sure, and the arson guys can narrow down those possibilities better than I can. Fortunately the repair work will be completed before the sea trials next week, but I needed to get the investigators here this morning before the cleanup work begins.''

''When did you make these arrangements?''

''Last night.'' He looked past her. ''I persuaded the night nurse to call some people I know.''

''I'm happy to hear you're making such a rapid recovery.'' Adriana wondered why Luke was so convinced the fire wasn't an accident. ''I'm sorry I couldn't be of more help with the tape. Other than Thorne and several Falcone employees, I don't recognize any of the other faces.''

''You knew more people than I did,'' said Luke with a slight smile. ''I've asked the shipyard's personnel department to review the film and identify anyone who isn't on the shipyard payroll. We should have enlargements of unidentified men and women in an hour or so if you don't mind hanging around a while longer.''

''I've got a meeting with one of the interior designers to look at some commissioned art pieces. I'll check back with you here when the meeting's over.'' Adriana looked at him closely. ''You're sure you'll be all right?''

''I'm fine, and I can always take a pill,'' he said.

As she hurried out of the office, Adriana knew Luke was still in a lot of pain. As hard as he'd tried to pretend otherwise, Adriana had detected a grimace or two he'd been unable to hide.

She'd arrived in Bremerhaven the day before to

personally meet with Marta Wilmont, a wonderful artist who had promised some magnificent paintings for the public areas of the ship. The majority of the artwork was now completed, and Adriana was anxious to see what Marta had accomplished. The next two hours passed quickly and Adriana was more than pleased with the final results, especially a series of hand-painted tiles that would decorate a section next to the main showroom. It was only when someone on staff mentioned lunch that Adriana glanced at her watch and recalled her promise to check back with Luke.

A receptionist in the main office directed Adriana to the cafeteria where she found Luke sipping coffee and studying some enlarged photos.

"Find anything?" she asked, sitting down beside him and picking up one of the photos.

"These three men were unidentified, but I've just learned from personnel that two of them are newly hired employees and their photos aren't in the computer system yet. The third man, however, is a mystery man. So far, no one knows who he is."

"What about the arson?"

Resting his arm gingerly on the table, Luke looked so serious that Adriana immediately knew the news was not good.

"The official tests and reports won't be available for another day or two, but I've been told that all indications are the fire was deliberately set."

"Which means we've got to find out the name of this mystery man." Adriana studied the man, his face partially concealed by a hat worn low over his forehead. The visible part of the man's face was thin and chiseled. His eyes were narrow slits and looked hard and cunning. "I'll call Nico. It's a long shot, but maybe he's seen this man before."

Luke stiffened. "Does the man look familiar? Do you think he's one of the men who tried to run your scooter off the road?"

Adriana fingered the grainy photo. "I didn't see anyone clearly that night. But this man's eyes seem so cold, so unfeeling, that I'll feel better if Nico takes a look and tells me I'm being foolish."

"I guess it can't hurt." Luke gathered up the pictures and stood up. "I'm going back to the office to look at more tape."

"Let me borrow this photo. I'll fax it to Nico." Adriana pulled the picture from the stack Luke held against his chest. For an instant she considered shredding it, as if the act of doing so would erase the possibility that danger had followed her to Bremerhaven. Instead, she tucked it into her briefcase. If she was lucky, the mystery man would prove to be nothing more than another unidentified shipyard employee.

Thorne was in the secluded office sitting at the desk Luke had recently occupied. He'd flipped on the TV/VCR combo and quickly realized Luke had obtained surveillance films from the shipyard. The comings and goings of everyone admitted to the shipyard had been duly recorded by hidden cameras, particularly around the ships. A quick review of the stack of tapes revealed that Luke had concentrated on the *Pisano,* and notably a few hours before and after yesterday's fire.

As the tape rolled, Thorne continued to look over Luke's notes, scribbled on a yellow tablet and tucked into the top drawer. Why did he think the fire wasn't an accident? Thorne wondered. Was there a basis for it?

Drumming his fingers on the desktop, Thorne curbed his rising anger and annoyance. He'd never anticipated Luke becoming a problem, a hindrance to achieving his goal.

"Find what you're looking for?" asked Luke, standing in the doorway.

"I was looking for you and was told I'd find you here," answered Thorne. "I stopped by the hospital last night as soon as I learned what had happened, but the nurse had given you a sedative and you were asleep." He paused. "I'm sorry you got hurt. How are you feeling today?"

Luke came into the room, his arm resting in a sling, and sat down opposite Thorne at the desk. "I'm doing as well as can be expected. It could have been worse."

"What's all this about?" Thorne picked up the tablet and let it drop back onto the desktop. "You don't seriously think the fire was anything but an accident, do you?"

"The arson squad I called in assures me the fire was set. I'll have the official report within a day, two at the most."

Thorne whistled. "Arson. You're certain?"

"It wasn't just a match. It was an entire book of matches."

Thorne swore. "But why are you taking such an active interest in this matter, Luke?"

"Didn't you ask me to watch over the marchesa?" Luke took a deep breath. "That's what I'm doing."

"Is it worth second-degree burns? Possibly your very life?" Thorne looked pointedly at Luke's bandaged arm and the square patch on his cheek. "The ship is insured and replaceable. You're not."

"What about Adriana? Is she replaceable?" Luke's tone was tinged with doubt and distrust.

Thorne didn't move, all his senses on alert. Luke was the brother he'd never had, the one person he would trust with his life. Like the ring resting close by his heart, Thorne had kept his private feelings and emotions regarding the Falcone family sealed off. He'd never discussed his plans and the reasons for them with anyone. Seeing Luke, bandaged and sedated in the hospital bed last night, had shaken him. He didn't want to lose Luke—either as a friend or as a company executive. But he recognized the possibility.

All he had to do was to divulge his motive to Luke.

But he couldn't say the words Luke needed to hear to end the widening gulf between them.

"Adriana is replaceable as head of the Falcone Line. That's all." Thorne knew his answer wasn't the one Luke wanted—or needed—and shook his head. "I can't tell you any more, Luke. I don't know myself."

Luke sighed. "What do you want me to do?"

"Get well." Thorne stood up and walked around the desk, placing his hand on Luke's shoulder. "I need you."

"Am I interrupting?"

Thorne swiveled around, surprised to see Adriana in Bremerhaven. He looked questioningly at Luke.

"She showed up yesterday," Luke explained. "I wasn't expecting her, either."

The marchesa wore beautifully tailored slacks, a blue silk blouse that almost matched her eyes and low-heeled comfortable shoes. She placed a soft-sided leather briefcase on the desk, gave Thorne a cursory glance and directed her attention to Luke.

"I faxed the photo to Nico."

"What photo?" Thorne asked.

"Excuse me?" Adriana's shoulders stiffened and

she looked at Thorne as he imagined she might a cockroach.

"Who's Nico?"

"A friend." She looked back at Luke.

"What photo?" Thorne demanded again.

"You haven't told him?" Adriana directed her question to Luke.

"Only about the arson results," Luke answered. "Not about the photo."

"I find it odd, Mr. Weston—"

"Thorne."

She ignored him. "—that a man who can't return a simple phone call can suddenly show up and demand to have his questions answered."

"You asked me to ignore you, and when I do, you get upset?"

"I certainly didn't mean for you to ignore my requests for relevant information. As I recall, we've become business partners."

"That's right," he said, admiring the way her blue eyes glowed with inner fire when she was provoked. "Now tell me about the photo."

"There were three people in the tapes that we were unable to identify. Personnel identified two of them as new employees, so we were left with just one—our mystery man. Security is working on it, but in the meantime I faxed the photo to a friend who has promised to check it out and call me back."

"Exactly who's this friend? Nico?"

"Nico knows someone who works for Interpol. He's asking them to run the photo through their database."

"You're both taking this very seriously, aren't you?" Thorne sat on a corner of the desk and crossed his arms. He saw Luke and Adriana exchange a glance and felt a spurt of jealousy at the degree of friendly intimacy between them. "Accidents are not uncommon at this level of shipbuilding, especially when the ship is full of different work crews and personnel," he reasoned aloud. "Despite your preliminary investigation, aren't you jumping to unwarranted conclusions?"

"I hope you're right," said Luke, still tight-lipped and distant.

"Of course I'm right." Thorne stood up, uncomfortable with the feeling he was the outsider, and equally determined not to let Adriana and Luke freeze him out. "I'm certain there's a perfectly logical explanation for the fire."

"In the meantime we've got to consider *all* the possibilities," Adriana said, looking directly at Thorne.

He held her gaze and saw the unspoken question in her eyes. "You do that," he said, angry that she would consider him responsible for a fire that had injured someone close to him, one of the few people he cared deeply about. But damned if he'd make it easy for her.

He was distracted by a timid knock behind him. He turned to see a young secretary standing in the open doorway. She fidgeted nervously and cleared her throat several times before she finally dragged her gaze from Thorne and settled on Adriana. "There's a telephone call for you, Marchesa. On line three."

The only phone in the room was located on the desk Thorne had appropriated. As Adriana thanked the girl and approached him, Thorne punched the phone button, picked up the receiver and handed it to Adriana, who managed to avoid touching his hand as she accepted it.

Thorne didn't budge, forcing her to speak knowing he was listening to the conversation. Adriana half turned away from him, but he knew she was conscious of him. When he heard her say, "Nico," he tensed, annoyed at the intimacy of her tone.

"Would you hold a moment, Nico?" To Thorne she said, "I'd like some privacy, please."

Thorne shrugged, but her impersonal tone toward him annoyed him even more than her casual dismissal of his arrival had earlier. He wasn't used to being ignored or dismissed, especially by a woman. He didn't like the feeling.

She lowered her voice and Thorne could barely understand the few words she spoke as he crossed the room and joined Luke. Both of them heard her sharp exclamation and gave up all pretense of ignoring her telephone conversation. Luke appeared as interested as Thorne was in the call.

When she hung up, Thorne's impatience surfaced. "What did he say?"

She appeared preoccupied, her mind obviously still on the telephone conversation. Absently she raked fingers through her hair, fussing and fluffing it and then moving on to adjust the collar of her blouse, smoothing the silk into place and straightening the cuffs before touching the gold clasp on her belt. She was shaken, thought Thorne, watching her attempt to restore order. She took a deep breath and looked directly at him before shifting her gaze to Luke.

"Interpol wants to know where Nico got the photo."

"Sounds sinister," Luke muttered.

Thorne noted the bleak expression in Adriana's eyes and the tension around her mouth. "What else?"

"The man in our photo resembles someone with so many aliases that he himself has probably long forgotten his real name." Adriana sat down at the desk and put her face in her hands, her pale gold hair falling forward and exposing her slender neck.

Thorne had to resist the impulse to go to her, pull her into his arms and comfort her. "What have you left out?" he said gruffly.

"The mystery man could be a known terrorist

named Feliks. He's thought to have been involved in a number of unsolved terrorist activities—in Rome, London and, most recently, in Egypt."

"Why is a terrorist interested in the *Pisano*?" Thorne crossed the room and sat down opposite Adriana at the desk.

Adriana's eyes were unguarded and her expression somber. "The group responsible for my husband's kidnapping and murder was linked to the Red Army Faction. This terrorist is thought to have been a member of that group."

"Are you saying this has to do with your late husband?" asked Luke, taking a seat beside Thorne.

Adriana shook her head. "I don't know why Piero was kidnapped. There were certainly many other men who had a great deal more money. Until I know the reasons Piero was targeted, the possibility exists that the Falcone Line or family is still at risk."

"Especially you," Luke said softly.

"An Interpol agent will be arriving to confiscate and examine the photo. We're to say nothing until he arrives."

"Bullshit." Thorne stood up. "This is all pure speculation."

"Speculation or not, I can't afford to take any chances," Adriana said. "As co-owner of the *Pisano*, Mr. Weston, neither can you."

"So what do you suggest, Marchesa?" Thorne asked, frustrated by the turn of events.

"We sit tight until this matter is resolved."

"You mean until we know who the hell this guy is?"

"Exactly." Adriana placed her hands on the desk and stood up, using the sturdy walnut table for support. "Until today, Interpol had taken him off their most wanted list."

"So he isn't a danger, after all," said Thorne.

"He hasn't been seen or heard from since the Egyptian bombing. Until they received our photo, Interpol believed Feliks was dead."

19

Superstitions

Bremerhaven

"Have you seen this man?"

Adriana looked at the photos the Interpol agent had spread on her office desk at the Bremerhaven shipyard. The agent was middle-aged, with a weariness about his eyes that made Adriana think that nothing she could say or do would surprise him. He looked like someone who had spent too much time walking on the dark side of life.

Oddly, she identified with him. Piero's death had brought her emotionally to her knees, and identifying her husband's nearly unrecognizable body had seared her mind and heart in ways that most of her acquaintances couldn't begin to understand. Adriana instinctively felt that this agent would have understood her feelings exactly.

She was tense and apprehensive without knowing why. This was one chore she wished she could delegate, but it wasn't possible. Trying to be detached and objective despite the knot in her stomach, Adriana studied the photos. There were only three and, in two, the man's features were indistinct, partly due to the graininess of the photo. All were black and white. In each case, the man appeared ordinary. Average height, average weight, average face. A man Adriana could easily pass in the streets without a second thought.

Except for one feature, she thought suddenly, leaning over to study one of the pictures more closely.

"See something?"

She'd been so intent and focused on every detail of the photos that she'd only vaguely registered the opening and closing of the door behind her. "Not exactly..."

"What is it?" The first question had been posed softly and quietly. This time Adriana heard the knife-sharp edge of the man's tone, and she recognized the voice.

"Nico?" Whirling, she saw him standing behind her, dressed casually in jeans, collared shirt and dark brown leather jacket. "What are you doing here?"

"I'll explain in a minute. First, tell me if you recognize him."

Folding her arms, Adriana took a steadying breath and realized she'd underestimated Nico Lintner. A mistake she wouldn't make again.

"You're one of *them?*" she asked, meaning Interpol and knowing the answer already.

"I'm a member of an elite Italian police unit and we work closely with Interpol." He nodded toward the photos. "Now tell me."

"I've never seen the man before," she snapped.

His eyes narrowed. "How can you be so sure?"

"His eyes are blank, shuttered like a camera lens. But, here in this photo—" Adriana pointed toward the close-up "—he's let his guard down. You can see the burning-hot fervor in his eyes."

Nico moved to stand beside her and picked up the photo she'd indicated.

"Is that what evil looks like?" she asked.

Nico shook his head. "For some the label is fanaticism, a total belief and conviction in their cause. For others, I'm convinced it's a form of madness—people totally disconnected from normal human feelings and emotions."

The knot inside her began to untangle and the force of it frightened her. Thoughts formed, swirling like dust devils until spinning away and leaving behind a stark reality. "Is this the man who killed my husband?"

Nico shook his head. "I don't know."

"If it was, would you tell me?"

"Probably not," he admitted with a shrug of his leather-clad shoulders.

"Nothing's changed." Angrily she snatched the

photo from his hand. "Secrets within secrets. Everyone working independently and no one getting anywhere. Egos, politics, boundaries. Meanwhile my husband has been in his grave for seven years and I don't know any more today about the reasons why he died than I did when I buried him."

Nico appeared stunned. Not so surprising, she realized, because when had he seen her even remotely out of control? She'd become a master at keeping her emotions in check, if not buried so far below the surface that she herself was barely aware of them. Somehow, over the years, she'd become more a mechanical doll, performing on cue.

Trying to fill the shoes that Piero's death had left empty.

Gesturing toward the two other photos Nico was now holding, Adriana continued, "That's the closest I've come in all these years to understanding my husband's death. And you deny me the right to know more?"

"You make it sound so simple, Marchesa, when the truth is anything but simple. To know more would place your life in even greater jeopardy. Why do you suppose I've been assigned these past months to watch over you?"

"Watch over me? Whatever for, Nico?" Another thought suddenly occurred to her. "That is your name, isn't it?"

"Nico, yes. Lintner, no." His dark eyes were apologetic. "We believe your life is in danger."

"Who would want me dead?" *I've been dead for seven years.*

"Possibly the same people who murdered your husband. Or others..."

"Others?"

He shrugged. "The fact remains that I witnessed several suspicious incidents that could have resulted in bodily injury to you, possibly death. Now the fire and a photo of a man believed to be one of the most dangerous terrorists in the world."

"Are you trying to frighten me, Nico? Surely you know I don't scare easily."

"Exactly my point. You should be scared. Your safety depends on taking these threats seriously. I can't help you as much as I'd like, but my unit will do what it can. Meanwhile you need to hire body-guards."

"Out of the question."

Exasperated, he ran a hand through his dark hair. "I know the police have urged you to consider this since your husband died and you've always refused. Perhaps that best explains why they wanted some-one like me around you."

"By whatever means possible? By pretending to be someone you aren't?" Her eyes narrowed. "What about Julia? Or was your investigation of her just part of the act?"

"Julia was considered irrelevant to our investi-gation. A dead end." He hesitated, as if weighing whether to tell her more. "Now we're not so sure."

Adriana didn't bother to mask the skepticism from her tone, "Why are you now unsure? Why should one more mystery bother you?"

"Before this, we were dealing with events in Italy. Now we've an international incident with possibly far-reaching consequences. You've recently sold an interest in this ship to an American, a man who you believe is connected to the woman Julia. Every angle, every possible association, now needs to be investigated."

"Does that include Thorne Weston?"

"I've already told you more than I should," he said, glancing toward the door. "The Interpol agent will soon return for the photos, which, by the way, are only copies. He's your official contact in this matter."

Hand on the doorknob, he hesitated. "Marchesa?"

"Forget something?" Her emotions were jumbled. Nico had been her safety net; now she felt adrift and abandoned.

"Take my suggestion and get those bodyguards. More importantly, trust no one."

Who's left for me to trust?

Miami

"I'm glad you could meet me for brunch," said Luke, grasping Nevada's arms and brushing her lips with his. Dressed in shrunk-to-fit jeans and a halter top designed to bring statues to life, Nevada looked hot enough to melt Alaskan icebergs. "You look spectacular."

"Thank you."

Luke pulled out a chair on the outdoor patio and Nevada sat down.

"Is that a blush?" Luke grinned, taking a seat opposite her. "Or too much sun?"

"Definitely too much sun." Nevada shook out the linen napkin and placed it in her lap. "I walked on the beach this morning. I was just thinking about eating when I got your call. How is your hand?"

"The bandages came off a few days ago." Luke flexed his fingers. "Still not very pretty to look at, but healing better than the doctors expected. Of course, I wasn't happy about Thorne ordering me to come back to Miami, but he was adamant. He's staying for the *Pisano* sea trials and wanted me to take care of some matters for him here."

"I tried to reach you several times in Bremerhaven. At first the hospital wouldn't put me through, and after you were released, I left several messages for you at the hotel."

"I got them but things were crazy. By then I knew I was returning to Miami, so I decided to wait until I could talk to you in person."

"I've heard a few rumors…"

"Thorne's trying to keep things quiet and I'd hoped he succeeded." Luke leaned forward intently. "What exactly did you hear?"

Nevada shifted in her seat, her attention seemingly captured by the dockside arrival of a large sailboat. When she turned back to him, Luke realized she'd been stalling for time. "I heard that you and the marchesa are quite an item." She paused, her dark eyes fixed on him, and added very softly, "Now who's blushing?"

"How could you possibly know…?"

"Thorne told me all about you and the marchesa."

"Thorne told you *what* exactly?" Luke exhaled slowly, wondering what had prompted Thorne to confide in Nevada. *I've been worried about all the wrong things.*

She shrugged. "Just that you hit it off with her."

"I was nothing more than a spy for him. Everything I learned about the marchesa I reported to him," Luke said, not bothering to conceal his irritation. "Adriana is a nice woman, Nevada, and she's been through some tough times. I think she's also in a lot of danger, and Thorne didn't like the fact that I was sympathetic and, yes, at times protective."

"Danger? What are you talking about?"

Luke glanced around and lowered his voice. "The fire was no accident."

A waiter arrived and took their drink orders. Luke waited until the man was well out of earshot before continuing.

"Interpol sent an agent to meet with us. It also turns out a member of an Italian police unit has been working undercover for the marchesa as a private investigator. Her husband's killers have never been found, and an international task force on terrorism hasn't ruled out the possibility that the Falcone empire might still be a target."

"But why?"

"It's widely known that the marchesa raised the necessary ransom money," Luke explained. "Just too late."

"So the kidnappers might try for the money again? Only this time kidnap her or harm one of her ships?" Nevada's eyes widened in shock and she sat back in the high-backed rattan chair. "It's diabolical."

"Terrorism is every shipowner's nightmare, Nevada."

"I remember that bomb in the wedding cake on the ship sailing off the coast of Africa. The pictures of the ship sinking were dramatic—and frightening."

"You know it wasn't the first instance of terrorism on the high seas, or the last. Although we've taken precautions to prevent anything serious happening in one of our American ports, we've got to be vigilant.''

The waiter returned with a mimosa and iced tea. While he hovered, Luke and Nevada decided not to order from the menu but to help themselves to the brunch buffet.

Then Nevada picked up her drink, leaned forward and clinked her glass to Luke's iced tea. "I'm glad you're back, Luke. I should also be thankful that you returned safely.''

Did you miss me? Are you sleeping with Thorne?

Luke was surprised not only by the desire to ask, but his need to know. On an already warm tropical day, Nevada was rapidly bringing his blood to boiling point.

Luke sipped his tea, hoping it would cool him off in more ways than one. "I had a great time in Italy, but it's always nice to come home. I got in yesterday afternoon and went by the office for several hours this morning.''

"The building is nice and quiet on Sundays, isn't it? No phones interrupting. Did you get some work done?''

"Let's say I made a start." Luke watched how the breeze from the bay lifted strands of Nevada's dark hair and then gently redeposited them. "Thorne asked me to oversee some additional security measures we've instituted for the *Pisano*'s inaugural cruise.''

Nevada lifted a spear of pineapple from her glass and began to nibble on it. Luke watched, distracted from the weighty thoughts troubling him. He was fascinated and tantalized by the way her lips, teeth and tongue sucked, nipped and enjoyed the taste of the fruit.

"I received a fax from Thorne several days ago regarding the invitation list,'' she said. "I've sent him a copy with the addition of several more names as he requested. I'll have a copy on your desk in the morning.''

"That's one of the things I need to ask you about. I left a note for my secretary to set up an appointment with you tomorrow so we can go over all the details. How are the RSVPs coming? Any difficulty with the invited guests boarding in New York for the cruise to the ship's home port in Miami?''

"So far, everyone seems excited about the cruise. We've got some terrific events planned in New York and even some celebrities coming onboard for the cocktail parties and dinners before we sail.'' Nevada put her napkin on the table. "I'm famished. Shall we eat?''

Luke followed her to the buffet inside the restaurant, conscious of the glances directed toward them, especially from the male customers. Nevada stopped momentarily to allow a waiter with an overloaded tray of dishes to pass and Luke took the opportunity to reach out and clasp her arm, his fingers sliding between her rib cage and the soft flesh of her inner arm. He felt the hitch of her breath and saw the surprise in the look she slanted at him before proceeding toward the buffet line, this time with him keeping pace beside her.

She handed him a plate and asked, "Hungry?"

Because she'd paired a strappy high-heeled shoe with the jeans, she was nearly eye level. Luke recognized the teasing glint in her eyes and answered the challenge by allowing his gaze to make one encompassing sweep of her luscious body. Licking his lips, he answered, "Starved."

She laughed and turned away, picking up a fork and helping herself to an array of cheese and fruit. Selecting a plump strawberry from the platter, she held it up for him to see. Biting into the juicy strawberry, she asked, "You do realize the brunch is an all-you-can-eat...."

Much later, Luke realized the strawberry had been his downfall. From that moment on, it seemed, he'd been able to think of one thing and one thing only. Even now, with the sun going down outside his high-rise and him sprawled on his king-size bed. Stroking Nevada's bare back, he wondered if he'd ever recover.

They had hardly eaten anything at the restaurant

earlier. By unspoken agreement, Luke had summoned the waiter, paid the bill, hustled Nevada into his BMW and driven like a madman to his nearby Key Biscayne condo. They'd made love the first time as soon as he'd managed to somehow close the front door behind him while his other hand had joined hers in tugging, pulling and unzipping. Within seconds, he'd buried himself deep inside her and felt her long legs wrap around him.

Now, hours later, Luke registered the faint arching of her spine and the corresponding thrust of her generous breasts against his bare chest. "You'll be the death of me," he whispered.

"I'm hungry."

Her mouth was pressed against his ear and her breath was hot and moist. Luke groaned, amazed at his own stamina as he felt himself harden. "I should go to Italy more often."

She laughed, low and sensual. "No, I mean I'm *hungry.*"

"Ah, *food.*"

"I haven't eaten all day." Nevada sat up, white sheet slipping and tangling around her waist and legs. "I don't suppose you have anything to eat in your refrigerator?"

"Grocery shopping is the last thing on my mind." Luke grinned, reaching for her. "My housekeeper won't be here until tomorrow. The refrigerator's empty."

"That's my cue to go home," Nevada said, evading his arms and slipping from the bed. She picked up her clothes and sauntered toward the bathroom.

Luke propped another pillow behind his head and wondered if Nevada was as serious as she'd sounded. He seldom brought women to his home for the simple reason it was difficult to get them to leave. A woman who didn't linger after lovemaking was such a phenomenon that Luke remained highly skeptical.

But when Nevada emerged from the bathroom fully clothed, she sailed through the bedroom as if they had not just spent hours locked intimately together. Her smile was no different from the one she gave in the Blue Ribbon Cruises office building—friendly, pleasant, affectionate. While he stared, Nevada said, "I'll check with your secretary in the morning to confirm our appointment."

Luke went from aroused to incredulous in the space of seconds. Vaulting out of the bed, he grabbed her arm. Immediately, he felt her body tense. "What was this?" he asked, gesturing toward the rumpled bed. "A little afternoon delight?"

"Works for me." She looked at his hand on her arm. "Let me go, Luke."

The order was issued with enough inflection to make it sound as if she'd belt him if he persisted in holding her. Luke was very astute at picking his battles, but even when all his instincts warned him to back off, he contemplated ignoring her demand. More surprising, he didn't want her to leave. Reluctantly releasing her arm, he became conscious that she was fully clothed and he was not. "I'll get dressed and we can go out to eat."

"No," she said with irritating coolness. "I've got chores to do at home. It's been nice, Luke, but you know all good things eventually come to an end."

"This is *not* over, Nevada." For once, he had no clue as to where the words came from, much less why. Just that her leaving so abruptly mattered to him.

She shrugged, an elegant gesture on her tall frame. "Perhaps not, but *today* is over."

As she walked through the condo, Luke followed her, tempted to restrain her and sure he could change her mind. Instead, he paused in the bedroom doorway. She walked like a woman who had just been more than sexually satisfied—slow and languid, a hand trailing over the back of his supple leather couch. As if she felt the heat of his gaze on her, she turned as she reached the front door.

"Just in case you're right about this not being over—" her eyes conducted a final frank exploration of his nude body "—I suggest you stock your fridge."

Bremerhaven

Adriana stood on the top deck of the *Pisano* with the captain and ship's officers, as well as several of the Falcone Line executives assigned to the ship. She'd insisted on holding the ceremony prior to the departure for sea trials.

The *Pisano*'s mast had been hoisted, ready for welding to the upper deck, and workmen stood ready to assist with its installation.

In her hand Adriana clasped a small jeweler's box. She took several deep breaths to still her racing pulse. By request, no photographers were present; every effort had been made to keep the ceremony quiet and private.

"What's going on?"

Thorne Weston's appearance on the deck beside her horrified Adriana. "Go away. This has nothing to do with you."

"Everything on this ship concerns me," he insisted, his mouth a grim line.

"It's a Stepping the Mast ceremony," Adriana said, her tone clipped, "for good luck. Be quiet and watch."

Ignoring Thorne's outraged grunt, Adriana nodded to the captain. She wouldn't allow Thorne Weston's unexpected appearance to spoil the significance of the occasion.

Slowly the workmen guided the completed mast into position. As the mast section was lowered—"stepped"—into position, Adriana opened the small box and removed the custom-made silver coin. Then she approached the mast and placed the coin in a small notch made in the base of the mast plating between the doubler and the deck plating. A group of workmen proceeded to guide the mast into position.

Someone handed Adriana a thick leather glove, which she put on before accepting a small welding torch. Her hand had barely grasped it when Thorne Weston's hand covered hers and she heard his furious voice rasp in her ear, "I swear you're an accident waiting to happen. At least let me help you with this."

She didn't bother to turn her head or even consider his offer. His help was intolerable. "Step away. I *must* do this alone."

For a fraction of a second, she felt his hand tighten over hers. Just as suddenly, his hand lifted and she no longer felt the press of his body against hers. Taking another deep breath, Adriana used the torch as she'd been instructed earlier. In less time than she'd imagined, she had successfully spot-welded the mast in place. A polite round of applause washed over her as she handed the torch back and removed the glove. With her bare hand, she touched the mast, shut her eyes and bowed her head.

Continue to lead the way, Piero. Thanks be to God.

When she raised her head and opened her eyes,

Adriana looked directly into Thorne's face, as dark as any thundercloud. Anger still radiated from him, and Adriana realized how accustomed he was to getting what he wanted and the effort it must have cost him to allow her to proceed with an event she had deliberately concealed from him.

"Explain this," he commanded, his lips barely moving.

Intuitively Adriana sensed that the slightest provocation—taking even a step away from him—would result in consequences. The men around them melted away, emptying the upper deck and leaving her alone with him.

"When I signed the first ship contract, I held one of Piero's good-luck Roman coins in my hand and later, according to ancient custom, placed that coin in a specially constructed pocket in the mast just before it was welded into place. For this ship, I had a special coin made with the Falcone falcon and inscribed with Piero's name, date of birth and..." She hesitated.

"Death."

"Yes." She took a moment to get a grip on her emotions. "It's a superstitious custom dating back to when masts were made of wood, and I've simply adapted it to fit the new system of building super-liners."

"Why?"

He was the only man she knew who could ask a

question that was really an order. "This ship is a part of Piero Falcone's dream and represents his vision of the future. The Stepping of the Mast ceremony insures the ship's good luck."

"Why didn't I know about it?"

"Would you have approved?" she asked softly.

"No. I'm not superstitious."

"Then you have your answer."

It was a face-off, she realized, holding his gaze. From somewhere deep inside, she dredged up every ounce of love and pride for the name she bore, for the man she had loved, and for the mission she'd willingly accepted as atonement for not raising the ransom money in time to save his life. Squaring her shoulders, she walked away, fully expecting Thorne to prevent her from having the last word.

But when she entered the elevator, she was alone and there was no sign of Thorne Weston anywhere.

Good Luck, he thought. *What a joke.*

Thorne waited for the elevator doors to shut before he stepped out of the shadows of the massive funnel and approached the mast. If there was some way he could have physically removed the coin, he would have done so. But he had learned something vital from the ceremony, something that had not only surprised him, but stunned him.

Adriana Falcone was as committed to expanding the Falcone empire as he was to destroying it.

The next day Thorne prowled the ship looking for Adriana. As he'd instructed, the captain had informed him when she boarded for their three days at sea. But that was hours ago. The *Pisano* was nearly out of the Elbe River and would be in the North Sea within the next ten minutes, at which time the sea trials would be officially under way. Since the marchesa wasn't in her cabin, Thorne was betting she'd found a vantage spot somewhere on the massive ship from which to observe the departure.

With effort, he had banished his anger from the previous day and now characterized his current mood as one of annoyance.

Annoyance that Adriana Falcone had insisted on coming along, when even those close to her had advised against it. Annoyance that he'd spent twenty minutes scouring the ship in an unsuccessful attempt to find her—and trying to ignore that with each passing minute he was feeling more and more annoyed.

When he saw her, his displeasure escalated. Of all places, she was standing in a nook on the Lido deck almost directly above his own suite on the deck below. Rather than looking at the view behind them as he had expected, she was concentrating on where the ship was headed—the open sea.

He continued to underestimate her, he realized with a fresh spurt of dissatisfaction. Plus, she looked too damn sexy. She was leaning on the railing, her shapely rear showcased in a pair of pants snug enough to tempt a eunuch.

"I hope you know what you're doing," he muttered, coming to a stop behind her.

She stiffened, her spine straightening visibly beneath the thin sweater she wore, and turned, blue eyes frosty. "Hello to you, too."

Friendly was the last thing he felt like being. "Walking around on a ship full of men in an outfit that tight is guaranteed to raise every man's blood pressure. If any work gets done, count yourself lucky. You're enough to ground a ship or steer it off course."

The sea breeze played havoc with her hair, the white-gold mass in charming disarray. Although her eyes were cool, the tight line of her mouth softened, making her look younger and more relaxed.

"Since when did the fine print of our partnership agreement include lectures from you—someone known to avoid any occasion where wearing a tie is required—on how I should dress?"

"Wearing a jacket and tie is different," Thorne said, ignoring her direct hit. "What happened to the pants you usually wear? They're looser, less revealing..."

"Look, Weston, I think you're the one with the problem. If it's high blood pressure, I hear a salt-free diet helps."

She turned her back on him and Thorne gritted

his teeth, slowly exhaled and leaned on the railing beside her. Above them, the sky was overcast, turning the water around them to an ominous dark gray.

Matches my mood exactly, he thought.

"Sea trials are a crucial test of a ship's equipment and also the ultimate test of the owner's massive investment," Adriana said, glancing briefly in his direction. "We're all uptight."

"It doesn't help when you add terrorist activity to the mix, either," he muttered.

"The ship's been gone over with the most sophisticated equipment. The most stringent security measures possible have been taken by the shipyard and authorities. Everyone on this ship has been vouched for. No one can even say for certain that the terrorist in the photos shown to us by Interpol is an exact match for the man in the film."

"Luke says they told him it was about an eighty-five to ninety percent possible match. These guys are often highly skilled at altering their appearance with wigs and makeup, often supplemented by plastic surgery when a more drastic change is called for. That's the reason a hundred percent identification is often nearly impossible."

"You've spoken with Luke?"

"He finally answered his phone when I called this morning. I was beginning to wonder myself."

"How is he?"

"Fine, he says. When I reached him, he'd just returned from buying out a grocery store."

Adriana frowned thoughtfully. "I didn't know he liked to cook."

"That's the point. He doesn't."

"So why…"

Thorne shrugged. "My best guess is that it's got something to do with a woman. I didn't bother to ask because, knowing Luke, she'll be history by the time I return to Miami."

"When is that?"

"Anxious to get rid of me?" She'd made it more than clear that she wanted him out of her life, while he had made it equally clear that it wasn't going to happen. "I'm returning right after these trials are concluded. And you?"

"Home to Genoa. Another payment is due to the shipyard and I'm overseeing the transfer. I assume that's one of the reasons you're heading to Miami."

"Among other matters."

"The installment is due before this ship is christened and leaves for New York," she reminded him. "We can't afford any delays. Your attorneys have assured me that your half of the money will be paid directly to our account at the shipyard."

"So why are you worried? You *are*, aren't you? Need I remind you that we're partners, and partners have to trust each other. Although, after yesterday, you've raised some questions in my mind."

"Don't go there," she warned. "We're partners because a piece of paper says so and for no other reason. As soon as I have the money to buy you out, I intend to do so."

"And in the meantime?"

"We coexist. You pay your money and I'll pay mine. That's the deal."

"And if *I* want to buy *you* out?" he asked, intently watching her reaction to his question.

"Not an option," she snapped. "As you well know."

Thorne grinned and saw immediately that it confused her.

"Damn you." She shoved away from the railing. "Sea trials. A terrorist. And a partner I consider the biggest threat of all."

He reached out and clamped a hand around her wrist, unable to resist touching her. "It should be an interesting three days, don't you agree?"

"Only if you jump overboard right now."

To punish her, he lightly stroked the inside of her wrist with his thumb and felt a stab of satisfaction at her indrawn breath. "Now? Wouldn't you prefer me to wait until we reach the North Sea where the waters are much more treacherous? Any chance of survival would be greatly reduced."

Her blue eyes widened as if considering his proposition. "No," she said with a toss of her head. "I opt for sooner rather than later."

Unreasonably the urge to teach her a lesson overrode his normal calculating thought processes. "Wouldn't you rather know what you'd be missing out on?"

He'd deliberately lowered his voice, knowing she'd shift toward him to hear. His timing was perfect. A gentle tug of the wrist at the exact moment she leaned forward, and she was in his arms.

Her hair smelled of fresh air while her body was soft in all the right places. Before she could react, he'd wrapped his arms around her, binding her to him.

He'd cast his line and now it was time to reel her in, but as anticipated, she fought him.

Perhaps that was the attraction, he mused as her struggles merely managed to make him want her more, overrode his usual controlled restraints and brought out the beast he normally kept tightly reined.

She was as uninterested in him as he was interested in her.

That in itself made her a worthy adversary. There was nothing that Thorne loved more than a challenge. To desire something unattainable, to get it, and then discard it.

His earlier moodiness evaporated and a blaze of desire seized him. Shifting a hand, he cupped the back of her head in forceful restraint, burying his fingers in hair as soft as silk.

He brought his mouth down on hers and knew the instant their lips met that he'd been wanting to taste her for weeks, that the desire to do so had been tormenting him and that she was at the root of his edginess, the cause of his sense of unbalance.

She continued to struggle, but then, as if knowing that doing so only prolonged the moment, she let her body go limp and focused her resistance entirely on preventing his invasion of her mouth. Clamping her teeth, she prevented the entrance his probing tongue sought.

Without retreating, he shifted his assault. In his mind, it was indeed an assault. And nothing less than victory would appease him.

His mouth on hers softened, the gentle caress of his tongue on her lips misleading her. She trembled, a movement so slight he might have missed it if he'd held any other woman in his arms. But his awareness of her was so heightened he felt every breath, every heartbeat. Shifting a hand to clamp her bottom, he pulled her against his loins, letting her feel the full force of his arousal.

Suddenly he felt the pressure of her hands, a barrier against his chest, lessen. Then those hands crept around him and clung. When her nails dug into his back, he felt a surge of satisfaction, of impending victory.

He deepened the pressure of his mouth, his tongue

probing aggressively for entry. She moaned—and shattered all his illusions.

Her mouth opened and he was sucked into a hot cavern of molten heat. His own rigid self-control ceased to exist. Thoughts of victory vanished. Possession was all that mattered.

His tongue thrust and his body ignited.

Silken hair, soft body dissolving into his, his hand cupping a perfect bottom.

He was on a trip to paradise.

Deliciously cool droplets of water on his heated skin merely heightened his pleasure. Seconds later he heard the first clap of thunder and dazedly returned to reality. Reluctantly he lifted his mouth and muttered, "We'd better get out of the rain."

She squirmed out of his embrace. Raindrops struck her uplifted face and left wet streaks on her pale face. "Do us both a favor, Weston," she said, backing away from him and looking at him as if he were Lucifer.

"Jump. Jump overboard *now.*"

20

Sea Trials

Miami

Nevada watched as staff members left the conference room, some checking their watches and others chatting with one another. It was almost quitting time for them, but it would be hours before she left her office and headed home. Luke, seated at the end of the oval conference table, made no effort to join the others, but remained comfortably relaxed in the dark green leather chair.

Nevada scooped papers into her briefcase, knowing that Luke's watchful eyes were cataloging every movement. Even separated from him by the length of a table, Luke was dangerous. Was he remembering—as she did nightly—the last time they'd been alone?

"The meeting went well, don't you think?" she asked him.

"Yes, very." He got to his feet, then straightened

his silk tie. "You've got everything under control for the *Pisano*'s promotional stop in New York."

Although she'd notified Luke of the meeting, it had been a formality. When he'd slipped into the conference room midway through her presentation and taken a seat at the end of the table, Nevada hadn't done so much as raise an eyebrow. After all, she had long since mastered the art of balancing conflicting professional and personal relationships.

"There's still a lot to do for the ship's arrival in Miami." Picking up her leather briefcase, discreetly embossed with her initials, Nevada walked briskly toward the exit. "I'll keep you informed. Right now I've got a mountain of telephone calls to return and some reports to review."

He waited until she was nearly abreast of him before stepping directly into her path. Hemmed in on both sides by a wall and the table, Nevada realized Luke intended to be difficult.

Keeping an arm's length between them, she stopped, welcoming the added height from the expensive high heels she wore with her tailored suit.

She'd deliberately avoided looking directly at him for the past half hour. *Keep it light, keep it casual.* The mantra she'd repeated ever since leaving his apartment five days ago ran through her mind as she looked him directly in the eye. "Don't do this, Luke," she warned softly.

"You can't keep avoiding me, Nevada." He

made no move to touch her, but his stance was confrontational, arms crossed, legs slightly spread. A muscle in his jaw twitched. "Are you still seeing Thorne? Is that why you haven't returned my calls?"

He's jealous.

Her breath hitched. Caught between a lie and the truth, Nevada merely shook her head. She thought she knew all the dance steps, but Luke was moving to music she'd never heard before, spinning her so fast she was out of step and perilously close to falling.

Unable to resist, she reached out and touched his arm, feeling his muscles tighten and bunch beneath her fingers. "Let's give it some time, Luke."

He stared at her. "All right," he agreed finally, his tone cool, impersonal, the sort he normally reserved for difficult business associates. "I'll wait for you to call me."

Nevada shifted her briefcase from her left hand to her right, welcoming its comfortable familiarity, as if a new dance partner had cut in and swung her back onto the dance floor, only this time to a rhythm and steps she knew.

Buttoning his suit jacket, Luke stepped aside and allowed her to pass. He waited until she reached the door before he quietly commanded, "Nevada."

She glanced over her shoulder, forced to look at

him once more and feel her heartbeat accelerate.
"Yes?"

"Thought you'd like to know. I went grocery
shopping."

The North Sea

Pisano

Adriana stirred, her mouth curving in a half smile
at the sound of Piero's whispered endearment.
Slowly her eyes opened and she blankly took in the
unfamiliar surroundings and then realized with a
sickening jolt that she'd been dreaming. Again.

She shuddered. Her dead husband's voice sounded
so real! No wonder she found the dream so unsettling.

Struggling upright in the comfortable chair, which
sat in one corner of her suite, Adriana glanced at
the paperback novel in her lap and the reading
glasses still clutched in her hand. She must have
dozed off, soothed, probably by the gentle cradlelike
movement of the enormous ship.

Adriana had retired to her suite immediately after
an informal dinner with the captain. The round table
seated ten, and Adriana had sat on the captain's right
and Thorne on his left. The other diners—officers
and technical representatives—had kept the dinner
conversation centered on the ship's performance, the

tests that had been completed and those still to be conducted. Adriana knew the purpose of this sea trial was to put the ship through every conceivable test, to check the maximum performance levels of every component—a degree of stress well beyond anything the ship would likely experience during its term of service.

Sea trials were nearly complete and the ship would return to the shipyard sometime late the following day. For the past two days Adriana had succeeded in dealing with Thorne Weston on a strictly professional level, never once allowing herself to be alone with him, although, she conceded, he had certainly made it easy for her. He seemed as determined as she in keeping their contact to a minimum. Less than twenty-four hours and she would be back on land—and closer to regaining control of her ship and putting Thorne Weston in her past.

Once in her suite and changed into patterned silk men's-style pajamas and matching robe, Adriana had retrieved a book from her half-packed suitcase. Pouring a glass of wine and settling down to read, she had hoped to spend the last night of sea trials engrossed in this current bestseller.

She wondered now if the psychological suspense of the book hadn't triggered her mind's fanciful flight when she'd dozed off. Relieved, for once, at finding a possible explanation, Adriana stretched and thought about climbing into bed. Glancing at her watch and seeing the time—nearly eleven—Adriana knew going back to sleep was next to impossible.

She stood up and crossed to the tiny built-in bar where she deposited her empty wineglass for the steward to whisk away in the morning. Her suite was comfortable, although, like everything else on the ship, still not entirely complete. As usual, however, the finishing details would take place during the crossing from Bremerhaven to New York, the first port where promotional events were planned.

Suddenly she felt the ship lurch and tilt dangerously portside. Adriana grabbed the cabinet and hung on. She watched in disbelief as the lounge chair she'd been sitting in tipped over and skidded, smashing into a wall. Everything on surfaces—ice bucket, her purse, the novel she'd been reading, her glasses—tumbled and rolled toward the wall. Thank God she'd closed the doors opening onto the balcony.

Outside her suite, Adriana heard shouts of alarm. She crouched down, clinging to the cabinet and wondering if it would hold.

She judged the list to be about fourteen to eighteen degrees. She felt the ship going in an ever tighter circle, doubly compounded by its high speed.

The gravitational pull was too strong and Adriana lost her grip, falling toward the portside wall and hitting it with bone-jarring force. Her head struck something sharp, and she felt a stabbing pain.

She grabbed a cushion from the overturned chair and used it as a shield. Her suite was in a shambles and she imagined the rest of the ship was suffering the same fate.

Holding her breath, Adriana focused on the ship's rhythm and knew immediately when the ship's officers corrected the problem. The vessel slowed perceptively, the tilting still pronounced but improving.

A disaster has been averted.

Now Adriana needed to know the cause.

As she struggled to her hands and knees, she heard pounding on her door and someone calling her name. Crawling across the suite toward the door, she grabbed the handle and pulled herself upright. The instant she unlocked the door, it flew open and she barely got out of the way.

Flattened against a wall, she pushed a handful of hair away from her face. Thorne, one hand gripping the door for support, hooked his free arm around her waist and anchored them in place.

"Are you all right?" he asked.

Grateful for the genuine concern in his dark eyes, she nodded. "What happened?"

"I don't know. I'd just come back from walking on deck when I got tossed across my cabin. Everything's a mess."

"Surely this wasn't a test, was it?"

"Hardly. We came too close to tipping over. I wanted to make sure you were unhurt before I went to the bridge for an explanation."

"I'm coming with you." Her hand wrapped around his muscular forearm.

"Absolutely not." He seemed to reconsider when he saw the stubborn thrust of her jaw. "You aren't dressed."

Glancing down at her robe and pj's, Adriana shrugged dismissively. "I'm covered up. Let's go."

She pushed against his arm and Thorne realized it was a waste of time to discuss the subject any further.

"Until the ship rights herself, getting to the bridge is not going to be a cakewalk," he warned. "Hold on to me."

Her blue eyes widened and he saw the cautionary yellow flags hoist. His mouth quirked. "You don't hesitate to go to the bridge of a nearly capsized ship wearing next to nothing, but touching me requires an act of Congress?"

Temper flaring, she shoved against the arm curled around her waist. "I can manage on my own."

"Fine." Abruptly he released her. She immediately started sliding away from him. Frantically reaching for an anchor, she instinctively grabbed his arm and pulled herself toward him. He didn't move to help her.

She panted and clung to his arm. "I hope you're satisfied."

"I'd be more satisfied if you agreed to wait here. I'll let you know what I find out."

"No, I'm going."

She never made anything easy for him, he thought, including the way he reacted to her. Her silk pajamas were loose and flowing, but in places they were too loose...

"Belt your robe," he said tersely.

"Excuse me?"

"Before we leave, belt your robe."

She glanced down and noticed the button that had become unfastened, allowing a more than generous glimpse of her breasts. Her fingers trembled as she buttoned her top and searched for the belt, then tied it snugly around her waist.

"Better?" she asked sarcastically.

Thorne shrugged. "I rather liked the view before, and I'm sure the ship's crew would agree with me."

"Well, I hate to deprive you." She paused. "Am I presentable enough now to accompany you to the bridge?"

Transferring her hands from his arm to the door handle, Thorne placed his own hand on her hip and propelled her gently through the doorway and into the corridor where the going was easier. Halfway to a staircase—Thorne decided not to risk using the elevator—he noticed a definite improvement in the ship's list.

"The guys must have figured out what was wrong," he murmured.

"Good," she said, shooting him a less than friendly look. "You can let go of me now."

"You know, you're a real pain," he said, but removed his hand from her hip and immediately missed the feel of her firm flesh.

"From you, that's a compliment."

He followed her up the stairs, assessing the visible damage without comment. Occasionally she slowed her steps and Thorne knew she was calculating the costs, both in time and dollars, of this new setback. A few steps from the top of the stairs, the ship lurched portside again. Thorne reacted immediately, reaching up and catching the marchesa when she lost her balance and started to fall backward. Inadvertently a hand cupped one of her breasts before he steadied and released her.

He was too much of a gentleman, he thought smugly, to comment on her reaction to his touch. Her nipple had stiffened and peaked beneath his fingers. The knowledge that the marchesa was not as uninterested as she pretended to be gave him a certain amount of satisfaction.

And leverage.

The bridge, which stretched the entire width of the bow with a panoramic view of the North Sea from its windows, hummed with activity. Numerous white-uniformed officers moved about under the direction of the captain, who paced the bridge, grimly studying papers and questioning various members of his staff. Catching sight of Thorne and Adriana, he gave some quick instructions to the crew before hurrying toward them.

After a quick exchange, Captain Robbiti gestured toward the wheel and said, "The ship was on automatic pilot—which is normal under these circumstances—while we practiced a tight anticollision maneuver. For some unknown reason, the steering mechanism jumped from autopilot into manual, and that made the ship spin tighter and tighter, and threw it into a deadman's turn."

Short and compact, the captain looked haggard under the fluorescent lights. "It wouldn't have been so bad if our speed had been slower. As it was, the first officer and chief engineer immediately took steps to correct the situation. The ship has sustained some minimal damage, mainly broken dishes and glassware."

"How could this have happened?" Adriana glanced from the captain to the wheel. "We've never had such a problem."

Captain Robbiti hesitated, looking at Thorne as if asking permission to speak his mind. Thorne nodded imperceptibly and hoped Adriana had not caught the exchange.

"I can't be sure," he offered, "but we think it might be a software glitch. As you know, all maneuvers are programmed into the computer that controls navigation. We're using a new program and there might be a bug in it, even though it was tested extensively before installation.''

Adriana glanced from the captain to Thorne and back again. "When will you know?"

The captain shrugged. "Likely not until we return to port and can examine the system further."

The ship was finally on an even keel. There was an almost tangible lightening of tension on the bridge and Thorne caught the sideways glances of several crewmen directed at Adriana. Instinctively he placed a protective hand on her shoulder and suggested, "Perhaps you should return to your cabin now."

Her shoulder stiffened and she stepped away, dislodging his hand.

"Thank you, Captain. I'll be in my cabin should you need me. Otherwise, I'll see you in the morning."

Without looking at Thorne, Adriana turned and left the bridge. Thorne smiled his thanks and shook the captain's hand before following her.

He'd nearly caught up to her when he noticed the blood dripping from his left hand. He wasn't injured, so he knew it wasn't his. Within seconds he'd reached Adriana and halted her with a firm hand on her shoulder.

When she tried to push it away, he said, "Why didn't you tell me you were hurt when I asked you?"

"I'm not—"

"You are." He held up his bloodied hand and said, "This blood isn't mine. Now stand still a minute." His gaze roamed her tousled hair and the shoulder where his hand had rested, but he saw no evidence of blood. Gently lifting strands of her hair, he ignored the fact that his hands were shaking. Behind her left ear, he found what he was looking for—a patch of blood-soaked hair and a nasty gash. A thin line of blood trickled down the back of her neck and disappeared under her collar.

He sucked in a breath, trying to banish the sight of the blood-matted blond hair. "Next stop is the infirmary."

For once she didn't argue with him, but simply lifted a hand and discovered the same telltale dampness. As he cupped her elbow and started walking with her toward the nearest elevator, he said, "You not only need a bodyguard, you need a keeper." Even to him, his tone sounded like a growl. "I've never known a woman so accident prone."

When they got on the elevator and watched the numbers descend, she leaned briefly against him. He knew the gash was beginning to really hurt and felt his insides clench.

"I fell when the ship tilted and hit my head on something," she explained. "I remember feeling a sharp pain, but it went away."

"Adrenaline." He helped her out of the elevator, wanting to hurry her while not wanting to frighten her. "As soon as you knew everything was all right with the ship, you relaxed and the pain you'd blocked kicked in.''

At the sight of the open infirmary and waiting doctor, Thorne felt a weight lift. After assisting Adriana onto a table and listening to the doctor explain that he'd had a rash of similar injuries due to the accident, Thorne paced the small facility. Although he hadn't smoked for years, he had an enormous desire for a cigarette.

''Thorne.''

He looked over at her, and the knot inside him tightened at the sight of the bloody gauze pads the doctor was discarding.

''I'm going to be fine,'' she said. ''Will you please wait outside?'' A corner of her mouth lifted in a small smile. ''You're making us both nervous.''

Once in the empty corridor, Thorne leaned against the wall and fought for control. The memories were assaulting him.

Golden hair spread fanlike on rock-strewn ground. Blood matting the blond strands and soaking into the ground.

A tidal wave of unspeakable agony threatened to overtake him. Using the technique he'd been taught to control the eruption, Thorne took deep abdominal breaths and superimposed an image of his favorite cay in the keys. From the bridge of his yacht, he watched the free-spirited dolphins as they swam alongside like a welcoming convoy.

''Thorne?''

He opened his eyes to find Adriana looking at him, pale and lovely. For an instant, he considered adding her face to his collection of mind-relaxing images. Although he felt empty and exhausted, the imagery had worked.

"All done?"

"Yes, no stitches, just a butterfly bandage and slight headache, which the two aspirin I just took should remedy." She tucked her hand in the crook of his arm. "You know, don't you, that even tiny head cuts bleed excessively? It's nothing for you to worry about—I'm fine."

"I'm glad you're fine," he answered. "I hope the room steward has straightened your suite. You should be in bed."

Neither of them spoke as they waited for the elevator. It wasn't until they'd stepped off on the veranda deck and were nearing their suites that Adriana asked, so softly that Thorne had to strain to hear her words, "You don't suppose that what happened with the ship tonight could be anything but an accident, do you?"

Impossible, he thought. "Don't begin thinking everything that happens is a conspiracy or threat. You've become paranoid."

"So you don't think—"

"No, I don't."

He scowled, both from the discussion and the glimpse into the opened doorway to his suite that revealed a steward working to restore order. "Let's hope he started with your suite," he muttered.

Adriana opened the unlocked door to her suite and felt a pleasant jolt of pleasure at the sight of a fully restored cabin. The strain she'd been feeling eased.

She glanced at Thorne. She'd decided that he was one of those tough guys who couldn't stand the sight of blood, so she'd cut him some slack since they'd left the infirmary. But she wasn't prepared to cut him much more, especially after implying she was slightly crazy for speculating out loud about the accident.

"You're welcome to stay until your cabin is ready," she offered politely. "It shouldn't take more than another ten minutes or so..."

She regretted issuing the invitation when his mouth curved into a sensual smile and his dark eyes swept her rumpled—but securely belted—sleepwear.

"So it took a crack on the head for you to finally invite me into your bedroom?"

Coconut Grove

It was two in the morning.

Scowling at the clock, Nevada placed the last tray of cookies on the kitchen counter and turned off the oven. The aroma of warm cookies chock-full of imported chocolate, coconut and rum—her secret ingredient—filled the kitchen.

Unable to sleep, she'd finally given up. She'd thrown on boxer shorts and an oversize T-shirt and, barefoot, come out to the kitchen, where she usually managed to work through problems.

Not so tonight, though, she'd quickly realized after examining her pantry. Luke had asked on more than one occasion for her to give the company's executive chef the recipe for her cookies. So naturally she'd wound up baking Luke's cookies tonight, instead of deep-sixing him from her thoughts.

Using a spatula, she transferred the last of the cookies to a plate to cool. As she did so, she recalled Luke's jealousy that afternoon. How often had she prayed to see that same look on Thorne's face? Instead, when confronted with any of her indiscretions, he'd simply looked the other way.

But not Luke. She'd never seen him as angry as he'd been that afternoon. It had given her a searing insight into Luke's soul. He was the man she couldn't stop thinking about, couldn't relegate to a category reserved for lovers, men who touched her body in exciting ways, but never her heart.

She'd given her heart to Thorne years before.

And only recently had it returned, even though it came with an affectionate kiss and what amounted to a murmured "Thanks for the memories."

When she was so vulnerable and least looking for anyone to fill the void in her life, she'd flirted with

Luke, never realizing he would be a threat to her carefully constructed life. Luke was her dear friend, a man she enjoyed teasing and someone who always made her feel all woman in his presence. A real ego booster whenever she'd often, in the past several years, needed validation. Luke had always given it to her, with no strings attached.

But everything changed after their night on Thorne's yacht.

She put the last cookie sheet in the dishwasher and turned the dial. She was ready now to tumble back into bed. Her calendar was filled for the following day, and she'd be lucky to get through her scheduled appointments without rudely yawning.

Switching off all but one kitchen light, Nevada hesitated by the door to the backyard. Brady hadn't shown up to eat for the past several nights and she'd grown concerned for the independent tom. It wasn't like him to miss a meal.

Stepping outside, she stared at the magnificence of a half moon and absorbed the quiet night stillness. Venturing down two steps, she winced as her bare foot stepped on a particularly sharp stone. Favoring the foot, she saw that the tin of food she'd put out for Brady was untouched. She crossed the tiny flagstone terrace, knelt in a patch of damp grass and softly called his name. She listened for the sound of him moving through the bushes, but there was only silence.

With a shrug, she stood and started to return to

the house when she heard a cat's meow. Plaintive, distressed, weak. Trying to identify the location, Nevada moved gingerly toward the south property line. Fifteen feet later, she almost tripped over Brady.

He was sprawled in the grass and looked battered and bloody. She scooped him tenderly into her arms, then rushed back into the house, easing the door open with her elbow. The light spilled on the bundle in her arms and she let out a cry.

One ear was almost severed, his eyes were swollen shut and patches of skin were ripped. Blood matted the black hair. Gently cradling him, Nevada snagged the nearby phone and punched in a number. The phone rang and rang and Nevada whispered a little prayer, sighing with relief when she heard the gruff hello.

"Luke?" she said, choking on a sob as Brady's tongue weakly licked her hand. "I need your help."

21

Dearest

The North Sea

C*arissima.*

Adriana stirred, her mouth curving in a half smile at the sound of Piero's whispered endearment.

"Caro," she murmured sleepily, curling into the heat of the lean body and distantly registering the steady heartbeat beneath her hand. Slowly, very slowly, her eyes opened and she realized with a breathless jolt that she wasn't dreaming.

The flesh-and-blood man in her bed wasn't a phantom.

Although his breathing indicated he was deeply asleep, she didn't dare move. She angled her head just enough to make doubly sure who it was she was hanging all over.

How had she wound up sharing a bed with Thorne Weston?

She flushed, embarrassed to realize she'd not only

flung an arm across the man's chest, but her hand was resting squarely on a puckered nipple. Her head was snuggled in the crook of his arm and she'd had the audacity to wedge a leg between his, and God in heaven, *what was that nudging against her thigh?*

She remembered Thorne entering her suite, pouring himself a drink and looking around with interest.

"You don't strike me as the frilly type," he had declared, surveying the king-size bed covered in a rich silk spread with lacy, ruffled pillows of all sizes and shapes mounded on the bed.

Changing from her bloodstained pajamas into a pair of aqua silk lounging pajamas, Adriana had emerged from the combination bath/dressing room. "You're partially right. It's really my decorator's idea of a feminine boudoir. She thinks I'm too serious, and perhaps ruffles and frills will help me relax. Since I'll likely spend very little time here, I agreed to experiment."

"So does it work?" Holding his drink, he'd sat on the bed, one hand caressing the silk spread.

As she'd watched his tanned hand resting against the pale apricot silk, Adriana felt a frisson of heat uncurl in her belly. "Are you conducting a test?"

"Yeah, I guess I am." He'd leaned back against several particularly ruffled confections. "How do you sleep with all these pillows?"

She'd laughed. "I don't. I toss most of them on

the floor. For once I'm in agreement with you. So many pillows are rather superfluous.''

In the infirmary, Adriana had worried that the mighty Weston would pass out. Somehow his weakness had made him seem more human to her, but she'd still felt uncomfortable seeing him reclining on her bed.

What was the matter with her? she'd wondered. Her bed wasn't sacred, a shrine to a long-dead husband. Or was it? Someday, she'd supposed, she would replace Piero in her bed, but the possibility seemed far in the distant future. She had too many goals to accomplish before that time came, if it did.

When Thorne had absently set his whiskey down on the night table, made a slight adjustment of his shoulders and hips on her bed and then closed his eyes, Adriana had wanted to protest. *Don't get too comfortable!*

But the words hadn't come. This had been the first time she'd seen Thorne Weston with his guard down, and she'd intended to take full advantage of the opportunity.

Settling into the comfortable lounge chair, restored to its position by the veranda doors, Adriana decided Thorne was just as handsome asleep as he was awake. The only difference that she could see was that his features softened; the angles of his high cheekbones were less pronounced and his lips were soft and relaxed.

Kissable.

The thought had just popped into her head. She wouldn't, couldn't allow herself to go down that road. It had taken two days for her to successfully erase the memories of his kiss after the Stepping the Mast ceremony. She had no time for diversions such as the one Thorne offered her, more so because she doubted his very motives. He didn't just want her, he wanted her cruise line. Piero's cruise line.

She'd turned her head away and felt a twinge of pain. The spot on her head had still been a little tender, but the aspirin had prevented a headache. She'd yawned and glanced at Thorne. She debated waking him and then remembered his concern for her safety and injury. She'd decided to let him sleep, but hadn't intended to fall asleep again in the chair.

So she'd risen, picking up a lap robe folded neatly at the foot of the chaise. She'd flipped on a small light in the bathroom and then partially closed the door, allowing just enough light to see her way to the bed after flicking off the switch controlling the remaining lights.

The king-size bed was large enough to allow her plenty of distance from Thorne, who, she'd assumed, would wake shortly and make his way to his own suite.

Covering herself with the soft blanket, she'd listened to the hum of the ship's engines and the steady breathing of the man beside her and fallen almost instantly asleep.

Now, she realized with a sinking sensation, Thorne Weston, who in truth seldom did as she expected, had not awoken and gone quietly to his own suite. Rather, he had taken advantage of her generosity and made himself right at home—in her bed! And she'd curled up in his arms!

"What's the meaning of *caro*?"

He wasn't asleep. And hadn't been for some time, perhaps even awake before she'd whispered in his ear.

Adriana tried to sit up, but Thorne's arm, wrapped around her shoulders and tucked beneath her arm and breast, tightened. Collapsing against him, she fisted the hand on his chest. Before she could carry out her intention of punching him, Thorne's fingers imprisoned her wrist.

She swore.

"Somehow, I don't think that's the answer to my question," he said with an indulgent chuckle. "So satisfy my curiosity."

"Why are you still here?"

"Why would I want to be anywhere else?" His fingers probed the softness of her breast. "*Caro*. What does it mean? I'm waiting..."

Horrified that she had uttered such a word to him, Adriana considered lying to him, telling him anything but the truth. As if reading her mind, he shifted and his hand inched higher on her breast. In a rush she said, "Dear. *Caro* means dear."

Silence.

Even his breathing seemed exaggerated, the bedroom was so quiet.

"I'm flattered."

"Don't be," she snapped, trying to tug her hand free from his grip. "If I'd known it was you, I'd never have said it."

His voice deepened. "Exactly whose ear did you think you were whispering into?"

There was no way she could tell this man such an intimate detail. Sprawled over his body in her own bed seemed less intimate—and less a violation—than divulging Piero's name.

"I don't suppose it's really any great secret, is it?" he drawled, his mouth close to her ear. "The tabloids claim only one man, Piero Falcone, has ever been able to melt the Ice Queen."

"Would you be quiet?" Her memories of Piero belonged only to her. As long as she had them, she didn't need any other man. But Thorne was trying to destroy them, crumble the walls she'd built so carefully.

"Tell me, Marchesa, exactly what made your late husband so special? Was he really so great in bed?" Without letting go of her wrist, he touched her chin, forcing her to look at him. "Did he spoil you for any other man?"

She struggled to get away, to shut out the words, but his arms imprisoned her. His low laugh told her that he enjoyed her distress, that somehow mocking her relationship with Piero gave him pleasure.

"What would your *caro* say if he knew how you reacted when I kiss you? You give off enough heat to melt—"

"Shut up!" she shouted, desperate to drown out his words.

"You're right," he whispered, his eyes glittering in the darkness. "It's time I shut up."

His fingers held her chin long enough for his mouth to slant over her lips in a kiss. A kiss meant to take everything from her and give nothing back.

Her legs and arms were so entwined with his that it seemed he was devouring her whole body, sucking her into himself until she ceased to have a coherent thought. She tasted blood and felt his mouth soften on hers, his tongue caressing her bottom lip and roaming over her clenched teeth until, with a reluctant moan, she opened her mouth.

His hands tore at her silk top, popping buttons until her breasts were exposed. She ground her hips against him and felt the press of his belt buckle against her flesh.

"Take off your pajama bottoms," he said.

Adriana pushed at the silk, mindlessly wanting only what his virile body promised. His hand, hot and intrusive, pushed between her legs and she writhed against it.

Reaching for his belt, her fumbling hands unbuckled, unbuttoned and unzipped. He moaned, a deep rumble that filled her with a nameless emotion.

Hands on her thighs, he spread her legs and pushed into her. "God, you're tight," he groaned.

"Don't talk." Adriana thought she'd die if he stopped, but needed no reminders of her years of celibacy. "Just take me."

With each stroke, he drove deeper into her body and, it seemed, into her soul. Her entire being centered on the heat building within her. Hands gripping his broad shoulders, she wrapped her legs around his hips and arched into each thrust.

The heat was unbearable and she exploded with a scream, which he muffled with his mouth. He swallowed her scream and tensed, absorbing her contractions and then, her satisfaction assured, he took his own, pumping into her two, three times.

Thorne rolled onto his back, pulling her with him. Framing her face in his hands, he searched for he knew not what. Satisfaction? Regrets?

When she averted her eyes, he knew he still shared her bed with a ghost.

"Well, one thing's for certain."

She lowered her head, nestling into the crook of his neck. "What?"

"I'd say your decorator was right on the money. These damn pillows did make a difference."

Coconut Grove

Nevada placed the basket of homemade banana bread on the kitchen table and watched with satisfaction as Luke reached for a slice.

"I still don't understand why you kept this place of yours such a secret," he grumbled. Biting into the bread, he raised his eyes heavenward. "This is delicious."

Returning from an all-nighter at the vet's, Nevada considered fixing breakfast for Luke before they both went to work only fair. But she hadn't expected the sight of him sitting at her kitchen table to give her so much pleasure. Despite being big and decidedly masculine, he didn't look out of place in her home, with its folk art, chintz sofas and teacup collection.

"I really appreciate your help with Brady." Refilling his coffee cup, Nevada allowed her free hand to rest on his shoulder but resisted the urge to drop a kiss on his cheek.

Luke watched her as she poured his coffee, his gaze so intimate that her hand shook. She replaced the pot and took a seat opposite him.

"We guys have to stick together," he said between forkfuls of scrambled eggs. "Actually, there's something rather admirable about a tomcat. Comes and goes as he pleases and screws every female in heat. Not a bad life.''

"Aren't you forgetting what happens to *old* tomcats?'' Annoyed, Nevada moved the basket of banana bread out of his reach. "I'd say he more than met his match and has the scars to prove it. Not to mention an ear that he'll be lucky to keep.''

"Well, I agree it might put a crimp in his lifestyle, but imagine what would happen if he changed. You know, kind of settled down to all the females in just one backyard. Why, he'd get fat and lazy and wouldn't be much use to anyone.''

Nevada reached across the table and whisked away his half-eaten plate of eggs. "You should have quit when you were ahead.''

He grinned. "What happened to those cookies you baked last night?''

She lunged for him and he caught her expertly, pulling her into his lap and kissing her until all thoughts of randy old tomcats ceased to exist.

The phone rang. "Who calls you this early?''

Reluctant to leave Luke's lap, Nevada stretched for the phone, picked it up and said, "Good morning, Thorne.''

Her smile was replaced by a frown. "Just a minute, please.''

Covering the mouthpiece, she whispered, "He wants to talk to *you*.''

"How did he know I was here?"

Taking the phone, Luke greeted his friend and then listened carefully before hanging up. "He'll be back in town tomorrow. There's been more trouble in Bremerhaven."

She looped her arms around his neck. "Did he ask why you were with me?"

"No." He kissed her lightly on the lips. "But he gave us his blessing, Nevada."

"Dawn." Her lips hovered over his. "Call me Dawn. It's my *real* name."

Bremerhaven

Adriana placed the powder blue cashmere cardigan in her suitcase and, after one last look around the cabin, zipped it shut. If only she could pack and zip up the events of the past twenty-four hours as easily.

The bed, stripped of silk spread and pillows, remained a poignant reminder of the hours she'd spent with Thorne. She knew he'd been surprised, first by her reluctance and then her ardor. He truly thought the Ice Queen had cracked—and just for him.

What he didn't, and couldn't, know was that her reserve had been simply due to loyalty to Piero. The closeness she'd shared with her husband had been special and, she knew, her personal salvation. Although a successful model, her life had been shallow and empty until she'd met Piero, whose love and affection had made her whole. Now she knew that denying her sexuality since Piero's death had been a mistake. Strong and virile, Thorne had awakened her to her own long-denied physical needs.

Hearing the knock at her door, Adriana smiled. Thorne had promised to return when the ship reached port. Since they were both staying in Hamburg for the night before catching separate flights the following morning, Adriana assumed they would spend the evening together. Even though she knew it was a foolish whimsy, she was excited and tantalized by the prospect of spending another evening with him.

She opened the door with a flourish and her smile faded. "Nico. What are you doing here?"

"I never really left, Marchesa." He glanced past her into the suite. "May I come in? I'd like to speak to you for a few moments."

"Certainly. I'd also like to know why you're here and not in Italy as I'd assumed."

"I was in Italy, but returned when I learned of the incident during the sea trials."

"You mean the deadman's turn?"

"According to my sources, Marchesa, it may not have been an accident."

"Sabotage?" Adriana sat down on the unmade bed and waved a hand toward the chaise. "How can that be, Nico?"

"I'll know more once the experts get through with their investigation. Right now, it looks like the software program contained a near-fatal flaw. The computer was programmed to shift from auto to manual pilot when tight evasive turns were executed. You were fortunate this ship didn't tip into the sea."

"But couldn't it still have been—"

"This kind of technical sabotage is not uncommon. They certainly have the resources to have done it. The real question is, did they have the opportunity."

Adriana took a minute to understand the implications of Nico's statement. "You think someone who works for me is helping them?"

He nodded. "It's a possibility that can't be ruled out. Someone certainly seems to have access."

"Who knows about this?"

"You're the only one I've told, and I'd appreciate it if you would keep this information confidential until the investigation is complete."

"All right, although I wish I could discuss this with one or two others."

"Believe me, it's best this way, Marchesa." He twirled his trademark silver-rimmed sunglasses in his hand. "When I got the call early this morning, I was in Rome. I visited Gemma Sacco yesterday and learned some interesting information."

A sharp rap and the sound of Adriana's door opening made them both turn.

"Adriana. Are you ready?" Thorne halted midway into the suite. A dark eyebrow angled upward. "Am I interrupting?"

Adriana quickly performed introductions, conscious of Nico and Thorne's appraisal of the other.

"Nico does some freelance work for me," Adriana explained. "We were just discussing one of his assignments."

"Well, I won't keep you. I just came by to say goodbye."

"But I thought—"

"Would you mind excusing us for a few minutes?" Thorne asked Nico.

Nico glanced from Thorne to Adriana. He cocked a dark brow inquiringly before he shrugged. "Certainly." With a curt nod to Adriana, he left the suite.

"You needn't have been so rude," Adriana said as soon as the door shut behind Nico.

"And you shouldn't have invited him into this cabin." He looked pointedly at the unmade bed. "Unless you want to broadcast what happened here last night to the whole world."

"You're right," she admitted. Thorne wore dress slacks, shirt and a soft suede jacket, and she noticed he'd dropped a leather garment bag by the door. "What exactly *did* happen here last night?"

He shrugged. "We enjoyed ourselves."

"Right again," she acknowledged with a stiff smile. "And Hamburg?"

"Canceled. I sent for my plane. I'm heading for Miami tonight." He hesitated, then reached for her. "And you?"

His hand rested lightly on the small of her back. "Nico and I are having an early dinner at the hotel," she said, instantly changing her plans. "I have an early-morning flight to Genoa."

His dark eyes narrowed, searching her face. "Do you need a ride to Hamburg?"

She shook her head. "No."

"So this is goodbye." His hand tightened, tugging her against him.

"Unless you forget to make the next installment on the *Pisano*, we will meet again for the ship's christening in a few weeks." She cupped a hand behind his neck, willing her fingers not to thread through his dark hair. "*Arrivederci*, Thorne."

Their lips met, cool and impersonal. She stepped away at the same moment his hand dropped from her back. He walked toward the door, picked up his garment bag and slung it over a shoulder before turning back to her. "I know you called him *caro*. What did he call you?"

She waited until he was halfway out the door before answering him.

"*Carissima.*"

Thorne walked out the door and didn't look back.

22

Genoa

"No excuses, Emilio." Adriana cut Emilio off in midsentence, surprising even herself. "You've known I needed to make another payment to the shipyard before the *Pisano* can be cleared for the crossing to New York. I don't care where you get the money, just get it and get it *now*."

Adriana walked out of Emilio's office and turned toward her own at the opposite end of the hallway. She was seething. Why was Emilio procrastinating? Their arguments over the past few days had been too reminiscent of Piero's kidnapping. Within days, a ransom demand had been received and Adriana had been confused by Emilio's reluctance to provide the necessary funds.

At first, she'd accepted his explanations—money not immediately accessible, bankers needing more time—until she'd finally realized the delays could cost her husband his life. She'd immediately sold whatever she owned outright, including jewelry, in order to raise the money herself. She'd been too late.

She was so close now to fulfilling Piero's dream. The idea that Emilio's frugality could jeopardize this achievement was unacceptable.

Entering her office, she paused at Carla's desk. "Get me a copy of the company's annual budget for the past two years, will you? Along with actual expenses. I also want a breakdown of this year's projections."

"You have—"

"I know what I have, Carla, but it doesn't tell me enough. Emilio moves money around like chess pieces. If he doesn't cooperate with me, he's going to find himself in checkmate."

Adriana figured it would take several hours before Emilio learned about her inquiries and collection of data. Crossing to her desk, with its neatly sorted stacks of papers detailing matters needing her immediate attention, Adriana smiled. Emilio would find it much more advantageous to make sure the shipyard payment was paid on schedule.

Adriana sat down at her desk and absently massaged her neck. Since returning from Germany three days earlier, she'd worked long hours. Anything to keep from thinking about Thorne and his cool goodbye. Although inexperienced herself, she'd seen enough of the world to know that some men viewed women as merely challenges. Had she been just another one?

Don't ever tell me I can't have something, he'd once told her. *It just makes me want it more.*

Well, he'd definitely had her, Adriana thought, putting on her reading glasses and reaching for the documents Carla had separated as first priority.

Just before Carla left for the day, she handed her a memo from Emilio acknowledging the transfer of funds to the Bremerhaven shipyard. About time, Adriana thought, relieved.

Although tired, she met Nico for a prearranged dinner at a nearby café. Over a plate of antipasto, Nico announced, "I've discovered that Piero purchased the Sacco farm and then deeded it to the family shortly after the war ended."

Adriana considered the matter. "As a favor to his wife? Ensuring her family's welfare?"

"Can't say for sure. When Luisa died, Piero, as the surviving spouse, was the principal beneficiary. There were a few small bequests, primarily several favorite charities, with the exception of a small bequest to her sister, Gemma."

"Has the farm always been the main source of income for the family?"

"That's the interesting part, Marchesa." Nico pulled a document from an inside breast pocket. "This is a trust fund established for Gemma Sacco in the late sixties and her principal source of income.

Although difficult to trace, it's been determined that Piero Falcone was the originator.''

"He never mentioned Gemma or his late wife's family to me,'' Adriana said. "There's no mention of this anywhere, especially in the archives.''

Helping himself to marinated eggplant, Nico asked, "What happened to Piero's personal papers and possessions after his death?''

"I'm not sure—everything was such a blur. The press...''

"Try to remember.''

"There were boxes of things sent from the office. They sat in a room at the palazzo before, I think, Donatella went through them. I assume anything of importance to the family wound up in the family archives.''

Gently Nico inquired, "What about Piero's personal things? Did Donatella go through them also?''

"No, I wouldn't let anyone touch his possessions.'' She hesitated. "I couldn't bear to stay in the apartment we'd shared at the palazzo, so I eventually moved to a smaller one and decorated it with only a few items from the larger apartment. Other than clothing, I boxed up Piero's things and put the boxes in the cellar, intending to go through them later. I guess I'd nearly forgotten about them.''

"Perhaps there's something there.''

"As I recall, it was mostly favorite books and a

few mementos. Certainly nothing important or valuable.''

A waiter arrived with their main courses, but Adriana had little appetite. A short time later, while waiting for their check, Adriana asked, ''Financially helping his first wife's family wouldn't be questioned. Why would Piero go to the trouble of concealing a trust account?''

''Gemma Sacco must have known something Piero wanted to make sure never came out.''

''Perhaps Julia's identity?''

''Whatever it was, the trust fund bought silence.''

Miami

Thorne stared at the zeros on the draft.

The financial controller's office had delivered the bank draft to him because, at Thorne's request, his authorization was required before the wire transfer of funds could take place.

Why was he hesitating to carry out a decision made months ago? It was not his nature to change course. But he seemed unable to banish the trusting look in Adriana's eyes when she had discussed this *Pisano* payment with him.

She had no clue that he hadn't any intention of paying it. Had never had any intention.

When she learned of this further duplicity, he

knew she'd be angry. He also knew she'd be hurt, and it was this knowledge that bothered him.

"Ready for lunch?"

"I wish you'd let Maria do her job." This was one time Thorne wished Luke had waited in the reception area outside his office. "I asked her to give you a call to see if we could make it tomorrow, instead."

"I came here directly from the port. Didn't get the message." Luke settled in a high-backed chair. "What's up?"

Thorne slid the check under his blotter. "I heard from the shipyard this morning. The *Pisano* incident was no accident. Someone tampered with the computer program. Whether or not the accident was intended to occur during sea trials is debatable."

"So the marchesa's in serious trouble."

"Looks that way," Thorne said.

"Have you paid the money?"

"Not yet."

"Are you going to?"

"I hadn't planned to."

"If you force her hand this way, don't you risk buying her problems, too? Whoever's after the marchesa might come after you, instead."

"I'm already a target, as you well know. It might just make me a broader one."

"So what's plan B?"

Luke knew him too well.

"I stay in the game. But on my terms."

As he reached for the phone, Thorne smiled for the first time that day. "Give me ten minutes, Luke, and we'll have that lunch after all."

Genoa

After nearly two hours of searching in the dark dusty cellar, Adriana found what she was looking for. She tucked the leather volume under her shirt, carefully replaced the boxes and turned off the overhead light.

The palazzo was quiet. Donatella and Emilio had returned earlier from a dinner party and retired to their own spacious apartment in another wing. Under the watchful eyes of generations of Falcone men and women, Adriana climbed the stairs to her apartment. She showered and changed into a comfortable gown and robe, then made a cup of herbal tea and picked up the leather-bound journal.

The sight of Piero's signature on the flyleaf made her throat tighten. Turning the page, she began to read.

Rome, 1942

The slap sounded like a small pistol shot.
I stared at the woman in my arms as if she'd gone

mad. That any woman, especially this one, would dare to slap me amazed me....

For several seconds he continued to stare at her. Then all the suppressed anger and betrayal he had buried while he toyed with her rose to the surface.

He shoved her away. The urge to beat her or make love to her warred within him. When she stumbled, he forced himself not to reach out and steady her. She caught herself on a nearby end table, but the loose chignon broke free and a cascade of glorious blond hair fell about her shoulders.

"Imagine, if you will," he said, "my return from war only to learn my wife has gone to France, against my wishes, to visit an aunt. This aunt, you understand, is, unfortunately for all, married to a Jewish man. I've been able to learn only that the entire household was caught in a raid and has since disappeared. Thinking my wife was likely dead, I was overjoyed to later learn she was here in Rome, with her parents."

He *had* been overjoyed to learn Luisa was safe. At least one corner of his crumbling world was intact. "A pass allowed me to come immediately," he continued, trying to keep his grief at bay. "I've just learned the truth. An *American* woman is impersonating my wife, who, we are all beginning to realize, may no longer be alive."

"I'm so sorry." Julia's hazel eyes beseeched him for forgiveness, and her bottom lip, he saw with an unexpected twinge of remorse, was swollen. "I never wanted to hurt anyone—"

"Well, you did!" The words spewed out like a volcano. "You've put my entire family in jeopardy with antics like the one today. Luckily I was able to prevent your discovery. My God, what were you thinking? This is wartime, not some game children play."

"I'm not a child," she said, a stubborn proud note creeping into what had, until now, been a repentant tone. "I fully understand the risk."

"Are you prepared to die?" Julia blanched at his harsh tone, but her gaze did not waver under his. "A woman as beautiful as you will not die quickly or painlessly. You would provide your torturers with much pleasure first."

"What is one life if so many others can be saved?"

He strained to catch her words, spoken softly but with unquestioned conviction. Despite all he was feeling—and trying not to feel—he admired her courage. Courage that, if she persisted in such dangerous activities, would be sorely tested in the days ahead.

He sighed, reaching for his cane. His leg was beginning to trouble him. Wounded seriously, he was considered permanently disabled by the doctors. But under his own self-imposed exercise regimen, his leg had healed beyond any doctor's expectation.

However, for his own purposes, he had chosen to keep his improved medical condition a secret. But surely there was a limit to the secrets one could keep, was there not? He stared at the woman who now faced him with an expression he recognized as boldly defiant. An expression he had seen most recently on men who faced a firing squad.

The safe-conduct pass allowing him to travel from Genoa to Rome and the petrol ration slips weighed heavily in his breast pocket. A decision had to be made, and quickly.

"Where did you take him?" he demanded.

"Who?"

"That airman. American, I suppose."

"I wouldn't know." Her hazel eyes looked guileless. "I left right away. Remember?"

"You can be made to talk." She would break easily. American women, as everyone knew, were lazy and spoiled. "Braver women than you have spilled their guts under interrogation."

"If you insist on finding out, *husband,* I suggest you report me."

Outwardly she bore some physical resemblance to Luisa. But there the similarity ended. Luisa was an obedient, submissive wife. With the exception of her trip to France, she always did as she was told. He doubted this woman ever did.

But she had played the role of Marchesa Luisa

Falcone too well. The result was that she had left him little choice.

"We'll leave in two days."

"Leave?" Her beautiful hazel eyes clouded with confusion. "You're going to report me?"

"No." Unable to resist, he reached out and touched her glorious hair. "I'm taking you home. To Genoa."

"I'm not going anywhere with you!" Pushing his hand away, she backed away from him. "I'm staying in Rome."

He ignored her protests. "Tomorrow we visit the jeweler. Until he can make a duplicate, you'll wear this ring." He removed the signet ring from his finger. She tucked her hands behind her back, but by using his body to trap her against a wall, he pried a hand free and pushed his ring onto her finger.

She stopped struggling and looked at the ring, which seemed massive on her hand. "Why must I wear this ring?"

"The gold falcon is the Falcone crest. This ring was my father's, passed from oldest son to oldest son. Luisa has an identical ring—smaller of course. It was her wedding ring. She wore it always."

"But I'm *not* your wife. I can't wear this ring."

"Genoa is not like Rome. The Germans control all of northern Italy. I obtained permission to come to Rome to bring you home. It's imperative that my wife returns with me. The Falcones have vital interests at stake in Genoa. Must I remind you that it was your decision to come to Italy, your decision to impersonate my wife? I'm afraid you've left me no choice. In Genoa, our lives will depend on your convincing performance. Now do you understand why you must wear this ring?''

Julia nodded, but Piero detected a stubborn thrust to her chin.

''As soon as I can manage it, I will see that you get out of Italy safely,'' he promised, surprising even himself. ''But for as long as you wear this ring, I demand one thing. If there is a bullet with your name on it, your death must honor the Falcone name.''

The look she gave him would have brought a lesser man to his knees. ''To die any other way would dishonor not only other women, but *my* family and country.''

Maybe, just maybe, he conceded with a glimmer of admiration, this impostor might prove much more useful than simply playing the part of a marchesa. But whether or not he shared other secrets with her, once they arrived in Genoa, only God knew the dangers they would face. If this young woman, just out of the schoolroom, failed to convince the Nazis she was his marchesa, it would cost both of them their lives.

23

The M.S. Pisano *Christening*

Bremerhaven

Adriana could easily have been an award-winning actress. For the past few hours, she'd certainly given the performance of a lifetime.

She'd arrived in Bremerhaven the day before, brimming with suppressed excitement. There were lots of reasons for her nervous anticipation, not the least of which was christening the *Pisano*. Although Donatella had been unable to attend the ceremony, Emilio had accompanied her along with several others from the Falcone headquarters.

Her only concern had been that the shipyard had not yet received Thorne's share of the money owed. The reports she'd received indicated that the funds were approved, the check authorized and the money ready to wire. Then she'd gotten caught up in the details of the christening, the crossing to New York and the extensive inaugural activities planned, both at Pier 92 in New York and the Port of Miami, and assumed the transfer had taken place.

She had also looked forward to seeing Thorne, attributing her anticipation to the questions she had hoped Thorne would answer regarding Julia and their relationship.

But the instant she'd glimpsed him in the hotel lobby, she'd known her reasons were much deeper. As she watched him cross the lobby, she noticed the deferential manner of the hotel staff, as if he were a head of state.

He was fire to her ice. He stoked all the senses she'd worked to hard to freeze. She could no longer lie to herself; she wanted Thorne Weston.

Until she learned he hadn't paid the money and her ship wouldn't be released until he did.

Incensed, she tried in vain to reach him at the hotel. She'd even asked Luke to intervene, but without success. Thorne had deliberately avoided her for the past twenty-four hours, yet had the audacity to show up for the christening. Posing for pictures beside her. Smiling for photographers. Charming her staff and, especially, Emilio. Somehow she'd managed to maintain the pretense of serene coolness, even when his hand touched her arm or conversation flowed around them.

She knew he wanted something and that he'd soon tell her what.

Everything was in place in New York and Miami.

The only glitch was Thorne's payment. She wondered what his price would be.

The ceremony was nearly over. Photographers were taking a few final photos. Adriana stood at a distance, knowing sooner or later he would choose the time and place. She wasn't surprised when he strolled toward her. She didn't give him an opportunity to initiate the conversation.

While continuing to pretend an interest in the formal proceedings, she demanded, "What do you want?"

"Besides you?"

"Excuse me. Let me rephrase the question. What do you *really* want?"

"What makes you think I want something *more* from you?"

"Look, you haven't paid your share of the funds we agreed upon. I'm told by your controller that you've delayed the wire transfer. Ergo, you want something. What?"

"I thought we'd go have lunch somewhere and discuss my terms."

"I think not."

He shrugged and walked away, smiling good-naturedly as he posed for another photo.

There were a number of colorful Italian descriptive words that suited him perfectly, thought Adriana. *Bastardo, Imbecile, Stupido,* came instantly to mind.

At Herr Schellin's invitation, she accompanied the shipyard president back to the shipyard offices for a glass of champagne and light refreshment. While they waited for the others to join them, Adriana slipped into an empty office and called the hotel to see if the Falcone Line's attorneys had arrived. Suspecting trouble, she'd summoned them to Hamburg as soon as she'd learned the status of Thorne's payment. She left instructions for them to wait at the hotel until they heard from her.

Returning to the large conference room allocated for the minicelebration, she wasn't surprised to see Thorne waiting outside in the corridor. "I think we should talk."

"I agree," he replied. Cupping her elbow, he walked her down the corridor away from the others. "I'm prepared to authorize the wire transfer..."

"If?"

His smile reminded her of a predator sensing the kill. "You sell me a fifty percent interest in the option you hold for the next ship scheduled to be built here."

"That's it?"

"Yes. And before you ask, it's not open for negotiation."

"My attorneys are at the hotel. I suggest you meet us there later this afternoon for my answer." She shook off his hand. "Now, if that's all you have to discuss, I'm going to have a glass of champagne."

As she left him, Adriana knew there was one more thing she had to do. Rather than return to Genoa, she was going back to Rome.

Only this time, she wasn't leaving until she had the answers.

Thorne watched her walk away and knew he was paying a higher price than he'd imagined when he'd embarked on the Falcone takeover.

He'd thought it would be so easy, but it was proving to be one of the most difficult moments of his life.

But he had only to remember the reason it was worthwhile, even if it meant hurting Marchesa Falcone.

Tuscany, 1967

The old truck chugged up the hill. Thorne wriggled his bottom to avoid the spring poking through the worn seat. Even though he was already ten years old, he couldn't see over the high dashboard unless he scooted forward, and he wanted to see where they were going. But a quick glimpse was all he could manage before the woman at the steering wheel beside him reached out a hand and gently pushed him back against the seat.

"Are we almost there, Signora Mazzini?"

It seemed he'd asked her a thousand times since leaving the farmhouse before the first rooster crowed that morning. He'd been anxious and restless since his sister, Julia, had left him a few days ago with the *signora,* one of her old friends. But the *signora* did not smile and laugh nearly as often as Julia, nor did she kiss and hug him, turning his insides to melted butter.

He wasn't sure why the *signora* had suddenly decided to bring him to meet his sister this morning. He thought it was because she thought he didn't like her food. It wasn't the food; he just wasn't hungry.

He missed his sister.

He never wanted to go back home. He wished he could always be with Julia. She really liked him; their mother, Inge Weston, didn't.

He shuddered at the thought of his mother. Closing his eyes tightly, he imagined his sister's smiling face. It was the only mind-picture that ever made him feel good.

The only one that made him forget his mother and the things she did to him, things he never talked about, not even to Julia.

"Relax, *bambino,* you'll see your sister soon."

The *signora* glanced at him with that look that made him worry. Had he done something wrong? The way she sometimes stared at him made him uncomfortable, but at least she never yelled at him or hit him. She just stared and when he noticed, she'd look quickly away.

Like now, he thought, as she looked back at the

road. He watched to see if her cheeks would turn pink as they sometimes did, but instead, lines appeared on her forehead and this time when she took one hand off the steering wheel, she made the sign of the cross.

"O Dio, O Dio, O Dio..."

Her foot stomped on the brake so hard Thorne flew forward, bumping the dashboard. In that instant, he saw parked cars and people standing in the road. The *signora* pushed her door open and scrambled out. Before slamming the door, she pointed her finger at him and ordered, "Don't move. Stay right here until I get back."

He scrambled onto the seat to see better. The *signora* ran, her dark blue skirt billowing around her legs. Finally stopping, she spoke with an elderly man, then ran to the edge of the road and looked over. Falling to her knees, she put her head in her hands.

Thorne saw her shoulders shaking and knew she was crying. A terrible stillness settled in his chest and he reached for the door, finally getting it open and tumbling out. He scrambled to his feet and hurried toward the *signora,* who was still sobbing.

No one paid any attention to him. He moved toward the edge of the road and looked down. The hillside was steep and at the bottom was a car, all smashed and broken, with smoke coming out of it. People were making their way down the slope.

Thorne squinted, watching several rescuers moving slowly toward the car and away from a partially visible body a short distance. He saw a bit of yellow hair sticking out from behind a big rock a little way from the car. And almost immediately he understood why the *signora* was crying.

He began to scramble down the hill, only dimly aware of the screech of tires behind him, car doors slamming and a man shouting orders. He kept his eyes focused on the long yellow hair and his need to get to that place. He tried running but kept falling, scraping his hands and knees until they bled. His clothes caught and tore on brambles, but he kept going; nothing would keep him from getting to her. As he got closer, his nose filled with the acrid smoke from the car, where two men were peering into the wreckage and saying words he didn't understand.

He skidded the last few yards, almost colliding with the boulder. He stopped his momentum with his hands, unaware and uncaring of the small, bloody prints he left behind. It was all a dream, he told himself. The only thing that felt real was the sound of his own gasping breathing and thudding heartbeat. He almost tripped hurrying around the boulder.

"Julia?" he whispered hopefully at the sight of the sprawled figure. Her beautiful blond hair blanketed the barren ground around her head. He knelt at her side, his small hand clinging to her hand, clenched at her breast. He leaned over her, knowing she must be hurt, because Julia never failed to greet him with a smile and love in her eyes.

But there was no smile, and no love in her eyes. Just a strange vacant look. Was she sleeping? He touched her shoulder and shook her ever so gently. Then he saw the blood matting her yellow hair.

Terror gripped him and he screamed her name, "Julia!"

She blinked, and for a second Thorne saw the light come into her eyes. It seemed to come from far away, growing brighter the longer she looked at him. Beneath his hand, her fingers quivered. She wore a ring he didn't recognize; it was loose and too big for her finger. Her lips moved and Thorne put his face as close to hers as he could, until he felt her breath on his face and heard the word she whispered over and over, each time fainter than the last until she spoke no more.

"Falcone...Falcone...Falcone."

Suddenly a strong arm clamped around his waist and attempted to haul him away. Squirming and thrashing, Thorne was determined that nothing and no one was going to separate him from his sister. Not now, when she needed him most of all.

He clung to her hand, his lifeline back to her.

He felt the strong chest at his back and the steely forearm holding him. The voice somewhere above his head was low, speaking a language he didn't know but whose meaning he clearly understood.

Go away. Get lost. You're a nuisance. You should never have been born. A mistake, a terrible mistake.

He'd heard the words from his mother all his life. He knew when he wasn't wanted, when he was in the way.

The man gave a quiet command to several younger men hovering nearby. One of the men moved and also wrapped an arm around Thorne's midsection. Both men pulled until, with a howl of despair, Thorne lost his grip on Julia's hand. The second man dragged him away, dodging Thorne's kicking legs and swinging arms and yelled for assistance. Soon Thorne was being held so tightly he could barely breathe.

Thorne continued to rage at the men holding him, struggling whenever their grips eased even a fraction. A part of him wanted to cry—and knew the tears would soon come—but another part of him, a new part, churned with a powerful rage. One that made him want to throw the men restraining him off the hillside and then rip the first man away from his sister, the man still kneeling beside her and moaning her name. He, Thorne, was the one who should be with her. Not that man.

His fury grew as he watched the tall dark man kneel over Julia, his head bowed, his lips moving soundlessly. His hand dared to touch her, stroke her hair and smooth her skirt down over her bare legs, ease a shoe back on a foot.

The moment Thorne realized the tall man intended to scoop Julia into his arms, he renewed his struggles, screaming, "No, no! Put her down, put her down!"

Ignoring him, the man scooped Julia up into his arms, her face nestled against his shoulder, her golden hair like a fall of sunshine, but for the blood. For an instant the tall man's eyes flicked over Thorne, and Thorne put a face on his own feelings, feelings he saw mirrored in the man's eyes.

Sorrow, deeper than any ravine, any ocean.

He spoke. More orders, Thorne realized as one of the men holding him nodded and said, "*Sí*, Signore Falcone."

The hands holding Thorne did not release him until the man reached the top of the ravine. He seemed to climb effortlessly, his strong legs and shoulders easily absorbing Julia's weight. One of her arms dangled and moved to the rhythm of the man carrying her.

Almost as if she were still alive.

So lifelike that Thorne imagined she waved a final time to him.

When the men released him, they pointed to the *signora*, who was carefully coming down the ravine toward him, and he heard the word *mama* and knew they thought he belonged to her.

But he knew he now belonged to no one.

The only person who cared had left him.

He remained standing where he was and heard again his sister's final words.

Falcone...Falcone...Falcone...

Thorne raised his eyes to the man who strode up the hill far ahead of him with the only person he had ever loved, and felt his rage turn to hate.

Falcone. Signore Falcone.

He was the man his sister had left him to go visit, and now the man had taken his sister from him.

Opening his palm, Thorne stared at the ring he'd been clutching. The ring he'd taken from his sister's clasp.

A gold ring with a black falcon.

He looked back up the hill, everything suddenly crystal clear.

Signore Falcone was the reason why his sister was gone—and never coming back.

24

Inaugural Cruise

Pier 92, New York City, 1999

"I don't think this is a good idea." Stepping off the elevator with Adriana, Nico glanced around the crowded Columbus Lounge and frowned. "Are you sure you don't want to forget about a drink and call it a night? You must be exhausted."

"Can't you forget who you are and what you do for a few days, Nico?" Adriana cast an admiring glance at him. He wore his tux with distinction. "I know you think I agreed to your suggestion to accompany me on this cruise because I'd finally decided I needed protection. But the truth is I thought you needed a vacation—and having you in my party of guests suited my purposes."

"I'm not sure Weston would agree with your 'purposes,'" Nico drawled. "I've been the recipient of several glaring looks this evening."

Adriana laughed and reached for Nico's hand, giving it a gentle tug.

Her gold chiffon dress shimmered in the subdued lighting as she moved through the room toward an empty table with a discreet reserved sign. Along the way, she smiled and murmured greetings to several of the men and women already seated or talking in small groups, but she didn't stop. This was a special occasion. She intended to sip champagne with Nico as the *Pisano* left New York.

The inaugural stop of the *Pisano* in New York had been a resounding success. Docked at Pier 92, the ship had been a whirlwind of activity for the past twelve hours. Invited guests, who would be sailing from New York to Miami, had boarded, joined later by a host of celebrities and local dignitaries, there for the celebratory party. After the receiving line broke up, Adriana had continued to circulate among her guests. The evening had begun with cocktails, followed by a six-course meal and culminating with Las Vegas-style entertainment in the main showroom. As soon as the last visitor had left, the captain readied the *Pisano* for the scheduled 1:00 a.m. departure.

Adriana collapsed on one of the cocktail lounge's plush circular couches. Nico took a seat beside her. Directly in front of them was a low marble table and, beyond it, the reason she'd chosen this particular spot. High atop the ship, the intimate Columbus Lounge offered an unparalleled view of the Manhattan skyline as the *Pisano* made her way down the Hudson river to the Atlantic. Ahead was the Statue of Liberty and Ellis Island.

Adriana savored the moment. The *Pisano* was the first Falcone ship to dock in New York, however briefly, and was another fulfillment of Piero's dream.

An attentive waiter arrived with the chilled Tattinger champagne she'd ordered, placing the ice bucket beside their table. With a flourish, another waiter deposited crystal flutes, napkins and an iced bowl of strawberries on the table. After a nod from Adriana, the first waiter poured the champagne, returned the bottle to the ice bucket and quietly left as Adriana raised her glass in a toast.

"To a successful cruise." She touched her flute to Nico's and took a sip.

"To a successful, *safe* cruise," Nico amended.

"Don't spoil this moment, Nico. I've been looking forward to this for years," Adriana said, settling back and crossing her legs. "You may not see me again until we reach Miami. I intend to relax in my suite, perhaps sit on the veranda with a good book. Tonight was just a dress rehearsal for the week-long events we've planned for Miami, followed by several cruises to nowhere."

"Well, at least you agree you should keep a very low profile. As you know, I would have much preferred it if you had remained in Italy."

"What we want and what we get are often two different things, Nico."

She debated telling Nico what she had learned on her impulsive return visit to see Gemma Sacco. After her flight from Genoa had arrived in Rome, she'd realized it would be hours before the flight to New York departed. She'd decided to make good use of her unexpected time in Rome, so she'd rented a car and driven to Gemma's farmhouse.

"It was Gemma who sent the diary entries to me," Adriana told Nico, setting her flute on the table and reaching for a strawberry. "When I arrived at the farmhouse yesterday, I had the feeling she'd been expecting me."

"I should have been with you," said Nico. "You might have been in danger."

"I wasn't, though, Nico." Her gaze on the view, she continued to speak, keeping her voice low. "Gemma sent the diaries to another daughter in Genoa who mailed them to me. When Gemma read that I had opened a cruise terminal in America, she began to worry and, when I showed up on her doorstep, she became more anxious about the secrets she'd kept for all those years. During the war, Julia had left her journals with Gemma for safekeeping.

Now Gemma isn't well, and she doesn't want to burden her children any further with the need to shield me from the truth.''

As the ship passed the Statue of Liberty, Adriana briefly filled Nico in on Julia's wartime deception.

"So Julia was Thorne Weston's sister." Nico's eyes narrowed. "Does he know about Julia's wartime pretense of being Piero's wife?"

"Gemma says he doesn't." Until she confronted Thorne, Adriana didn't intend to tell Nico the other things she'd learned.

Gemma had told her how Julia died, and that Julia's brother, Thorne, had watched her die. And blamed Piero Falcone for her death.

"The ring." Elbows resting on his knees, Nico leaned closer to her. "Do you know how Thorne Weston got your husband's ring?"

Adriana shook her head. "No. During the marriage arrangement, Julia wore a ring Piero had made for her, but she left everything behind with Piero when she left Italy. Gemma has no idea how Thorne acquired the ring."

"So Piero deeded the farm to Gemma as a way to buy her silence? So that Julia's role posing as his wife would be kept quiet?"

"Yes. When Luisa was found alive in a concentration camp, she was near death. At first he wanted to shield her from the truth, although, when she got stronger, Piero told her another woman had pretended to be his wife. After Germany's defeat, there were still those in Italy who were Nazi sympathizers. Piero wanted to protect Luisa from any repercussions due to his own partisan activities and never spoke of Julia to anyone.''

Not even me, Adriana thought.

After reading on in Piero's journal, agonizing pages written sometime shortly after Julia's death, Adriana knew without a doubt that Julia had been the one true love of her husband's life. Reading the account written in his own hand, she understood for the first time the underlying sadness she'd sensed in Piero when she'd first met him at a dinner with friends.

She'd attributed the melancholy to the loss of his wife, Luisa. Instead, it had been Julia he'd truly mourned, an American woman who had pretended to be a dutiful Falcone wife, often entertaining Germans in the Falcone palazzo, and then risking her life countless times beside Piero as a spy on nighttime assignments in the hills around Genoa. Eventually, the pretense had become a reality.

And sharing a bed more than a duty.

"Would you excuse me, Marchesa?" Nico glanced at his watch. "I promised to meet some friends. I can return in half an hour."

"That won't be necessary, Nico. I'm just going

to finish this glass of champagne, and then meet
Donatella and Emilio in the Emperor lounge for the
midnight show. I'd actually enjoy a few minutes by
myself.''

He bent and kissed both her cheeks. ''I'll say
hello to my friends, Mario and Vittorio, for you.''

Adriana watched him leave, his reference to
''friends'' making her suddenly uncomfortable.
Mario and Vittorio were security people he'd hired
to accompany him and were posing as guests. Adriana didn't want to be reminded of them and hoped
she'd never have occasion to meet them.

A burst of laughter made Adriana look up just in
time to notice that Thorne Weston was seated several tables away from her. His party was large and
seemed to include several tables. Adriana recognized Luke, who appeared to be totally absorbed in
conversation with a striking dark-haired woman
called Nevada.

She also recognized the women on either side of
Thorne. One was the Grammy Award-winning
singer who'd entertained guests at the party earlier
in the evening. The other, so Adriana had been told,
was a daytime soap opera star, who had been seated
with Thorne at dinner.

Thorne's financial interest in the *Pisano* had not
been widely known, confined to the financial community. But when he'd boarded for the cruise to

Miami, several news organizations covering the event had immediately begun speculating about the romantic possibilities. In an effort to defuse the tabloid rumors, Adriana had instructed her publicist to release the information regarding their joint venture. Nico's pretending to be her attentive escort and Thorne surrounded by a bevy of beauties also helped.

So why did the sight of Thorne enjoying himself with two beautiful women make her heart feel squeezed as if held in a vise?

Thorne looked up, his gaze colliding with hers. Adriana felt suddenly breathless. She shuddered, realizing time and distance had not vanquished her attraction to him. Her gaze fell to his mouth as she remembered how it had felt against her own. The knowing twist appearing at its corners indicated he'd correctly read her thoughts. With an effort, she dragged her gaze away and back to her champagne, the strawberries and the view.

Only now, she discovered, her champagne tasted flat, the strawberries bitter and the view outside had lost its appeal. Gathering up her small beaded bag, Adriana got up from the couch and deliberately chose an exit path that wouldn't bring her anywhere near Thorne's party.

It didn't do any good. Adriana could feel him

watching her—a prickling at her nape—all the way
to the elevator. Rather than wait for it, she detoured
for the stairway, disappointed rather than relieved
when the heavy door closed behind her.

Less than twenty-four hours after the New York
departure, Luke looked at the stars in the sky and
counted his blessings. He was glad to be alive, glad
to be in love, glad to be on a beautiful ship with the
woman of his dreams. Dressed in a tuxedo for the
formal dinner, the first at sea, Luke had been headed
for the midnight entertainment in the showroom.
Waiting impatiently for an elevator, he'd decided to
detour across the Lido deck, been struck by the
splendid solitude of the night and plunked down on
a lounge chair.

Stop and smell the roses.

Determined to practice what he'd been preaching
for the past week, Luke located the Big and Little
Dippers and searched the sky for other constella-
tions. Thorne had been tense and withdrawn ever
since his last trip to Bremerhaven. Adriana had been
reclusive, spending the entire day in her cabin, or so
he'd been told by Nico, who, although still not
overly friendly, did seem like a decent sort of guy.

Of course, Thorne couldn't stand Nico. A fact
Luke found both amusing and interesting.

Thorne was bent on acquiring everything bearing

the Falcone name—except the most valuable Falcone possession of all.

Grinning, Luke pushed himself out of his chair. Nevada would be wondering where he was, and she was one lady he didn't want to keep waiting.

When Luke stepped out of the shadows, he nearly collided with a crew member. "Excuse me," he muttered hastily.

The brief flash of hostility he saw in the man's eyes rattled him. He frowned.

It can't be. Can't possibly be that same guy.

Thoughtfully, Luke strolled in the opposite direction, mulling over the incident in his mind. He just couldn't be sure, and the uncertainly troubled him.

If he was wrong, he reasoned, no big deal.

But if he was right, they were in big trouble.

"That's who I saw. If it's not Feliks, he's the guy's twin brother." Luke stabbed the picture in Nico's hand. "What do we do now?"

"Let's not panic or jump to conclusions. If we're wrong, it's going to be embarrassing. Let's find the captain, and see if he recognizes this man as a crew member. If so, we'll look at his files before we confront the guy."

Before leaving his cabin, Nico slipped out of his jacket and checked the .38 in his shoulder holster, then put his jacket back on. "Let's go."

In the corridor, Nico rapped on a cabin door beside his and spoke briefly to the occupants. Turning back to Luke, Nico explained, "They're with me. If I don't check back with Mario and Vittorio within ten minutes, I've instructed them to contact the FBI in Miami."

When they reached the bridge, an unfamiliar officer barred the door. "Off-limits," he told them with just enough of a smirk to indicate he enjoyed their discomfort.

"We need to speak with the captain. It's urgent," Luke argued.

"Oh, I'm sure it is," said a voice behind them.

Luke glanced over his shoulder and saw Feliks. Hands shoved him through the door to the bridge, which had now opened. When Nico reached for his gun, the officer landed a punch that knocked Nico to his knees.

"They say it's urgent, Jorge," Feliks said. "Take his gun and check them both for weapons."

Feliks looked at Luke, then turned his gaze to Nico, lingering assessingly on him. "I had a feeling about this one all along."

"I warned you," said the man he'd called Jorge, yanking Nico to his feet.

Luke looked at the other men on the bridge, realizing they were not all ship personnel. Two of them held Uzis. The first officer, who had a gun pointed at him, picked up a special talk-back radio and handed it to Feliks.

"That's it," Feliks snapped. "We've secured the engine room. Put these two jerks with the captain. It never hurts to have more than one hostage."

The first thing Luke saw in the captain's cabin was bloodstains on the carpet. "What have you done with Captain Robbiti?" he demanded.

"If you don't shut up, you'll soon join him." Herding them into the bathroom, Jorge handcuffed Luke and Nico to the fixtures.

"What is it you want? You can't get away with this," Nico said.

"Shut up," Jorge snapped, clipping him in the chin with his Uzi. He made his way to the cabin door, then stopped and switched on a stereo, turning up the volume. "Scream all you want," he said with a sick grin.

As Jorge stepped out and slammed the door, Luke saw a body slumped on the shower-stall floor, nearly hidden by the plastic shower curtain.

"The captain," Nico said. "Let's hope he's alive."

"And if he isn't?"

"We probably won't be alive much longer, either."

"Like hell." Luke struggled to free himself. "I've no intention of checking out now—or anytime in the foreseeable future.'' *Not now when I've got so much to live for.*

From the back of the Emperor lounge, Nevada could see everything. Including Thorne seated at a table with the Falcone group. Adriana looked so lovely that Nevada was reminded of her childhood when kids had teased her for being tall, big and awkward. Since then Nevada had never felt beautiful, although lately when Luke whispered the words to her she wanted desperately to believe him.

But now Luke had disappeared. She'd been waiting for twenty minutes and the show was about to begin.

She left her drink on the table and went to find him. With the exception of punctuality, Nevada thought with a dreamy smile, the guy was just about perfect.

It didn't take Nevada long to learn Luke had been last seen with Nico, the Italian friend of the Marchesa's, and headed for the bridge. Why would he decide to take a stranger for a tour of the bridge when he knew she was holding a table for them? Especially when she'd been feeling rather vulnerable and needed to hear Luke tell her once again that he loved her.

On her way to the bridge, Nevada noticed the

door to the captain's quarters was ajar. When she tapped on the door, it opened.

"Captain Robbiti," she called softly, stepping inside. Lights were on, and loud music blared from a stereo in the bedroom. As far as she could see, the cabin was empty. She grimaced, wondering how an Italian captain had become so fond of country-and-western music. As Nevada turned to leave, she inadvertently tripped over a footstool. She swore as she felt her nylon rip. Her curse was broken by shouts and banging from the bathroom.

When she opened the door, she gasped and dropped to her knees. "Luke, are you all right?"

"Just get us out of these cuffs, Nevada."

"You're lucky I once dated a magician."

Nevada pulled a nail file from her evening bag and released the men. Luke gave her a hug and Nevada welcomed the comfort of his arms. Nico immediately checked on the captain and announced, "He's alive, but unconscious. We can't help him now, but if these guys return and find him here and us gone, he could be a dead man."

"We can't leave him here," Luke said, picking up the captain. "We'll put him in your cabin, Nevada."

With considerable effort, the three of them reached Nevada's cabin just down the hall and made the captain as comfortable as possible.

"The doctor will be here shortly," Luke said, hanging up the phone. "You stay here with him, Nevada, unitl I come back for you."

"Hell, no. I'm coming with you."

For the past half hour, Adriana had felt odd. At first, she'd attributed the feeling to being in close proximity to Thorne, who had accepted Emilio's invitation and joined them at their table in the Emperor showroom. But after several minutes, she'd realized it wasn't the tingling physical awareness that permeated her body whenever he was close, but a different feeling, an unsettling feeling.

Suddenly, Adriana realized what had been subconsciously bothering her, what had bothered her since first meeting Thorne. Why his eyes looked familiar. They were just like Piero's. Her mind scrambled to sort out her thoughts.

She rose unsteadily and excused herself.

"Leaving so soon?" Thorne asked, his tone amused.

"I need to talk to you," she said, touching him on the shoulder. "After the show."

Adriana somehow managed to smile at several people who spoke to her as she left the showroom. She wouldn't confront Thorne with her suspicion until they were alone, and not before she'd had time to think more clearly.

Deep in thought, Adriana hurried along the promenade deck to the nearest ladies' room. She was about to enter when Nevada grabbed her arm.

"There are terrorists onboard."

Instantly Adriana asked, "What makes you so sure?"

Quickly and concisely, Nevada told Adriana all she knew. "You'll be one of their targets, along with Thorne. Also, we can't rule out the two U.S. Senators, from New York and Florida. Nico is rechecking the passenger manifest and collecting any others that might be high on their list of hostages."

Nevada's hand tightened on Adriana's arm. "We've got to hide you."

"I'm not hiding from anyone. Come on. We've got work to do. Where are Luke and Nico?"

"They're meeting me in one of the provision rooms."

"We're wasting time," Adriana snapped. "Follow me."

She pressed a panel in the wall and it opened into the ship's interior. Throughout the ship, there were such concealed doors that allowed crew members easy access to passenger areas. Adriana avoided the engine room almost dead center in the ship and headed aft. Within minutes, they arrived at the storeroom.

By the time Luke and Nico joined them—along

with both senators and their wives—Adriana was dressed in a skimpy showgirl's outfit.

"We've got to warn Thorne," Adriana said. "He's in the showroom."

"How are we going to get him out of there?" Nico asked.

"Leave that to me," said Adriana, glancing at Nevada. "Can you give me a few tips?"

Thorne blinked. And blinked again.

No, he wasn't seeing things. The nearly naked showgirl on the stage was Adriana. She looked beautiful and he fought the urge to jump up and cover her with his jacket. What the hell was she doing on stage?

She looked right at him and crooked her finger, beckoning him. Was she trying to tell him something, strutting around the stage, driving half the male audience into a frenzy? And, if so, what?

When Adriana left the stage, Thorne excused himself with a promise to rejoin Emilio and Donatella shortly. Thorne hurried out of the showroom and toward the dancers' dressing room. Ducking through a hidden panel, he found Adriana waiting for him.

"It took you a few minutes longer than I thought to get the message." Adriana stripped off her headdress, running her fingers through her hair and covering herself with a short robe. "There are terrorists on board. Nico's notified the FBI in Miami, and he and his guys are busy getting passengers out of the way. Nico has a plan. I need your help."

"Where's Luke? Is Nevada safe?"

"Yes, she's checking on the captain and Luke is with Nico." Adriana answered all his questions as she hurried him into the bowels of the ship.

Slipping out of his Armani suit and into a waiter's uniform, Thorne realized he'd made a serious mistake in underestimating the terrorist threat to the Falcone Line. He had no one to blame but himself for the danger to the ship and her passengers.

He was going to make sure the bastards didn't succeed.

Nico arrived at the storeroom with a passenger and crew manifest in hand. "As far as I can determine, there are two men in the engine room and three on the bridge." He handed SIG-Sauer guns to Thorne and Luke and said, "You take care of the engine room, Luke. You can help my men and me with the bridge, Thorne."

"We've changed course," Adriana said. "I think they're headed for Cuba." Adriana glanced from Nico to Thorne. "Can they get there before help arrives?"

"It's going to be close," Thorne said, glancing at his watch and looking at Luke and Nico.

"Kiss me for luck?" Thorne pulled Adriana into his arms and kissed her. "Stay right here until I get back," he ordered, his hands gently removing her arms from around his neck. "Everything will be fine."

"Stay safe," she said, conveying in her eyes what she felt in her heart.

He nodded and left the room.

Thorne didn't have a moment to think about Adriana's words or the emotion he'd seen in her eyes—the *love* he'd seen in her eyes.

When Thorne knocked on the door to the bridge with a tray of food, he wasn't afraid. The fear didn't kick in until the ruse worked and he and Nico secured the bridge, with the help of Nico's men who smashed through the bridge windows to help them. It was like taking candy from a baby, Thorne thought when he called the engine room and Luke answered. The element of surprise had worked—this time—in their favor.

The first officer was too injured to tell Thorne who had masterminded the plot. After a brief but effective discussion with Thorne, Feliks confessed that his orders came from someone on the ship, an old member of the Red Army Faction.

Thorne went looking for Adriana. He hurried to Adriana's cabin and found Emilio.

Bound and gagged, Emilio had been bashed on

the head and was only semiconscious. "Gone. She's gone," he mumbled.

Thorne realized the danger wasn't over at the same moment he realized Adriana was missing.

Numb with shock, Adriana stared at the gun barrel aimed at her heart. She sat on a bed in a vacant cabin. Donatella stood several feet away. The gun held steady, her eyes burning with an unholy light.

"You're just like her." The words spilled from Donatella's mouth, a stream of pent-up bitterness and hate. "*She* tried to take everything away from me, too. But I fixed her."

Adriana shivered as she finally realized the menace that had been concealed for so long by black cashmere, haughty superiority and the Falcone heritage.

"Did you cut the brakes on Julia's car?"

Donatella's dark eyes narrowed. "How did you know?"

"I found Piero's diaries," Adriana admitted. "He was devastated by Julia's death. He knew the accident was no accident. He tried to find Julia's killer, but you hid your trail very well."

"Julia got what she deserved. If she hadn't interfered with my plans, I would have married Stephano and now this—" she gestured with the snub-nosed revolver "—would have been mine. Instead, Julia found the note I left for Piero, and Stephano walked into the ambush I'd set up for his brother. Piero should have died *then*—and not years later.''

The hair rose on Adriana's nape. The horror of Donatella's words exceeded anything she could have imagined. Wrapping her arms around her waist, tears welled in her eyes and began to trickle down her cheeks. It took several attempts before she could speak. "*You* killed Piero?''

"Fool! I didn't *personally* kill him.'' She leaned forward and Adriana recoiled from the undisguised hatred in Donatella's eyes. "But I had it done. You'd convinced him to start a family and I couldn't take the chance that there'd be another heir.''

"*Another* heir?''

For an instant, Donatella's features softened. "Before I came to the Falcone palazzo to live, I'd secretly married a partisan and we had a son. When my husband was killed, I gave the boy to others to raise and arrived on the Falcone doorstep to claim my son's heritage. I've waited all these years and it will soon all be mine—and my son's.''

"Your *son?*''

"My son, Dante, is the first officer on this ship. He's been under your nose all this time, waiting for the right moment to assume control. He's going to rescue us all from a terrorist takeover of this ship and emerge a hero. But not before killing the handful of terrorists on this ship—along with you and Thorne Weston.''

Adriana felt her breath hitch. Would Thorne realize the first officer was really a terrorist? Would he let his guard down around him and place himself in even greater danger? *My God, I love him,* she realized. I've loved him all along. And now I may never get the chance to tell him so. Or to tell him the truth about who he is.

''Why Thorne?'' Adriana asked even though she knew the answer.

Donatella glanced at her watch. ''Dante should have telephoned by now.'' Keeping the gun pointed at Adriana, Donatella punched in an extension number on the phone.

''Who is this? Let me speak with Dante.'' Donatella cursed and slammed the receiver down. She motioned with the revolver. ''Let's go.''

Adriana rose, feeling the gun's cold steel pressed against her side. ''Where are we going?''

''Dante isn't on the bridge. I need to know why.'' She shoved Adriana into an empty elevator and punched the button that would take them to the bridge.

Adriana's safe.

Thorne saw her walking toward him and—in that moment—nothing else mattered. Not ships, fortunes or painful memories. She was the only possession belonging to Piero Falcone that he had the slightest interest in claiming for his own.

Hurrying toward her, Thorne noticed the stricken expression on her face and wanted to reassure her that everything was under control. His need to hold Adriana in his arms was all-consuming.

Thorne reached for Adriana and saw the gun in Donatella's hand now pointed at him.

"What—?" Thorne looked from the gun to Donatella's face and had his question answered. "You're behind all this?"

"You've figured that out a little too late." Her mouth twisted. "You're just in time to die with the marchesa. Turn around."

Thorne glanced at Adriana. Shoulders back and head high, she looked every inch a true queen of the seas, proud and courageous. *Good girl,* he thought. For a fraction of a second, her lips curved in a tight smile, and he knew she'd do what he asked.

Thorne stepped to the side, forcing Donatella to swivel automatically in his direction and away from Adriana. "Run!" he ordered and lunged for the gun. Grabbing Donatella's wrist, Thorne twisted the revolver from her grasp.

"Dammit." He glared at Adriana, "I told you to run."

"I don't take orders from you!"

Donatella struggled against his hold. Thorne demanded, "Why?"

"You were in my way. I wanted it all."

Nico stepped forward and led Donatella away.

Thorne felt a hand on his shoulder and turned. Adriana slid into his arms, wrapping her own around him and holding on tightly. "I love you," she whispered.

Thorne's arms tightened around her and his lips covered hers. He was overwhelmed with emotion. "And I love you."

Adriana's hand touched his cheek, a loving caress echoed in the depths of her blue eyes. "Take Piero's ring off the chain around your neck and wear it always."

"Why?"

"Julia gave you that ring because she knew it belonged to you."

"She didn't give it to me...I took it."

"Julia knew the ring passed from father to firstborn son. She was your mother, Thorne, and Piero was your father. You're the Falcone heir."

Epilogue

The Wedding Gift

Genoa, Italy

Three months later, Thorne stood in the palazzo foyer. He wore the fede ring on his hand. The ring—identical to one given to Julia by Piero to pose as his wife—was Julia and Piero's legacy to their son.

It had taken time for him to sort out the past, to put to rest all the truths and untruths.

He finally understood why his puritanical mother had always considered him—her supposed change-of-life baby—such a burden. And why she'd delighted in punishing him for every infraction; why she'd never loved him. She'd enjoyed the role of the martyr, raising her daughter Julia's illegitimate son as her own and making them all pay every moment for her sacrifice. It was now all so clear. Why his mother had never seemed like a mother; why Julia had seemed much more than a sister.

He fingered the new wedding band on his left

hand and watched the woman coming down the palazzo steps toward him. She was the reason he refused to dwell on the past and looked forward to each new day.

Nevada and Luke followed his wife down the steps. Their wedding was planned for the following month in Miami.

A week before, Thorne and Adriana had been married in a joyous ceremony attended by family and friends at the Falcone palazzo. With Adriana at his side, Thorne planned to run the Falcone Line and Luke was taking over the helm of the Blue Ribbon operation. Already there was talk of combining the two cruise lines. But, for the time being, Thorne wanted to keep things simple and operate them separately. He wanted to spend time with his bride.

"Ready?" Adriana asked.

"As ready as I'll ever be," replied Thorne. The painting of Adriana and Piero had been removed from its prominent position in the foyer. In its place was another, hidden underneath a draped cloth.

"I took the painting of Genoa's harbor—the one you'd hung in your office and a gift to you from Julia—to a noted restorer for cleaning. The name P. Falcone proved that it was painted by Piero. During the war, many old masterpieces were hidden in the nearby caves around Genoa for safekeeping from the Nazis. Piero mentioned in his diaries that he'd hidden some by painting over them in a rather simplistic but convincing style.''

Adriana stepped forward and pulled the cloth from the painting.

In the stunned silence, Luke said, ''My God, it's a da Vinci.''

''It's been missing from the Falcone collection since the war.'' Adriana looked at Thorne. ''Your father would want us to hang it where it belongs.''

Adriana linked hands with Thorne, who looked from the painting to the woman he planned to spend the rest of his life with, loving her every moment. ''So would Julia.''

A trilogy of warm, wonderful stories by bestselling author

DEBBIE MACOMBER

Orchard Valley, Oregon

It's where the Bloomfield sisters—Valerie, Stephanie and Norah—grew up, and it will always be home to them.

When their father suffers a heart attack, they gather at his side—the first time in years they've all been together. Coming home, they rediscover the bonds of family, of sisterhood. And, without expecting it, they also find love.

ORCHARD VALLEY

THE PERFECT SINNER

The Crighton family saga continues in this riveting
novel from *New York Times* bestselling author

Penny Jordan

Prominent lawyer Max Crighton has it all—money, power, the perfect
home life. But he's putting it all at risk by his reckless and
dangerous behavior.

Then Max is brutally attacked. And the man who comes home from
the hospital is a stranger to his wife, Maddy, to his children and to
himself. Has the perfect sinner truly repented?

"Women everywhere will find pieces of themselves
in Jordan's characters."
—*Publishers Weekly*

MIRA

On sale mid-June 1999 wherever paperbacks are sold!

By the bestselling author of *Romancing the Stone* and *Elusive Love*

CATHERINE LANIGAN

THE LEGEND MAKERS

The steamy jungles of the Amazon offer the perfect escape for geologist M. J. Callahan, a woman running from her own haunted past.

But the jungle has a dangerous secret of its own—of a past expedition from which there were no survivors. As she and the two very different, very compelling men in her party approach the heart of the jungle, truths are revealed, betrayals uncovered, and M.J. is forced to confront her own demons before history repeats itself.

On sale mid-June 1999 wherever paperbacks are sold!

From one of the world's most popular authors comes a novel that masterfully explores one man's attempt to climb beyond his station in life and the tragic consequences it will have on his family.

THE UPSTART

CATHERINE COOKSON

Businessman Samuel Fairbrother wants a home more in keeping with his recent wealth. The thirty-four-room mansion he purchases comes with a staff—a headstrong staff. In particular, butler Roger Maitland considers his new boss nothing more than an upstart. Soon Samuel and Roger are locked in a battle for supremacy of the household and for the loyalty of Samuel's own children. And Samuel is at a disadvantage.

As the years pass only Janet, the eldest daughter, remains. In her lies the only hope of reconciling the scattered family—even if she has to defy both her father and convention to do so.

NOT FOR SALE IN CANADA

On sale mid-July 1999 wherever paperbacks are sold.

Wanting her became an obsession as powerful as his need to expose her...

She has no memory of her life before being captured by the Apache. Then suddenly she is given a name, a past—Anna Regent Wright, the long-lost Regent heiress, has come home at last.

But there is no doubt in Brit Caruth's mind that Anna is an impostor. And though this beautiful stranger has a hold on his body, he'll be damned if she'll get her hands on an inheritance that the Regents have long said was his....

Wanting You

NAN RYAN

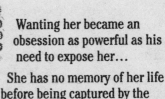

MIRA